THE RIDICULOUS RIVALRY

When Adrienne Castle saw Lady Pamela Tremayne, the woman whom Lord Dominic Creighton was pledged to marry, it was easy to reckon Adrienne's chances of turning Lord Creighton's head and winning his heart.

Lady Pamela was extraordinarily beautiful, while Adrienne thought herself only passably pretty. Lady Pamela was skilled at dancing, riding, playing the pianoforte, while Adrienne knew she possessed none of these elegant accomplishments. Lady Pamela flaunted a wardrobe that made her the fashion-plate of society, while Adrienne was certain her clothes made her appear ill-dressed and schoolgirlish.

Adrienne, in short, had absolutely nothing that could possibly win this competition . . . except a great deal of desire—and even more daring. . . .

The
Last Waltz

SIGNET Regency Romances You'll Enjoy

The Last Waltz

by
Dorothy Mack

A SIGNET BOOK

NEW AMERICAN LIBRARY

NAL BOOKS ARE AVAILABLE AT QUANTITY DISCOUNTS WHEN USED TO
PROMOTE PRODUCTS OR SERVICES. FOR INFORMATION PLEASE WRITE TO
PREMIUM MARKETING DIVISION, NEW AMERICAN LIBRARY, 1633 BROADWAY,
NEW YORK, NEW YORK 10019.

SIGNET TRADEMARK REG.U.S.PAT. OFF. AND FOREIGN COUNTRIES
REGISTERED TRADEMARK—MARCA REGISTRADA
HECHO EN CHICAGO, U.S.A.

SIGNET, SIGNET CLASSIC, MENTOR, PLUME, MERIDIAN, and NAL BOOKS
are published by New American Library,
1633 Broadway, New York, New York 10019

First Printing, March, 1986

1 2 3 4 5 6 7 8 9

PRINTED IN THE UNITED STATES OF AMERICA

1

"You mean to do *what*?"

Miss Anthea Beckworth's normally placid countenance was distorted into an expression of consternation as she stared openmouthed at the other occupant of the shabby room. Her companion met the agitated glance briefly before returning her attention to the shirt she was hemming with swift, even stitches. Her soft voice was as cool and matter-of-fact as her face.

"You heard me, Becky."

A lifetime's intimate knowledge of the girl sitting opposite caused the older woman to groan inwardly at this point, but she tried to infuse confidence into her brisk tones. "Nonsense, Adrienne! What you contemplate is totally impossible."

"We are nearly out of funds," the other pointed out. "Granted, the rent for this magnificent establishment"— the girl swept a contemptuous eye around the poorly furnished and dimly lighted room—"is paid for the next few months, but what then? And how do we find the wherewithal to feed and clothe two growing boys? We might sew until our eyes drop out of our heads, but we'll never be able to save enough this route to pay for our passage to England."

"We can always appeal to Lady Creighton."

"No," said the girl, rejecting the tentative suggestion out of hand.

"It's what your father wished, after all."

A fierce aquamarine glare bombarded the older woman as the girl raised her head from her stitching. "Papa's relatives cast him off twenty-five years ago, and after he married Maman they refused all further contact with him.

5

I would liefer starve in a ditch than appeal to any member of such a family.''

"Lady Creighton never cast your father off. They were friends from childhood, devoted to one another. It was her husband who forbade her to correspond with Matthew. The earl was a very possessive man and irrationally jealous of the attachment between the cousins.''

"I don't choose to seek charity from any member of my father's family. They are a stiff-rumped, arrogant lot and I'll have nothing to do with them.''

As the girl resumed her sewing Miss Beckworth marveled anew that soft lips and a delicately pointed chin could take on such a mulish set, but she knew that look of old. "*I* am a member of your father's family," she reminded Adrienne with exaggerated humility. "Must I too be cast off after all these years?''

Sudden laughter drove the scowl from Adrienne's face. "For your sins it is your fate to be forever enmeshed with the Castles. Besides, you are merely a connection of Papa's, scarcely a relative at all." As quickly as it had arisen, her mirth departed. "You are *our* family, Becky," she said with transparent affection, "and what we should ever do without you I shudder to contemplate. Poor Maman could never have coped on her own with creditors and tradesmen and three raucous children, not to mention Papa!''

They were silent momentarily, each lost in her own memories of the gentle, ineffectual woman who had been so unfitted for the life she had chosen by allying herself with a man infected with the gambling fever and imbued with a wanderlust.

"When your father presented his bride to me I saw at a glance that Juliette would be disastrously ill-suited to an unsettled life, which his looked like being. She was so delicate, ethereal almost, and couldn't understand what had happened to her country, why her family had had to flee from France. And when her parents both succumbed to influenza in England, she turned to your father as though he were her savior. Little did she know!''

"Papa did give one a marvelous sense of security—at

least before one grew up," Adrienne said thoughtfully. "He was so big and exuded an air of such confidence, it was natural to believe that one's fortunes would inevitably improve tomorrow—or the next day at the very latest." She shook her head musingly and looked with curiosity across at the sober-faced woman in the cane-backed chair. "But you *were* grown up, Becky. What prompted you to throw your cap over the windmill, as it were, and attach yourself to us?"

"I don't quite know." Miss Beckworth's expression was abstracted and she took some time before expanding on this statement. "I was fond of Matthew, of course, but I was aware of his weaknesses. The thing was, Juliette, your mother was not. She was expecting a baby when I first met her, and she was clearly still a babe herself. I was at a fairly low ebb myself just then. The man I was betrothed to had been killed in 1793 during the siege of Toulon, and—"

"I didn't know you'd ever been betrothed, Becky!" cried Adrienne, looking at her companion in quick sympathy. "I suppose I just took your presence for granted since you've always been part of my family. Losing your fiancé must have been a terrible blow. Did you never wish for a life of your own later when your first grief had abated?"

A self-mocking smile teased at the corners of the older woman's mouth. "There never seemed to be a 'later,'" she admitted ruefully. "At your father's request I came to stay with them temporarily to help Juliette, who was unwell during much of her pregnancy. Then you were born and she hadn't a notion how to care for a baby, apart from being in a weakened state to begin with. I actually did return to my home briefly, after Matthew engaged a nurse —the first of several, as it turned out, and all equally unsuitable. I called on them a few weeks later and was appalled at the chaotic state of that household. Juliette couldn't manage the servants, Matthew couldn't manage Juliette, and you were being neglected amidst the tumult. There seemed only one thing to do."

"So you moved back in and managed everybody, fortunately for us."

Miss Beckworth did not respond to the smile that

accompanied this cheerful summation; indeed, her expression grew more somber as she confessed with a twinge of bitterness, "If I could ever be said to *manage* anyone, it certainly wasn't Matthew or he would have altered his way of living before bringing us to this pass. Nothing I said on the subject of gambling over the years had the least influence on him."

"Please, Becky, do not be blaming yourself!" Adrienne reached across the table to grip her companion's hand in a comforting clasp. "You know he wished to stop gaming, tried to stop times without number, but he was trained for no profession and could see no other way out of our difficulties. With people like Papa, gambling is an obsession, almost a . . . a *sickness*."

As the young girl prepared to release her companion's hand, Miss Beckworth leaned forward and gripped tighter, holding the aqua eyes with an accusing hazel gaze. "And yet you have just proposed to set up as a gamester yourself!"

"Becky, it's not the same thing! I have no intention of turning gamester permanently, but there is no other way we'll be able to accumulate enough money to get the four of us to England."

"There is Lady Creighton."

"Never!"

Miss Beckworth sighed, reflecting with unhappy conviction that however much her charge resembled her delicate mother physically, she was in essence her father's daughter, every bit as stubborn and willful as Matthew had been.

"What gives you to assume you will be able to win the necessary money by gaming? Your father spent a lifetime trying to win a fortune and died in debt."

Adrienne dismissed this reasonable argument with an airy wave of her hand. "I intend to go about the task in a methodical fashion," she explained eagerly. "Success in faro or roulette is too dependent on chance, but piquet is another matter. I don't wish to brag, but you will allow that I am a better piquet player than ever Papa was. Did he not take me with him on several occasions when our finances were at their worst, and did I not win enough each time to tide us over the crisis?"

Miss Beckworth's glance slid away from the expectant girl and she bit her lip to keep from articulating her opinion of a man who introduced his innocent daughter to the evils of gambling and the society of gamesters.

"So you see," continued Adrienne, taking silence for agreement, "there is no reason for all this concern."

This blithe statement caused Miss Beckworth to close her eyes for an agonized moment, but she rallied and protested strongly, "No *reason*? Setting aside for the present the very real possibility that you will meet your match at cardplaying, being seen in a gambling hell will sink you quite beneath reproach and ruin your chances of contracting a respectable marriage at the very least. And heaven only knows what personal indignities or actual danger you would be subjected to in such places!"

So far from daunting the young girl, this dire prediction evoked a gurgle of laughter. "A pauper with two brothers to establish in the world is totally ineligible for marriage in any case," she retorted, undismayed by the prospect of continued spinsterhood. "But I have no intention of frequenting *hells,* Becky. The two places Papa brought me to were perfectly respectable; indeed, one was a private home, and there were women playing in both."

"Unescorted females? Girls of your tender years?"

"Perhaps not quite so young as I," admitted Adrienne with a scrupulous regard for the truth, "but several seemed to be without escort, though I have no way of knowing for certain."

Miss Beckworth sniffed. "Women of the demimonde, most likely, and ruinous for your reputation to be seen in their company."

"But I shouldn't *be* in their company, and what good will an unblemished reputation be to us if we are starving?"

"Now, that is pure fustian, Adrienne," declared Miss Beckworth tartly. "We are not going to starve, and well you know it. I have my little annuity, and our sewing brings in a pittance at least."

"It won't get us out of Brussels!"

At the ring of desperation in her companion's tones, Miss Beckworth's glance sharpened and her hands ceased their mechanical motions with the needle. "It's Luc, isn't it? You were not discontented with Brussels until the troops began to arrive in the area. But truly, my dear, I am persuaded you alarm yourself unnecessarily. Given the circumstances, most boys his age would be army-mad."

"Perhaps. But most boys would not be constantly begging for permission to be allowed to enlist at *fourteen* —or threatening to run off to join without permission!"

"They would send him packing in a trice."

"Yes, ordinarily, but these are not ordinary times, are they?"

The older woman had resumed her stitching but the younger cast hers down and began a restless pacing in the small apartment. "The Bruxellois are convinced that Bonaparte will invade, and from the talk in the shops, a significant proportion of them would be happy to see him victorious. Now that Wellington has arrived, I fear war is inevitable, and in times of war no one is going to be overly particular about checking on a volunteer's age. And you will admit that Luc appears older than his years."

"He is well-grown certainly, but his countenance betrays his extreme youth."

"Some of the young troopers who come into town look scarcely older."

As it was clear to Miss Beckworth that her charge was determined to clutch her worries to her bosom, she wisely curtailed her ineffectual efforts to provide comfort. Conversation lagged for a time, but Miss Beckworth, despite her head bent attentively over her stitchery, was keenly attuned to the activity in the room. She knew when Adrienne pulled the curtains together to eliminate the one-inch space that was generally present in the center, and when the girl straightened the painting of the Grand Canal that hung over the mantel. Sparks cracked in the fireplace in response to some halfhearted stirring and several ornaments were redistributed on a tabletop. At one point the girl bent down to retrieve an object that her impetuous movements had swept off a table. A covert glance at the smooth young face revealed that Adrienne's thoughts were far removed from the actions of her fingers. Miss Beckworth was already braced against shock when the girl broke the silence to propose eagerly:

"Becky, what if I disguised my identity? If I am unrecognizable as Adrienne Castle, there can be no possible objection to my going to a gaming club to win our passage to England."

Several objections occurred to Miss Beckworth, but she swallowed them, merely inquiring in an expressionless voice how her companion planned to disguise herself.

"Well, I would venture that one's coloring is the most distinctive thing about one, would not you, Becky?"

"Yours is," agreed the other with a faint smile that drew forth an answering sigh and a rueful grimace in the pier glass on the part of her companion.

"Why could I not have inherited Maman's beautiful blue-black hair as Luc and Jean-Paul did, instead of Papa's carrot top?"

"It's not carroty, it's a marvelous dark auburn," corrected the other. "Recollect also, while you are bemoaning your fate, that you did *not* inherit your father's freckles along with his hair color."

"Heaven be praised!"

"Your coloring is undeniably distinctive, but tampering with one's hair color is chancy business at best."

"A wig wouldn't be tampering. Do you recall that old wig of yours that we used to play with when we were children? I believe it is still in one of the trunks."

"You want to escape notice, not attract it! Hairstyles like that towering erection went out of fashion twenty years ago."

"But the hair is abundant and can be cut and arranged in a modern style with very little trouble. You have such clever fingers, Becky."

"Oho! So it is *my* fingers that have been selected to effect this transformation," said Miss Beckworth with a quizzical look. "I am honored."

Adrienne dimpled mischievously. "Well, neither of us has any illusions about the cleverness of my fingers," she retorted. "Except for rudimentary sewing ability, can you dredge up a single feminine accomplishment to my credit?"

This lighthearted challenge served to depress Miss Beckworth's spirits still further. "I would be ill-advised certainly to claim any outstanding success in imparting to you those accomplishments that are considered indispensable to a lady's education," she confessed, after rapidly passing under mental review her charge's musical and artistic attainments.

The latter paused in her perambulations about the room to recommend in kind tones that Becky not refine overmuch on the situation, since she herself did not consider that to be accorded an accomplished female was an accolade to be devoutly coveted in any case. "Of what use to me would be the ability to simper and sing and assume missish airs? And as for making interminable sketches of every tree or building that crosses one's path, I hold that to be a sheer waste of time, when one may easily obtain such from professional artists, should one desire a memento of a particular scene. It is of much more practical worth to learn how to stretch a joint to make three meals and how to get raspberry stains out of one's best table covers, and so I shall tell anyone who—"

"Adrienne, *please,* I beg of you, do not air such sentiments in company if you ever wish me to hold my head up again!"

The girl chuckled, having succeeded in drawing the expected reaction, but she made amends with a quick hug as she passed in back of Miss Beckworth's chair on her tour. "I shouldn't tease you at this hour of the day, Becky. You are too fatigued to retaliate. The candles are nearly guttering. I'm for bed. I'd like to search out that wig first thing in the morning."

Adrienne wished her companion good night with an admonition against staying up late to continue sewing. Though she nodded in acknowledgment, the older woman did not immediately follow the girl from the room. Her unseeing gaze reflected a degree of troubled concern she had taken pains to conceal earlier. She had no intention of publicly confessing that she regarded their present situation with even graver misgivings than Adrienne. The girl's fears were all centered on the remote possibility that her young brother might succeed in escaping their guardianship and joining the army. In the eight months since Matthew's death, life had gone on in the same quiet style for the children despite their grief. The natural optimism of youth and the experience of a lifetime spent living on the fringe of financial disaster had protected them from sharing the growing worry that overshadowed her own days and nights. Only at this moment did she acknowledge that she had spent these last months drifting along trying to deny any anxiety about the future that threatened to overwhelm her if she brought it into the light. Tonight Adrienne's absurd proposal to try to make their fortune by cardplaying had torn the self-applied scales from her eyes.

The shock of Matthew's death from a sudden pneumonia must be her only excuse. He had been a hale-and-hearty man of barely forty-eight, who, as his daughter said, radiated confidence and optimism. His unexpected death had cast her asea without the resolution to do more than drift along from day to day. She must hold herself extremely culpable for this present state of affairs. Matthew's financial dealings had ever been complicated, of course, but within a month or two of his demise the bald evidence of their penury had come to light. After his debts had been paid there had been practically nothing left on which to live. Her initial suggestion that they should remove to their own country had been casually rejected. Except for Adrienne, who had been born there, none of the children had even seen England. So here they had remained while the unwelcome suspicion that their resources were insufficient gradually and inexorably became hard fact. Certainly it was more than time to make a push to improve their situation, but as she gathered her sewing materials together and desposited them neatly in her workbox, Miss Beckworth was a long way from sharing Adrienne's optimistic expection that cards could provide the means of effecting a change for the better. Indeed, her shoulders were bowed beneath an additional load of worry as she snuffed the candles and scattered the coals in preparation for quitting the room.

covered with numberless coats of varnish as a Christmas
surprise a few years previous. Miss Beckworth was so
skilled in the art of using her hands...

2

It proved impossible to remain pessimistic for long in
the face of Adrienne's enthusiasm for her scheme, especially since Miss Beckworth soon found herself deeply
involved despite her reservation. Well before the house-
keeping chores were completed the next morning, the girl
erupted into the bedchamber they shared, triumphantly
holding out a moth-eaten item that Miss Beckworth took
no delight in recognizing as her once-prized wig.

"I was up in the attics at first light rooting about in our
trunks," Adrienne explained, pausing to brush a trail of
dust from her dark skirts.

Miss Beckworth watched unmoved as the dust settled on
the surface she had just polished. She ignored the molting
object being offered her in favor of removing the dust
from her spotless table.

"See, there are mounds of hair left, some of it very long,
more than ample to cover up the bare spots."

The older woman paused in her labors to cast a look of
extreme disfavor at the tangled mass of golden tresses
falling over Adrienne's wrist. "You overrate my talents if
you believe I can make anything of that deplorable
article."

"Now, Becky, let's not give up before we begin."

"I assume that is the royal *we* I am hearing?"

"I'll fetch your workbox and finish cleaning in here,
shall I?" offered Adrienne, ignoring the dryness in her
companion's tones as she relieved her of the polishing
cloth. She whisked out of the room, to return in seconds
carrying the large wooden box decorated with the Egyptian
design motifs that she had glued on each surface and

covered with innumerable coats of varnish as a Christmas surprise a few years previously. Miss Beckworth was installed in the armchair near the window, the wig in her lap, before she could express any additional doubts about the feasibility of the proposed renovation. And after a thorough examination of the remains, her expression of fastidious distaste was transformed into interest, reluctant at first but soon fired with the zeal of creativity as she became intrigued with the challenge presented by the object in her lap.

It was readily apparent that the wig must be almost totally reconstructed, for Adrienne's report of bare spots had not been exaggerated. It took the better part of the day to cut, gather, and restitch sections of hair to the cap to eliminate these areas before any thought could be given to restyling. In the course of the day Luc and Jean-Paul wandered in and out of the bedchamber and sitting room where Miss Beckworth resettled as the sun moved in the sky. Characteristically, neither boy displayed more than a minimal interest in feminine activity. Luc was intent on relating snippets of information about the arrival of the Fighting 52nd in the area, and Jean-Paul, as usual, had his head stuffed full of some scientific experiment or other reported in the books he devoured with unnerving regularity. The women were more relieved than otherwise at this state of affairs, since each had her own reasons for preferring to keep the proposed gambling sortie a secret for the time being.

Though she could not like the scheme, Miss Beckworth summoned all her experience and counsel to her charge's benefit for the simple reason that it partially appeased her notions of propriety to ensure that Adrienne should be disguised beyond the possibility of detection. Consequently she created a classic hairstyle, smoothly sweeping the golden tresses up high off the face to serve as the greatest achievable contrast to the girl's own short curls that ordinarily refused to be tamed. Adrienne's one decent evening dress was a youthfully styled celestial-blue muslin trimmed with deeper blue grosgrain ribbons at the hemline and high waist, but since most matrons insisted on wearing similar gowns, no matter how inappropriate to their figures or status, this could not be considered a sure indication of the wearer's youth. Miss Beckworth was cautiously satisfied with the effect of her handiwork until Adrienne broke into a smile of triumph on being told that she looked several years older, which action brought twin dimples flashing into play in her cheeks to augment the rather distinctive one in her chin. Her duenna groaned as the illusory maturity gained by the hairstyle was instantly routed.

"Pray, try to remember not to smile like that, dearest. You look about sixteen. For purposes of identification, three dimples might as well be three scars!"

Adrienne composed her features into sober lines on the instant and promised to remain cool and unamused no matter what hilarity transpired during the evening. Spotting the mischief sparkling just beneath the prim exterior, Miss Beckworth was a prey to strong doubts as to the girl's ability to play a sober role for any length of time. She groped for additional measures to alter her outward appearance and finally hit upon the trick of lightening the straight brown brows that gave character to Adrienne's face, with an application of gray powder. The young girl's potent attraction lay more in her vivacity and vivid coloring than in any classic arrangement of features, and Miss Beckworth considered that the washed-out effect achieved by the powder rendered her looks fairly insignificant.

Despite all her precautions, Miss Beckworth spent an uneasy evening awaiting Adrienne's return from the gambling club. The boys had retired before their sister left, so her sentence was a solitary one. The ticking of the clock on the mantel progressed from a background murmur to a rhythmic cacophony with threatening undertones as the hours crawled past. She sat with her sewing in her lap, her fingers engaging in periodic flurries of activity that died to a halt after a few minutes as her eyes roamed involuntarily and unseeingly about the empty room. By midnight she had abandoned all pretense of working, setting aside the white heap of sewing in uncharacteristic disarray. One o'clock found her eyes fixed with decreasing efficiency on a volume of poems while they strayed with increasing regularity to the relentlessly ticking clock. It was close to two, and fears of bodily injury had long since replaced earlier apprehensions about discovery and disgrace, when quiet sounds from the main entrance downstairs brought her to her feet in an agony of relief and trepidation. Before her shaking legs could carry her to the door, Adrienne burst into the room waving her reticule in triumph.

"I won almost twenty-five louis!" the girl declared, seizing her companion's upper arms and whirling her around in an exuberant victory dance until the latter begged for mercy and staggered into a chair. Adrienne tossed the bulging reticule into her lap and bent down to pick up the sewing she had scattered in her impromptu gyrations. She dropped into a chair herself, sprawling in a graceless attitude that earned her an automatic rebuke from Miss Beckworth. The older woman surveyed the sparkling face of her charge, enhanced at the moment by a slight becoming flush on her high cheekbones, put there by excitement.

"Did you find it a simple enough matter to engage an opponent in a game of skill?" she inquired in tones that she strove to make casual.

"Well, not at first," confessed Adrienne. "It was different when Papa brought me. He introduced me to all his acquaintances and mentioned that I enjoyed playing piquet. Most of the gentlemen were quick to challenge me to a rubber to test my skill. I felt just a little awkward tonight without an escort, and judged it the better part of valor to remain in the background while I reconnoitered the situation, as Luc would say."

"And how long did this reconnoitering take?"

"After an hour or so I began to feel a trifle conspicuous." Adrienne stopped abruptly and shot her companion a look from under her lashes before racing on. "There was a man who had tried in vain to interest one of his friends in a game of piquet—they were bent on gaining a seat at a faro table. He was wandering around from table to table watching the play and drinking glass after glass of wine, so I took my courage in hand and asked if he would do me the honor of playing *me* at piquet.''

Miss Beckworth was scandalized. ''You invited an *inebriate* to play cards with you?''

''He wasn't an inebriate, Becky, not even really bosky. He was just an ordinary gentleman slightly on the go. When we began our contest he switched to soda water and was actually more sober at the end of play than the beginning. Also, twenty-five louis the poorer, not that he seemed at all upset to be bested by a female. In fact, he was quite complimentary about my abilities,'' she finished with a grin.

Miss Beckworth sat up a little straighter, made uneasy by the too-innocent face confronting her. ''What nationality was this obliging gentleman?''

The blandness dissolved into giggles. ''He was Bruxellois, and we spoke entirely in French. I told him my name was Madeleine Giroude. During the whole evening, no one showed the least sign of recognizing me, Becky, so you may be reassured.''

A satisfied Adrienne went off yawning to her bed, but Miss Beckworth was not reassured. She remained sitting where she had landed for another half-hour, mentally forming and rejecting plans to reduce the risks to the girl. The problem was that Brussels was full of visiting English of all social classes. She herself could not accompany Adrienne to the gambling clubs without giving away her identity, and there was no one to whom she could entrust the duty. Such acquaintances as they had made in Brussels were either cronies of Matthew's or persons residing in the immediate neighborhood. The former would be sure to think the situation a lark, too diverting not to share with others, and there was no one in the latter category who could fill the bill, their neighbors, though pleasant enough, being mostly persons of inferior rank and as poor as themselves. Not for the first time in the last half-year did she experience a cold chill of loneliness and a prickling sensation of impending disaster.

This presentiment was strengthened three days later when Adrienne returned from her second visit to the gambling club. The girl smilingly presented her winnings—only ten louis this time—but Miss Beckworth was quick to detect a diminution of the tearing spirits with which Adrienne had greeted her on the previous occasion. A show of sleepiness designed to put her companion off the track had quite the opposite effect, as deviousness was not a quality in Adrienne's behavioral repertoire. Careful questioning elicited the reluctant admission that, as an un-escorted female, she had begun to attract a deal of unwelcome attention. She reiterated her belief in her ability to fend off such advances, citing the fact that she had been able to give the slip to two gentlemen professedly eager to escort her home by stealing out to take the sedan chair she had earlier engaged for the return trip while the gamesters' attentions were directed elsewhere for the moment. The blithe assurance that she had paid the chair-men well not to reveal her destination to anyone utterly failed to quiet Miss Beckworth's alarms.

"What gives you to think that men who have accepted money from one person who wishes to buy their silence will not then accept money from a second who desires information?"

Adrienne's eyes widened in protest. "Jacques and his brother are not like that! Indeed, Becky, they appeared to be very honest fellows who were quite sincerely concerned for my safety."

Her companion discovered that Adrienne's disappoint-ment was connected with her mediocre showing at piquet that night. It seemed the gentleman she had played the first time had again been present and desirous of an oppor-tunity for revenge, which request she had been happy to grant, having assessed his play previously and found it inferior to her own. The outcome had been a repeat of their earlier encounter, and she would have come home enriched by seventy louis had she not succumbed to a challenge issued by a dark-browed Englishman who had systematically relieved her of her winnings. Fortunately, she had established a time limit at the beginning of play. Her opponent had been obliged to release her before she was quite run off her legs, but her confidence in her ability had received a severe jolt.

Miss Beckworth waved away Adrienne's apologetic murmurs. "You say your opponent was an Englishman? Of what age?"

"I should suppose him to be a few years younger than Papa," replied Adrienne, a bit puzzled.

"Did he display any undue interest in you—any *personal* interest, I should say?"

Adrienne chuckled in understanding. "Not at all. I might have been the pig-faced lady for all the interest Mr. Emerson took in me." Her expression darkened. "There were others, though, younger men, who did display a tedious curiosity. I told them all my name was Mademoiselle Giroude and pretended I understood no English. It answered quite well. Fortunately for me, our countrymen are not exactly noted for their linguistic abilities. A poor dab of a girl whose only asset is an ability to play piquet and who cannot even speak English will not long hold the attentions of such dashing young bucks."

Miss Beckworth, who did not agree with Adrienne's slighting self-portrait, was patently unconvinced, but her efforts to persuade the girl to discontinue her reckless scheme proved unavailing. To her arguments that each additional visit would increase the general curiosity about the mysterious lady gamester, Adrienne would promise only to alternate her visits to both establishments to lessen the chance of detection. The conversation ended with her agreement to wait a few days before making her next excursion, this time to the house of Madame Mireille, whose clientele was perhaps a bit more select.

A comprehensive glance around the brilliantly lighted rooms off the entrance hall of Madame's large house alerted Adrienne to some recent changes in the once-staid establishment. The dark heavy tables and chairs that had formerly graced the rooms had been replaced by spindly-legged items of gilded wood whose seats were upholstered in crimson to match the new draperies at the long windows. Blinking in the glare of hundreds of candles placed strategically around the rooms, the girl could see it would be idle to hope for a dark corner in which to enjoy a private contest. The recent influx of military personnel in Brussels had obviously brought prosperity in its train; all was sociability and noise these days. A number of nationalities were represented by the patrons, judging by the variously colored uniforms present among the players sitting around the faro tables or circulating between the rooms. Adrienne cast a jaundiced eye on the rather youthful assemblage, her instincts telling her it would be more difficult to arrange a serious game in this atmosphere of bonhomie.

And so it proved. After a period of seemingly aimless wandering about the rooms trying to make herself as inconspicuous as possible, she did manage to engage a gentleman in a hand of piquet but was not left to enjoy the contest in peace. Not being blind to the interest an unescorted female would arouse in such a setting, she had been careful to approach a soberly dressed civilian of indeterminate age. Unfortunately her antagonist turned out to be a jolly Bruxellois whose hearty laughter attracted an audience after a short time. By dint of a strong-minded performance of complete indifference, she was able to ignore the comments of the onlookers, but her concentration, so vital to success in piquet, suffered as a result. The score seesawed for an hour or so until Adrienne became disheartened and brought the game to a close as gracefully as possible, bidding her partner a cordial adieu.

It was as she was tying the strings of her hooded cloak under her chin a half-hour later that it became evident that lack of pecuniary gain was to be the least of her problems that night. In order to avoid the importunities of a pair of young Belgian officers bent on conducting her to a private party and disinclined to accept a polite refusal, she had lingered in the ladies' retiring room as long as she dared, though it was still too early for her sedan chair to be waiting. Now she stood on the stairway landing until the entranceway should be free. Breathing a sigh of relief, she slipped out the door and ran lightly down the steps, intending to wait in the shadows until her chair arrived.

She had barely gone a step when two figures materialized on either side of her, taking her arms and propelling her forward.

"Told you she'd try to give us the slip," one said with a silly laugh that proclaimed how deeply he had been imbibing of Madame's supply of wines.

"She's just shy, that's all. Come along, little darling. We can promise you a good time tonight." There was a hint of coercion in the amiable tones of the second man that sent a tremor of fear along Adrienne's nerve endings.

She dug in her heels, pulling the men off balance for a second while she tried unavailingly to free her arms. "I have no intention of going anywhere with either of you. Unhand me instantly or I'll scream loud enough to empty Madame's establishment."

"Now, now, my dear, we can't have that. Can't allow you to make a scene," said the second voice.

"She's not very friendly," complained the one with the giggle.

"Oh, a drink or two will do wonders for her good nature."

Adrienne was opening her lips to scream when a rough hand went over her mouth. She struggled frantically, kicking out behind her, and had just managed to bite the fingers pressing against her mouth when a new voice rang out, followed by the sound of quick footsteps on the stairs as someone leaving the gaming house rushed to her assistance.

Still flailing about in a concerted effort to break out of the hold, Adrienne was too intent on aiming a lethal elbow at the body of her assailant to catch everything the newcomer said. She had a confused impression that his French was very accented and his voice sounded *amused*! The words "*chère amie*" came through clearly, however, and the instant she was free she rounded on her rescuer, who was watching the rapid departure of the Belgians.

"How *dare* you tell those oafs I am your mistress!" she

flared, turning a blazing glance on the fair-haired giant at her side.

"Your pretty gratitude overwhelms me, ma'am," he replied with a mocking bow. "I beg pardon for such indelicacy, but I didn't wish to hit two men obviously in their cups, especially when I am a guest in their country."

Adrienne had calmed down by now. Fortunately the street was not too well lighted, but by his voice and costume she knew her rescuer as a British military officer and she did not wish to rouse the curiosity of an Englishman. In a voice struggling to be cordial she thanked him for his timely intervention. He bowed again and made a motion to hail a passing cab, which she stopped by grabbing his arm. Still in her role of grateful receiver of favors, she informed him sweetly that she had already contracted for a sedan chair, which was due any moment.

"I intend to see you home," the stranger said shortly.

"That won't be necessary." Adrienne spoke through gritted teeth, but her lack of enthusiasm for his company had no effect on the good samaritan at her side. When it became apparent that she would not be allowed to undertake the journey on her own, she pretended to feel queasy after her ordeal and insisted on walking to avoid telling him her exact direction while her brain scrambled around trying to discover a way to give her escort the slip.

It had been an ill-fated outing from the start, and now Adrienne's cup of bitterness was to overflow as she was forced to endure a homily on the evils of gambling and the folly of going about unescorted. Not that she listened to her insufferably pompous attendant as he struggled to express himself in halting French; she was too intent on escaping him. In high dudgeon that disguised a rising panic, she refused to dignify his remarks with any reply, merely indicating by hand signals which way they should turn.

Her chance came when they had almost reached the street where the Castles had lodged since their arrival in Brussels. A man stopped her escort to ask directions. Adrienne took instantaneous advantage of his momentary inattention, fading back a step and running around the corner they had just negotiated. She slipped into the shadows of the first deep entranceway, not a second too soon, as her erstwhile rescuer came pounding past. Her muttered prayers that her luck would hold a few seconds longer were answered as she managed to race ahead and attain the safety of her own building unchallenged.

On the night of Adrienne's third gambling adventure, Miss Beckworth did not even attempt a show of working. For an hour or two she simply sat unoccupied and almost unmoving, her face a study in concentration and doubt. From time to time her lips moved soundlessly as though rehearsing a speech, and she had already made one or two tentative movements indicative of an intention to rise out of her chair, movements that had ended by her sinking back onto its seat, when her face assumed an expression of fixed determination that was translated into an abrupt spring from her reclining position. She proceeded directly to a small table under the window, from the drawer of which she extracted a sheet of paper, and after some slight searching, a pen and some ink. Her movements still reflected purposefulness as she resumed her seat by the table bearing working candles, where she carefully mended the pen and began to write.

After a few moments, though, her resolution apparently faded, the pen faltered and paused above the last word. Another long moment went by during which Miss Beckworth sat staring into space with her bottom lip gripped in her teeth before she set the pen down and rapidly scanned the words on the paper. She reread them twice more, made an abortive motion toward the pen, then seized the paper and crumpled it into a ball. After this action she reverted to staring into space and was actually caught unprepared by the sound of a key in the lock. A hasty glance at the clock revealed that it still lacked twenty minutes to midnight as the girl in the blond wig entered quietly.

"You are early tonight."

Adrienne grimaced and sank wearily into a chair. Avoiding her companion's eye, she began to remove the pins anchoring the wig in place.

"Is anything wrong?"

"After a time it gets hot and gives me the headache."

If this explanation was intended as a red herring, it failed in its intention. "Were you losing?" pursued Miss Beckworth, watching the girl's face closely as she removed the wig and shook out her hair, running her fingers repeatedly through the damp, flattened curls until they stood out on end.

"I lost a few louis, nothing to signify."

"You did very right to leave, then," declared Miss Beckworth. "To continue playing once one begins to lose is fatal, my dear."

Under the approving glance of her companion, Adrienne shifted uneasily. "That wasn't quite the way it was," she confessed. "Normally I should have beaten my opponent. No, truly, Becky, I was the better player," she insisted, interpreting the other's expression as one of doubt, "but there was too many onlookers about, watching and making conversation, which I thought exceedingly ill-mannered of them; it quite destroyed my concentration."

Miss Beckworth sat very still for a moment, staring searchingly at the young girl, who fidgeted under that stare, her fingers moving nervously among the tresses of the wig in her lap.

"Adrienne, this isn't going to answer," she said at last. "It is only a matter of time before someone makes improper advances to an unprotected girl and . . ." She broke off as the guilty color sprang to Adrienne's cheeks, before continuing grimly: "You may as well open the budget and tell me everything that happened tonight."

Eventually the whole story did come out under close questioning. Miss Beckworth's mind was a parade ground of changing pictures, one more horrifying than the next, to judge by her dismayed countenance. Adrienne leaned over to pat the hands clasped together with white-knuckled pressure.

"Relax, Becky. It was a close-run thing, but it is all over now."

"Yes it is! You must see that you cannot continue with this foolishness any longer. Not after tonight. It is simply too dangerous! You must stop!" Miss Beckworth looked imploringly at the girl, who had risen to her feet during this impassioned speech.

"I am truly sorry to disoblige you, Becky dear, but I *cannot* stop yet. It is the only way to get the money." Adrienne's voice was gentle, but it was the almost sorrowful expression on her face that convinced Miss Beckworth that further argument would be fruitless. She watched blankly as the girl left the room.

The sound of the door clicking shut released her from the spell of immobility, however. She jumped out of her chair, strode over to the window table, and removed another sheet of paper from the drawer. This time there was no hesitation in her manner as she again took up her pen. She had covered the entire sheet with her controlled copperplate script before she so much as raised her head from the task to look over the mantel clock. Half after midnight. It seemed incredible that less than an hour ago she had been so uncertain of her course as to be incapable of action. There was nothing uncertain in the hand that wrote the direction on the sealed letter and then carefully concealed the result in her workbox. Within another thirty seconds she had extinguished the candles and followed Adrienne into the bedchamber.

3

It was a brilliant and warm morning, but Miss Beckworth was scarcely conscious of the lovely spring day as she drank her coffee in nervous little sips and darted assessing looks at her companion when Adrienne's attention was engaged elsewhere.

Like most of the English in Brussels in the spring of 1815, the ladies avidly followed every movement of the field marshal in whose capable hands their continued safety rested. This morning Adrienne was reading an account of the first large entertainment given by the Duke since his arrival in the city three weeks before to take command of the allied forces.

"My goodness, Becky, not only was there a concert and a ball followed by supper at the Salle du Grand Concert, but he hosted a dinner party *before* all this at the Hôtel de Belle Vue, which was attended by their majesties the King and Queen of the Netherlands!"

"King William has been quite visible since his arrival. I suppose it gives his new Belgian subjects an opportunity to get to know him."

"Oh, Becky, it says here that Madame Catalani performed at the concert. How I should love to hear her sing!"

"I had that privilege a few years ago in Vienna. She has a magnificent voice."

Silence descended while Adrienne continued reading a list of the distinguished guests in attendance at the Duke's ball. She mentioned several prominent names and experienced a vicarious satisfaction in learning that her friend recalled meeting one or two in the dim past. "I never knew you were so well-connected, Becky," she said with teasing admiration.

Miss Beckworth shrugged. "It's all water over the dam at this juncture." She glanced across the table in time to witness Adrienne's unsuccessful attempt to stifle a gasp as her fingers clutched the paper convulsively.

"What is it, my dear?"

"N-nothing. I was afraid I was going to sneeze. I see Sir Reginald and Lady Armbrewster were also present at the ball. Did you not once say you were acquainted with them?"

"No, I did not, and if it was the mention of Colonel Lord Creighton of Wellington's personal staff that brought on your sneeze, perhaps I should tell you I read the account earlier."

For a minute Adrienne was deprived of further speech; then she rallied. "Oh! Well, nothing could be more unlikely than that we should encounter Lord Creighton, such a quiet life as we lead."

A guilt-ridden Miss Beckworth caught the note of uncertainty in Adrienne's breezy tones and sighed. She had known it wasn't going to be a simple matter to explain. "I'm afraid nothing could be more *likely,* my dear. In fact, I am in the expectation of receiving a visit from Lord Creighton momentarily."

"Momentarily?" Adrienne bounded up with a hunted expression and cast her eyes around the room as if seeking a hiding place, before common sense came rushing back. She subsided onto her chair once more as Miss Beckworth made soothing noises.

"Not literally, child, but I received a communication from Lady Creighton yesterday in which she stated that she had written Lord Creighton by the same post and had directed him to call at his earliest convenience."

Tears shimmered in Adrienne's eyes. "How could you do this, Becky? You know I wish to have nothing to do with this man who forbade his wife any contact with her own cousin!"

"There was really no option, dearest, if we are to remove to England soon. Besides, Colonel Lord Creighton is Lady Creighton's *son*, not her husband, who died some time ago, and indeed, Adrienne, she wrote me the most comforting letter with not a trace of condescension. She is most willing, nay eager, to assist us in our difficulties. Here"—reaching into a pocket in her plain morning gown for an envelope—"read the letter for yourself. I am persuaded you will agree that she is sincerely well-disposed toward us."

Adrienne, who had been growing increasingly agitated during this speech, snatched at the envelope and removed two sheets of pressed paper. "Does she give her son's direction?" she muttered to herself, casting a quick eye over the first sheet of paper before discarding it to scan the second. "Ah, yes, Rue Ducale. It must be near the park." The second page joined the first on the table as the girl pushed her chair back with a decisive motion.

"Adrienne, what are you about? Where are you going?" Miss Beckworth's voice sharpened as her charge dashed into the bedchamber and emerged in a few seconds wearing a shawl and tying the strings of a bonnet haphazardly under her chin.

"To see Lord Creighton, of course."

"Adrienne, you cannot call on a gentleman unchaperoned!" her companion moaned. "What will he think of you?"

"I can, and it doesn't signify what he thinks of me." The girl's hand was on the entrance door when she looked back over her shoulder, a most unfeminine determination molding the contours of her mouth and jaw. "I daresay he'll be too relieved to have us off his hands to notice the proprieties in any case."

"Adrienne, *no*! Come back!"

The reverberating slam of the door all but drowned out Miss Beckworth's urgent commands even in her own ears. After a long moment during which she stood staring at the wooden portal, she sank back onto the chair and transferred her blind gaze to the sheets of paper lying on the table.

"A Major Peters has called, my lord."

The man sitting behind an ornately carved desk looked up in startled irritation, his fierce concentration on the sheet of paper in his hand having prevented his hearing the butler's preliminary knock. The frown darkening his brow vanished as he perceived the identity of his caller, however, and he came eagerly around the desk to grasp the extended hand of the smiling man who approached in the wake of the butler, cheerfully oblivious of the waves of disapproval emanating from the latter at such presumption.

"Ivor, by all that's wonderful! When did you arrive?"

"I came in Lord Uxbridge's train."

"I didn't see you last night at Wellington's affair. Uxbridge was there."

"*I* don't travel in such exalted circles, Dominic, dear boy."

A snort of derision escaped the dear boy's throat as the Earl of Creighton paused to give an order for refreshments to his waiting butler. This accomplished, he turned to find his guest gazing in an attitude of thunderstruck admiration at the neat blue frock coat that looked as if it had been molded to its owner's powerful shoulders, and the tightly fitting white net pantaloons of a staff officer.

"My, aren't we the dapper dog nowadays! You've come a long way from the Peninsula days when we were lucky to have a whole uniform on our backs, and if we did, it was sure to be covered with mud."

"Lord, yes! The mud of Spain will be one of my enduring memories." The earl waved his guest to a chair in front of the fireplace before seating himself nearby. "Speaking of dapper dogs, the Duke himself was cast into the shade by Uxbridge's magnificence last night. There's nothing that sets off a dress uniform to more advantage than the furred pelisse of a hussar flung dashingly back over one shoulder. He was the cynosure of all eyes, absolutely slayed the ladies."

"I can well imagine. Everyone watching to see how old Hookey would receive him, no doubt."

"Well, naturally Wellington wanted Conbermere to command the cavalry again. He was pleased with his performance in the Peninsular campaign."

"And the Horse Guards in their infinite wisdom send him instead the man who ran off with his brother's wife five years ago. Incidentally, Lady Charlotte will not be joining her husband in Brussels."

"That helps, of course. The Duke received Uxbridge quite cordially, but it would be awkward in the extreme to be forever running into his former sister-in-law at fetes, and we are very social this spring, let me tell you. Be prepared! Are you on Uxbridge's staff? What do you think of him?"

"I haven't found him as difficult to deal with as rumored. He's got a reputation as a damned fine cavalry commander."

"He'll need to be."

"It's inevitable, then? Boney means to attack?"

"I should think so. He's routed Angoulême. What's left to stop him? The old king certainly isn't about to do anything effective from Ghent. And even if Napoleon's protestations about wanting peace are gospel, the allied powers choose not to believe him. They've all refused to receive his overtures and will certainly make a push to remove him from the throne."

"There is some talk of abdication in favor of his son, is there not?"

"Not from Bonaparte, and he has the wholehearted support of the army. I just hope the Duke has time to assemble an adequate force before the French cross the border."

"The War Office being dilatory as usual," finished Major Peters with a grin.

There was a brief lull in the conversation then as the butler appeared with a tray bearing a decanter and glasses. While the business of supplying the gentlemen with wine was being accomplished, Major Peters looked about him, idly at first, and then with widened eyes as the noble size and luxurious appointments of the room struck him.

"Come into a fortune, have you, Dominic?" he queried when the door had shut once again behind the butler. "This place beats a bivouac in Spain all hollow, but I'd have thought you'd be bunking in with the rest of the bachelor staff." He fixed a pair of bright dark eyes agleam with merry speculation on the face of his friend. "Doing the social bit up brown, are you? Or perhaps you're thinking of tying the knot, hmmmm? I hear half the matchmaking mamas in the kingdom are here in Brussels with their hopeful daughters, not to mention a similar number of designing widows."

The earl set his glass down with a sharp little click and thrust himself back in the overstuffed chair with an impatient movement before addressing himself to the first of his loquacious friend's observations. "This house is an accident, really. My mother was planning to come over this spring, so I made the arrangements to hire this place for her before I went back to Vienna for the Congress. Then of course Boney escaped from Elba and I advised her not to make the trip." His eyes warmed with sudden laughter. "For once she took my advice and stayed safely at home. Having leased the house, it would have been foolish to leave it empty when I was posted here, especially since Mama had already sent her majordomo over last month to get it ready. He hired the local servants, and I go on very smoothly here—at least I have done until now." The scowl reappeared on the earl's brow as he stared into his wineglass.

"That will teach me to jump to ridiculous conclusions," Major Peters said, smiling blandly as quick suspicion appeared on the features of his host.

"Now, I wonder whose tongue has been wagging?" The earl's voice was very soft.

"Well, I did happen to get a letter from Corny, written when he was in Vienna," Major Peters admitted.

The earl held up a hand. "Enough said. John Cornelis is worse than an old woman for gossip. He happens to be correct this time, however. I *am* engaged, though no announcement's been made yet. It just happened this week."

Major Peters sprang out of his chair and surged forward to pump the hand of his friend. "Let me be the first to felicitate you, dear fellow. Who is the lucky girl?"

"Didn't Corny tell you that too?"

"You tell me," said Major Peters gently.

"I met her in Vienna last winter. Her name is Pamela Tremayne, Lady Tremayne, and she is a widow, though *not* a designing one." Under his lordship's baleful glare the insouciant major preserved an innocent countenance and uttered soothing noises. Satisfied, the earl continued. "The boot is on the other foot entirely. She is constantly surrounded by admiring suitors, and deservedly so. Ivor, she is the most glorious creature! It isn't just that she is beautiful, she has more wit and charm and just sheer presence than any woman has a right to possess. I had to beat my way through the pack to get near her. I still can't believe my incredible luck that she should prefer me to all the others who pay court to her."

Major Peters, indulgently observing that his friend had fallen into a rapt contemplation of his good fortune, had no difficulty at all in believing that an impecunious widow (information he owed to the maligned Corny) would prefer Dominic to many another suitor. Even before the embellishments of title and fortune had been added at his father's demise two years previously, the tall, handsome figure of Colonel Norcross had caused flutters in many a feminine dovecote. His pleasant manners, allied to a genuinely kind nature, made him a universal favorite with the ladies, while his male acquaintance respected his courage and integrity. The really astonishing thing was that he had escaped the lures cast out to him by numerous pretty daughters with knowledgeable mothers behind them until the advanced age of nine-and-twenty. Had he not been actively engaged with the army since Cambridge days, and generally under conditions unconducive to conducting a courtship, most likely he would have succumbed before now. These reflections Major Peters kept to himself, saying merely, when his host's attention returned from Utopia, that he looked forward to the pleasure of meeting Lady Tremayne.

"She *is* in Brussels at present? She doesn't reside in Vienna?"

"Oh, no. She has been accompanying her brother, Sir Ralph Morrison, and acting as his hostess. They arrived in

Brussels a couple of weeks ago." At the flicker of some passing emotion on his friend's face, Lord Creighton laughed dryly. "I see Sir Ralph is not entirely unknown to you?"

Major Peters denied this. "I've never set eyes on the fellow personally, but I'm acquainted with someone who had . . . dealings with him in London last year, if it is the same person. Bit of a mushroom, what?"

"If that were all! Bit of a loose screw, rather. He's a gambler who doesn't confine his activities to the track and the tables. Always involved in some moneymaking scheme or other, mostly unsuccessful, I'm told, leaving investors wiser but poorer. Pamela, needless to say, has no idea of her brother's unsavory reputation. I'll be much relieved when I can remove her from his sphere."

"Er, yes, quite so. You say the betrothal's not been made public yet?"

"No. I've been planning to announce it at a small dinner party next week—to which, by the by, you are hereby invited—but my dear mother has just considerably complicated my life."

"Has Lady Creighton decided after all to descend on Brussels, Bonaparte or no Bonaparte?"

"Much worse than that. She's just landed me with the responsibility for an orphaned family."

Major Peters blinked. "Your mother is an intelligent, charming, and very enterprising woman, but I must confess that it is not immediately apparent to my meager intellect how she, situated outside Brighton, can have embroiled you, here in Brussels, in the affairs of another family, orphaned or otherwise."

The earl released a snort of exasperated laughter. "If you can say that, Ivor, then you don't half-know what Mama is capable of, especially when her compassion has been aroused. Distance means nothing to her at all. In this instance, however, it is precisely her distance that is my undoing. I was reading a letter from her when you were announced. It arrived yesterday, but I had so little time to dress last night for the Duke's affair that I put it aside to read this morning. As best I grasped the matter, it seems that a cousin for whom Mama had a great fondness in her youth, and whom I seem to recall hearing my father describe as the black sheep of the family, upped and died some months ago here in Brussels, leaving three orphaned children. His wife was French and has been dead for several years. The children have been in the care of another family connection until now. This woman has written to Mama detailing the plight of the family and requesting her assistance in getting the children over to England. Mama, of course, with her penchant for lame ducks, is determined to take them under her wing and has commanded me to make their travel arrangements. I am quite willing to undertake this commission, you understand, but in the meantime, what am I to do with three half-French brats?''

"Nothing at all, your lordship, because the half-French brats hereby decline to accept your protection!"

Neither man had heard the door open, but the frosty feminine voice brought their heads spinning around in unison to stare toward the entrance to the room where Moulton, the butler, his posture rigid with disapproval, stood just behind a slightly built young girl with flashing eyes under a bonnet tied a bit askew, who was fairly quivering with animosity, though her voice has been coldly controlled. The earl and his guest straggled mechanically to their feet as Moulton defended his lapse.

"I told the young lady that I would inquire whether you could receive her, my lord, but she followed me into the room."

"It's all right, Moulton, you may go." Lord Creighton gestured in dismissal, though his eyes never left the girl's face. "I'll see Miss . . . Miss . . ."

"My name is Adrienne Castle," supplied the girl with her chin at a dangerous elevation.

"I'll see Miss Castle now. Won't you be seated, Miss Castle?"

The girl's expression of frozen disdain did not alter by a degree at this display of smiling courtesy on the part of her host. "No, thank you, my lord. I shan't be here long enough to sit. I have come today solely to request that you convey my thanks to your mother for her kind offer of assistance, while you explain to her that it is not at all needed or desired. I will be grateful if you will say all that is proper from me to Lady Creighton in declining her offer. Good day, my lord.''

The girl sketched a curtsy and headed directly for the door through which the butler had vanished just seconds before. In her haste she knocked against a side table, sending a meerschaum pipe which had been reposing there crashing to the parquet floor. A quick glance to ensure that there was no breakage, a quicker apology, and she was through the door in a whirl of skirts.

''Wait, Miss Castle! Come back!''

But Miss Castle did not wait and she did not return.

The earl bolted after her but was back in seconds to find Major Peters in the act of replacing the pipe on the table. He shook his head as his friend's eyebrows rose questioningly. ''She had already made her escape. I could scarcely chase after her down a public street in broad daylight.''

Major Peters' eyes gleamed with amusement. ''Not yelling 'Stop, thief!' at any rate, and somehow 'Stop, pipe breaker!' does not have quite the same ring to it.''

''Is the pipe broken?'' asked the earl indifferently.

His friend nodded. ''The bowl is cracked. If, as I gathered, Miss Castle is one of your orphans, she seems to have solved your problem for you quite expeditiously by declining your aid.''

The earl's brows met in a straight line. ''*Solved* it? If the other two are in the same mold as that hoyden, I should say my problems are just beginning.''

''You cannot very well force assistance on people against their will,'' observed Major Peters.

''Can I not indeed?'' scoffed the earl. ''You don't imagine I shall leave a child like that on the loose in Brussels, do you? I'll be paying a little visit to the Castles in due—'' He broke off as his friend murmured a comment. ''What did you say?''

''I said Miss Castle didn't strike me as being a child,'' responded the other mildly.

''Of course she is!'' His lordship's voice rang with impatience. ''A mere schoolroom miss, or should be! And will be brought to heel in good time, but at the moment"—glancing at his watch—"I must show my face at headquarters. Care to accompany me, Ivor? Gordon should be there, and Somerset too."

Major Peters signified his agreement with this course and the two left the earl's residence to stroll around the park to army headquarters on the Rue Royale.

4

Indignation carried Adrienne out of Lord
Creighton's house at an impressive speed, which she might
have maintained all the way back to the dingy street where
their lodgings were located, had she not been compelled to
slow down by a severe stitch in her side. Glancing around
for the first time at narrow houses leaning crookedly
against each other, she realized she had put considerable
physical distance between herself and Lord Creighton in
the past fifteen minutes. A vertical pleat between her
brows was the outward sign that she had been less successful in attaining comparable mental distance.

Becky thought her impetuous and full of foolish pride
for dashing off this morning, but it had struck her as vital
to prevent Lord Creighton from discovering their circumstances. She would *not* permit any member of her father's
family to sit in judgment on Matthew Castle! It had been
her intention to decline any offer of assistance in a dignified formal manner, complete with punctilious expressions
of gratitude designed to convince Lord Creighton that
pecuniary assistance was both unnecessary and unwelcome. She had carefully rehearsed her little speech
during the half-hour it took to reach the large stone
residence facing the park. The impressive facade and the
even more impressive individual who opened the door to
her knocking had the effect of robbing her of some of her
composure without in any way impairing her determination to complete her mission, so that when the lofty butler
had run his arctic eye over her unimpressive person and
desired her to remain in the hall while he ascertained
whether his lordship was at home, she had followed him
impulsively, fearing that an unfavorable report to his

master would result in Lord Creighton's refusal to see her. In proof of the old adage that eavesdroppers never hear good of themselves, she had arrived just in time for the phrase "three half-French brats" to assail her ears, with the result that punctilio, dignity, and even basic good manners had fled before the roaring fury that accompanied her humiliation.

Adrienne's steps slowed even more noticeably and the scowl deepened as she reviewed the scene in Lord Creighton's house. The only thing she could be thankful for was the fact that Becky had not been present, for she would have expired of mortification at her former nurseling's lack of civility. In her own defense it must be acknowledged that the provocation had been great. The taunting description had flicked her on the raw, but it was her first sight of Lord Creighton that had completed her undoing, for to her horror, the man addressed by the butler was the officious individual who had come to her rescue last week outside Madame Mireille's gambling establishment. She could only hope she had not betrayed her recognition of him. The need to master a sudden breathlessness so she might say her piece and make her escape had driven her to the brink of rudeness. It was no good telling herself that Lord Creighton's slighting reference absolved her from any duty to preserve the rules of civility. The shameful realization that she had behaved like a badly brought-up child took a firmer hold on her spirits as she increased her distance from the earl's residence.

Adrienne was so engrossed with recalling the scene just enacted that she bumped into a stout woman with her arms full of vegetables.

"*Je vous demande pardon, madame,*" she murmured, restoring a couple of turnips to the indignant woman before hurrying on.

She would take her oath that Lord Creighton had not recognized her. An irrepressible chuckle bubbled up as a picture of the two men she had recently left flashed across her mind. They had worn identical expressions of startled consternation at her unheralded appearance, but after she identified Lord Creighton, all her attention had been focused on him. She would not recognize the second man were she to meet him around the next corner, but, unhappily, the earl's handsome features were stamped on her memory. When she recalled his stubborn insistence on escorting her home on that other occasion, her heart spiraled down into her shoes and her feet dragged accordingly. A nagging fear persisted that she might have been twice as rude and still not have succeeded in diverting him from what he considered to be his duty.

A solid thump from behind brought Adrienne back to a sense of her surroundings. She apologized sweetly to the irate, gesticulating Bruxellois who had walked into her when she stopped dead. His dark eyes warming with unmistakable interest as he took a second look at her acted as a spur to set her quickly on her way again. Her ruddy hair seemed to hold a fascination for Belgian gentlemen and she had learned to take evasive action at the first sign of interest.

Miss Beckworth was in a state of nervous agitation when Adrienne arrived back at their lodgings, but she found the girl's answers to her many questions strangely bland and unsatisfactory. Yes, Adrienne had succeeded in obtaining an interview with Lord Creighton. What had she said to him? Why, just what Becky must have known she would say. She had declined to acccept any financial assistance, and yes, naturally she had expressed their deep sense of gratitude to Lady Creighton for her kind intentions. When it came to relating Lord Creighton's reaction to this turn of events or describing the man himself, Adrienne's replies became still more vague, until Miss Beckworth, under the influence of a sudden attack of intuition, decided that perhaps she'd rather not press for more detailed responses after all. The heightened color of Adrienne's normally pale clear skin had not escaped her notice, nor, during the rest of the day, did the girl's heightened awareness go unobserved. She appeared to suspend breathing while each new sound from beyond their entrance door was identified. Miss Beckworth bided her time and forbore to comment on this strange behavior, her instincts having informed her that the issue of acceptance of assistance from Lady Creighton had still perhaps to be resolved to the satisfaction of all parties.

Fortunately for the wear and tear on both ladies' nerves, this state of unresolved tension was not destined to be long-lasting. The women were already at their sewing the next morning and Luc was seated at the table working on his Latin grammar when a knock at the door signaled an end to the waiting. Anyone wishing to beat Luc to the door would have to be quick off the mark indeed, for the reluctant scholar welcomed any and all interruptions to his studies. Today he had no competition for the privilege of being first to greet a caller, since neither lady showed any inclination to bestir herself. Miss Beckworth's fingers continued their rhythmic motions, but a glance from under her lashes informed her that Adrienne's efforts had ceased and her complexion was drained of natural color as an authoritative masculine voice declared:

"I am seeking Miss Beckworth. Is this her residence?"

"Yes, *sir*!"

"Would you ask her if it is convenient to receive me? I am Colonel Lord Creighton."

Luc's eyes were popping as he accepted the colonel's card while throwing wide the door. "Yes, s-sir! She's right here. Becky!"

Watched by the silent, apprehensive girl, Miss Beckworth put aside the shirt she was hemming and rose gracefully from her chair to greet the tall man who entered after tucking the cocked hat of a staff officer under his left arm.

Pride and humiliation expunged all signs of animation from Adrienne's features as she saw the swift glance their caller cast round the shabby apartment before concentrating his polite attention on the woman advancing to meet him. She thought she detected a flicker of relief in his eyes before the polite social mask was back in place. The conviction that Becky's air of quiet good breeding came as a welcome surprise after her own unconventional eruption into his life yesterday did nothing to assuage her sore spirit, but her chin lifted in mute defiance.

"Lord Creighton, I am Anthea Beckworth," Becky was saying in her pleasant voice. "How do you do?"

Lord Creighton took the hand she offered in a warm clasp as he examined the slim attractive woman looking at him from clear hazel eyes containing an appraisal as frank as his own. He judged her to be a year or two under forty, and liked what he saw. She was good-looking with regular features and fine-grained, unlined skin, and was dressed with neatness and propriety. A lace-trimmed cap framed thick blond hair, and she wore her simple morning dress of dark blue cotton with an air of distinction. He gave her a wholehearted smile that was endearingly boyish.

"It is a pleasure to meet you, Miss Beckworth. My mother informs me that since their father died my young cousins have been in your care."

"Cousins?" Luc raised startled eyes to Lord Creighton's. "Are we cousins?"

"We have been in Becky's care since birth," Adrienne corrected haughtily.

"Adrienne, my dear, if you would clear those shirts off that chair so we might offer Lord Creighton a seat?"

Carrying out Becky's practical suggestion gave Adrienne a chance to let her heated cheeks cool. Her runaway tongue was like to earn her a scold when his lordship departed.

While the small party was disposing itself more comfortably, Luc simmered with impatience and finally burst out, "Are we really your cousins, sir? I did not know we had any relations—none that owned us, at all events."

"We are distantly related to Lord Creighton," his sister cut in before the gentleman addressed could speak for himself.

His lordship, however, was not content to have it so. "Despite your sister's reluctance to acknowledge me, we are quite nearly related," he said, smiling in a friendly fashion at the eager youth. "Our parents were first cousins." He turned the smile on Miss Beckworth. "I believe you and I meet somewhere on the family tree also, ma'am."

"A mere connection only," replied the lady, returning his smile.

The earl's expression became serious. "For our present purposes I am persuaded it would be best if we did not draw attention to the distant nature of the connection, do you not agree, ma'am?"

Before Miss Beckworth could express her probable agreement, Adrienne demanded to know what his lordship meant by "present purposes."

The earl smiled at the truculent girl and said gently, "I am referring of course to my mother's plan to assist in your return to England."

"*England*!" exclaimed Luc, pinning an accusing glare on his sister. "You *couldn't* be so . . . so *paltry* as to think of cutting out of Brussels just as the fun is about to start!"

Adrienne cast an imploring glance at Becky, but it was Lord Creighton who came unexpectedly to her rescue. "Surely it must always have been an object with Miss Beckworth to see an English family resettled in England, where you have ties. And there is your education to be thought of as well. How old are you, Cousin . . . ? I beg your pardon, but I do not seem to recall hearing your name."

Luc pronounced his name and grudgingly admitted his age while both women hastened to apologize for the oversight. Lord Creighton returned his attention to the boy, addressing him as an equal. "My name is Dominic, by the way. I can see that it must seem vastly exciting to be in the area where fighting might ensue, but I must tell you that it is no such thing for civilians. It becomes excessively crowded and uncomfortable beforehand as well as vastly expensive as commodities grow scarce. And if there should be any fighting, you would not be in a position to see it, only the suffering that comes afterward, and that, let me tell you, is not an edifying sight."

"I want to join the army!" Luc insisted with a mulish glint in near-black eyes. "Wellington will need all the soldiers he can get to beat Bonaparte. I'm big enough to fight."

For a moment the earl's gentle manner was replaced by sternness. "You may be big enough, but you are not old enough to make that choice. There may not even be any fighting in the end. No one really knows what is going to happen. Meanwhile, this is an unsettled existence for all of you." He appealed to Miss Beckworth. "How much time would you require to arrange your affairs and pack up, ma'am? There is a packet leaving Ostend on Monday. Could you be ready by then?"

"Why, yes, I should think—"

"Becky, *no*! We *cannot* allow Lord Creighton to assume our obligations. It may take a little longer but we'll get to England on our own." Adrienne ignored the colonel entirely while she pleaded with her companion.

The earl watched the young girl's *gamine* features grow impassioned, those incredibly colored eyes all but drowned in tears she refused to shed. Without understanding it, he was touched by her pride and desperation. His voice was gentle as he inquired, "Are you of age, Miss Castle?"

"I shall be shortly," she returned, not taking her eyes from Miss Beckworth, who sat twisting her hands in her lap in indecision.

He tried to conceal his surprise. "How shortly?"

"My birthday is in August." She supplied the information impatiently, her attention still on her companion.

"Is your guardianship of my cousins legal or unofficial, ma'am?" asked the earl, addressing the older woman.

Miss Beckworth smiled briefly. "Unofficial. If you had known Matthew Castle you would not have found the question necessary."

"If you have it in your mind to try to assume guardianship, my lord, let me warn you that Becky and I will not permit it. I do not think you would be able to prevail at law before I reach my majority."

Lord Creighton smiled at the defiant girl facing him. "I wish you will try to rid your mind of the notion that I intend to involve myself in your affairs except to act for my mother in the matter of arranging your transportation to England, which was, you will allow, the reason Miss Beckworth contacted Lady Creighton originally."

Color flooded into Adrienne's cheeks at this polite setdown. She opened her lips to retaliate, but Miss Beckworth intervened.

"Adrienne, dearest, I am persuaded we must accept Lord Creighton's kind offer. Our situation here in Brussels is not going to improve materially." She cast a lambent glance at the youth, who was following the conversation closely, before returning her serious gaze to his tense sister.

Adrienne took her meaning, and quite suddenly her resistance collapsed, leaving her completely dispirited. "Very well. It shall be as Lord Creighton directs." She picked up her sewing and sat back in her chair, withdrawing herself from the conversation. Luc offered a few more protests that were speedily overborne by the earl, who then insinuated himself into the boy's good graces by promising to send him reports of the military situation as it developed. Looking up in surprise, Adrienne searched his lordship's face and could not doubt his sincerity. His clear blue eyes were regarding her brother with sympathetic understanding. When they headed in her direction she dropped her own and hastily resumed her stitching, though her thoughts remained with this incomprehensible new relative, who was now discussing the practical aspects of the prospective move with Becky.

"*Ouch!*"

All heads turned to the girl, who colored up in confusion as she sucked her punctured finger.

"Are you much hurt?" inquired Lord Creighton, reaching automatically for her wrist.

"No, no!" She shook her head vigorously and pulled her hand away. "It was my own fault entirely and just the merest prick—really, my lord," as he seemed momentarily disinclined to accept her description of the injury.

"Adrienne is what is meant by the phrase 'accident prone,' " laughed her brother. "She is forever tripping over cracks or dropping things." His engaging grin took the sting out of the words, although his sister replied by sticking out the tip of a pink tongue before turning her back on him.

"A good soldier knows how to avoid an unnecessary skirmish," said Lord Creighton, rising from his chair with a mocking smile. "I shall take my leave of you before this degnerates into a family quarrel. By the way," he added, struck all at once by something missing, "I thought there were three of you. Was I misinformed?"

Adrienne answered with less constraint than she had so far demonstrated in his lordship's presence. "Our brother, Jean-Paul, is suffering from a feverish cold, so we are keeping him in bed today."

"I trust he will be recovered before Monday," replied the earl easily as he moved toward the door escorted by all three residents. "I shall look forward to meeting him then. How old is Jean-Paul?"

"He's twelve," said Miss Beckworth, offering her hand to the departing caller. "You know how children are, ailing one moment and better the next. I have every confidence that we can be ready to catch Monday's packet. Good day, my lord, and thank you."

The earl responded suitably and left to set in motion the mechanics of removing a family of four and their belongings across the English Channel. He did not in the least begrudge the effort required and was glad he had been on the spot to ease the transition for the orphans. He had been moved to sympathy by their plight, sight unseen. Meeting them had added admiration for the courage and independent spirit of the two eldest, and appreciation for the devotion of Miss Beckworth. His mother would certainly find much with which to occupy herself in trying to arrange a future for this volatile family if his brief acquaintance with the two eldest members was anything to judge by. They would need clever handling, and he congratulated himself that he had accomplished what he had set out to do in the face of determined opposition.

The earl went around feeling inordinately pleased with himself until six o'clock on Saturday evening. That was the hour at which Moulton admitted a sober and scared Luc Castle to the study where Lord Creighton was enjoying a glass of Madeira and a chess game with Major Peters.

"Luc! Is anything wrong?" The earl got slowly to his feet as the boy stood hesitating in the entrance.

"I beg pardon for intruding, sir, but we . . . we won't be

able to take the packet on Monday. Becky said I should let you know.''

"What's amiss? Has your sister refused to budge?"

"It's Jean-Paul. He's much worse, sir!" blurted the boy. "The doctor's been twice and he thinks he's got something called rheumatic fever."

"Is that serious? I've never heard of it before."

"I have, and it can be serious if not properly treated," said Major Peters to his host.

Luc swallowed with difficulty. "Becky says he'll get better, but I know she's worried. Adrienne too. She's been crying after the doctor left. She denied it, but I can always tell when Adrienne cries because the tip of her nose gets red and she glares at me."

"Here, son, sit down for a minute." The earl put his hands on the boy's shoulders and eased him into a chair. A glance at his friend sent Major Peters to a side table, where he poured something into a glass. He passed it to the earl, who pressed the glass into the youth's hand. "Drink this, Luc."

The boy took a gulp of the liquid and gasped. "Ugh!" He put the glass down hastily, but the earl picked it up and offered it again.

"It's only brandy, Luc. It will warm you a bit. When you've finished it I'll take you home." When his cousin had reluctantly accepted the glass, the earl walked over to the fireplace and pulled the bell. He addressed his friend in low tones. "I hope you'll forgive me, Ivor, but I think I'd best check up on the little boy myself. This lad's fagged to death, though he doesn't know it. I assume you've gathered by now that he is one of my newfound cousins whom I was about to pack off to England?"

"Miss Castle's brother?"

"One of them. It's the younger one who's ill. I don't know what this will mean for— Oh, there you are, Moulton," as the butler entered the room. "Send round to the stables for the carriage right away, if you please. I shall be going out as soon as it arrives." He glanced across to the other side of the fireplace where Luc was sipping at the brandy, his nose wrinkling in distaste, his eyes fixed on empty space. When the boy put down the glass a few minutes later and turned toward his host, the earl explained:

"My carriage will be here directly, Luc. I am going to drive you home."

The boy jumped up in distress. "Oh no, sir, you must not put yourself out for me! I can walk home perfectly well. I'm only sorry to have interrupted your game." He indicated the chessboard with a nod and sent a look of shy apology toward Major Peters, who was regarding him in a sympathetic fashion.

"No apologies needed, lad. I was twisting and turning in a trap and was delighted to get off before the ax fell."

Luc mustered up a slight acknowledging smile as he edged toward the door, protesting that he could not drag his cousin out at dinnertime.

"Whoa, Luc! I want to see Jean-Paul in any case, so we may as well go together. Another time will serve to give Major Peters his usual drubbing." The earl made his cousin known to his friend. While the two were in the process of exchanging bows, Moulton returned with the news that the carriage was at the door.

As the three exited the study together, Major Peters expressed the civil hope that the news of Luc's young brother would shortly be better. A worried look descended on the boy's brow again.

Lord Creighton said bracingly, "I am persuaded Jean-Paul will quickly respond to the devoted care of his sister and Miss Beckworth. Children make amazing recoveries from feverish ailments, you know."

He was repaid for this unsupported assumption by a visible lessening of the tension that held Luc in its grip. The boy even managed a polite mumble of farewell as he and his new cousin took their leave of Major Peters outside the door and climbed into the waiting carriage.

5

A scant half-hour later Lord Creighton too would have welcomed an authoritative pronouncement on the remarkable ability of children to overcome feverish ailments. By then he had met his youngest cousin under the most unpropitious circumstances, and, to his admittedly untrained eye, the boy looked exceedingly ill.

A listless Adrienne had opened the door to them. One glimpse of her pale, subdued countenance confirmed the seriousness of the situation. Lord Creighton would have given much at that moment to be greeted by the defiance and antagonism she had displayed at their previous meetings rather than the dull acceptance that characterized his reception this evening. To his queries about her brother's condition she replied readily that although his temperature had not been so elevated as to cause immediate concern, his whole body was racked by pains, now more acute in one joint, now in another. He drifted in and out of consciousness, sometimes seeming not to recognize his family. Her voice faltered at this point and a film of tears clouded her vision momentarily. She didn't even notice that the earl had taken her hand in his and was uttering awkward murmurs of sympathy while she fought for control. His request to be permitted to see Jean-Paul brought her back to the present. An expression of surprise crossed her features and lingered when her eyes dropped to their linked hands, but after a slight hesitation she drew hers out of his clasp and led the way to the sickroom.

The chamber where Jean-Paul lay was small and cramped. The dim light admitted by a single window in one corner was augmented by a branch of candles on a stand near the double bed that dominated the room. A tall painted chest opposite the bed and a wooden chair occupied by Miss Beckworth completed the meager furnishings. All this Lord Creighton assimilated in one swift impression before his eyes gravitated to the restless figure in the big bed. At fourteen, Luc Castle was half a head taller than his sister and solidly built, so the earl was unprepared for the small frame and childish appearance of the youngest member of the family. His heart went out to the flushed little boy thrashing about uncomfortably, his blue-black hair soaked with perspiration. He was aware that Miss Beckworth had glided over to join him. His eyes still on the child, he asked quietly, "Is there any improvement?"

"No, but I do not believe he is any worse, either."

They had kept their voices to mere breaths of sounds, but Jean-Paul's restless muttering intensified and he sat up suddenly.

"I'm so thirsty, Becky. Becky, where are you?"

Miss Beckworth was at the boy's side, gentling him back down onto his pillows before his hoarse mumbling could be repeated. "I'm here, my dear, and Adrienne has prepared some lemonade for you to drink."

"Adrienne?" The child opened near-black eyes like his brother's and focused on his sister filling a glass from a pitcher on the candle stand. "My throat hurts, Adrienne, and my knees ache like the devil."

"Drink this, my pet; it will help your throat. Soon it will be time for some medicine the doctor left that will make your legs feel better."

"*No!* It tastes bitter and it doesn't help." Jean-Paul shook his head fretfully and his eyes fell on the silent spectator standing at the foot of the bed. "Who's that?"

"This is our cousin Lord Creighton, whom I told you about," Adrienne replied lightly. "You would not wish him to think you have not got good botton, would you, refusing to take your medicine like a baby?"

Lord Creighton intervened as the patient scowled and looked mutinous. "I am not partial to bitter-tasting medicines myself, Cousin Jean-Paul, but if one wishes to get well *quickly,* one must screw up one's courage and obey the doctor."

"I don't like him, he's a quack," replied the boy in querulous tones.

"You don't really believe that Miss Beckworth and your sister would entrust your care to a quack, do you? You will wound their feelings if you suggest such a thing."

"I . . . I didn't mean that exactly," muttered the child, discomfited.

"Of course you did not, my dear. Here, drink your lemonade." Becky put the glass into the boy's hand and he drank it obediently, his feverish dark eyes surveying his visitor over the rim with a touch of resentment. "I ache all over," he complained.

"You will soon feel more the thing. Try to sleep now, my pet. You will feel better when you wake up."

While Adrienne soothed the little boy and made him more comfortable in the bed, Miss Beckworth led Lord Creighton out of the room.

"Are you satisfied with the medical advice you are receiving?" he inquired abruptly when they were beyond hearing distance. "Should you like me to call in another doctor?"

"Well . . ." Miss Beckworth hesitated. "Dr. Martin was recommended by our landlady. He seems competent enough, but I confess I would welcome another opinion."

"I will send Dr. Hume around to look at him tomorrow morning." Lord Creighton's assurance brought a relaxation in the tense lines of Miss Beckworth's pale countenance. She pushed a weary hand through her hair, smoothing back a strand that had come out of the simple knot at the nape of her neck.

"You cannot stay here," continued the earl, ignoring the woman's instinctive protest. He glanced around the bare, cheerless room, his eyes coming to rest on several boxes testifying to the fact that a beginning had been made on their packing before Jean-Paul's illness had brought that activity to a halt. "You can't cater to his comfort in this place. I will make arrangements to have you all conveyed to my house immediately. Then we may—"

"Lord Creighton, *please*! That is not necessary or advisable. Jean-Paul is too sick to be moved at present, and I assure you Adrienne and I will take the greatest care of him.''

"I beg your pardon, ma'am. My clumsy tongue does me a great disservice if you thought I meant to imply that he could receive better care than you and his sister will provide, but you have no facilities here, no space. You and Miss Castle will be completely done up before long. You look exhausted now. And where does Luc sleep?''

Before she knew what she was about, Miss Beckworth found herself replying to his compelling manner. "He and Jean-Paul share a room, but naturally we have moved Luc out for the duration of his brother's illness. We have made up a pallet for him out here.''

Lord Creighton was shaking his head. "It won't do. None of you will get any rest under this arrangement. I will carry Luc home with me this evening at least and return him in the morning. We will see what the doctor says then about moving Jean-Paul.''

Luc protested that he was needed to help nurse his brother and run errands for the women, but after a thoughtful interval Miss Beckworth agreed that she and Adrienne would be easier in their minds about him if they knew he were sleeping in a proper bed and eating regularly while they were so taken up with the care of his brother. She declared that they needed nothing to be fetched before morning, when Luc would be back again to assist.

Lord Creighton expected to have to defend his suggestion against arguments offered by Miss Castle before he could put it into operation, but Luc, who had gone into the room he shared with his brother to pack a change of clothing, emerged in short order with a small valise. When questioned, he replied casually that Adrienne, on hearing the proposal, had merely cautioned him not to trouble his cousin's household unnecessarily before returning to her task of bathing Jean-Paul's forehead with lavender water.

Had fast-moving events permitted advance planning, it is probable that Lord Creighton would have turned his cousin over to his reliable butler with orders to feed the boy and make him comfortable for the night. As matters stood, however, they had not covered half the distance between the two residences before he had decided to cancel his plans for the evening in order to remain at home with his guest. Luc looked as miserable as he remembered feeling his first night at Eton. The boy's spirits required supporting, and strange servants in a huge barracks of a house would contribute little toward hoisting him out of the dismals. The earl devoted his energies and not inconsiderable charm to soothing his cousin's unspoken fears for his brother before and during the consumption of a tasty meal his cook retrieved from the threatened debacle of the master's unscheduled disappearance and equally untimely reappearance over an hour later. When Luc had regretfully declined a third helping of chocolate mousse on the ample grounds of satiety, the two retired to the library, where Lord Creighton was surprised to find himself extremely hard pressed to defeat his young cousin in a lengthy game of chess. The lad went off to bed presently, much buoyed by the unstinting praise for his grasp of tactics expressed by this splendid new relative for whom he was already halfway to a case of hero worship. He was nearly asleep before his head hit the pillow.

After his guest had retired, the earl sat on in the study for a time, sipping occasionally at a glass of brandy while he pondered the situation into which he had been propelled. Between escalation of the military preparations in the area, and this unexpected responsibility for three half-grown cousins (he conveniently lumped Adrienne in with her brothers for purposes of classification), and his recent betrothal, life was suddenly fraught with interest. Here in the privacy of his own dwelling—in possibly the last moments of pure privacy he would know for an indeterminate period of time—he could admit that, had he been consulted, he would have opted for a bit less interest and more routine. His duty was clear. These pathetic newfound cousins could not be permitted to remain in their squalid surroundings under the present circumstances. His mother would expect him to provide for them, and provide for them he would, even if it meant running roughshod over his prickly female cousin's highly developed sensibilities. He must see about getting another medical opinion first thing in the morning and removing that poor child to his house as soon as medically feasible. He gathered that the boy was not in any immediate danger of his life. If he were well bundled up, a short ride in a well-sprung carriage should not set his recovery back. Miss Beckworth and Miss Castle would have servants to assist them here. Both were looking worn to a frazzle under the strain of nursing Jean-Paul. Surely Miss Beckworth was of an age to provide adequate chaperonage for Adrienne under his roof, and herself was enough older than he to give rise to no malicious whispers on that head. It was a trifle awkward, of course, but the best solution he could contrive in the present emergency.

Lord Creighton's brow furrowed as he realized his personal plans would have to be altered. His engagement dinner party must be postponed for a time. It would be inappropriate to have any kind of revelry in the house until he knew Jean-Paul to be on the mend. He must arrange to call on his fiancée first thing tomorrow, or at least as soon as he had contacted Dr. Hume and sent him to the Castles'. He hated to disappoint his lovely Pamela, but she would appreciate the necessity. The frown smoothed out of his forehead as he pictured Pamela's beautiful smiling mouth and soft amber eyes. His own eyes brightened with eagerness momentarily as he glanced at the clock on the mantel. Ten-forty-five. Perhaps it wasn't too late to try to catch up with her on the social round. Anticipation faded as he tried in vain to recall which receptions she had planned to attend this evening, and was entirely extinguished when his glance fell on his informal dress and crumpled cravat. By the time he had changed into suitable attire . . . He sighed, settling deeper into the overstuffed chair. Better leave it till tomorrow. He would have something definite to tell her by then.

It was nearly noon when Lord Creighton entered the drawing room of the modest lodgings Sir Ralph Morrison had hired recently. If he was disappointed to find both tenants in occupation at the moment, he concealed his feelings behind a social smile that warmed as his gaze rested on the beautiful face of his fiancée.

"Good morning, my dear." He bent over her hand, keeping it in his after pressing a kiss on her palm while he greeted his future brother-in-law with a bow. "Servant, Sir Ralph."

The bow was reciprocated by the immaculately turned-out gentleman raising a glass of sherry to his lips. Lady Tremayne's lips moved into a provocative pout that increased her appeal, if possible. Her voice had a slightly breathless husky quality that never failed to intrigue him. "I should scold you, Dominic, for failing to appear at the Montroses' last night, conduct vastly unbecoming to a newly betrothed man, but I shall demonstrate my forgiving nature by inviting you to lunch instead."

"Thereby intensifying my feelings of guilt," said Lord Creighton with a rueful smile. "I hope your evening was enjoyable."

"Without your saving presence I'm afraid I found it tedious." Long curling lashes swept up, enhancing amber-brown eyes of a rare brilliance that sparkled invitingly in a face of classic perfection. A wealth of dark brown hair arranged today in a coronet lent regal grace to her proudly held head.

"And yet you contrived to amuse yourself tolerably well, I observed, my dear." The insinuating sauvity of Sir Ralph's voice acted on the earl's ears like chalk squealing across a slate, but his sister replied indifferently:

"You know I always contrive to amuse myself, Ralph, but Creighton's presence eliminates the need for contrivance. Can you stay for lunch, Dominic?"

Lord Creighton responded with a gratified smile to the eagerness in his fiancée's manner. "Thank you, I'll be delighted."

If he hoped to discover Sir Ralph with a previous engagement that would allow him to rejoice in Lady Tremayne's exclusive company, Lord Creighton was doomed to disappointment, for the former got lazily to his feet when luncheon was announced and followed the engaged pair into the small dining room. There was nothing for it, since he could not remain past lunchtime, than to acquaint Pamela with the changes in his situation in the presence of her brother. He needed more time than would be provided by a quick private farewell to explain the sequence of events that made it necessary to postpone their betrothal dinner.

Although he had every confidence that she would understand and approve his actions, he found himself unsure of exactly how best to phrase the news, which was bound to prove upsetting at first. A wry smile twisted one corner of his mouth as he confessed:

"I fear I am about to require more proof of your forgiving nature, my dear."

For a second Pamela's lovely features seemed to freeze into lifelessness; then she smiled blindingly, dispelling the illusion. "Are you about to tell me you cannot after all escort me to the Amberlys' rout party tonight?" she asked in tones of mock despair as she sliced a piece off one of the cheeses the butler had left when he cleared the remains of their luncheon. She offered it to Lord Creighton, who accepted it automatically, saying in surprise:

"Had we made plans to go there tonight? I'm glad you mentioned it, for I had not remembered. Certainly we shall go if you would like it, my dear." He shook his head. "No, what I have to tell you is the result of a promise I made to my mother to act for her in the assistance of some young relatives." He recounted the story of his mother's letter and his first meeting with his unknown cousins, omitting any reference to Adrienne's impulsive call at his house, before describing his plan for their journey to England. His listeners made no interruptions, giving him the courtesy of their complete attention until he came to Luc's visit acquainting him with Jean-Paul's illness.

"So you see, all my plans for their removal are now in abeyance until the boy is fit for travel." His brow darkened with worry. "He is a very sick youngster at the moment. I had Hume go over him this morning, and he confirms the Belgian doctor's diagnosis. I am having him brought to my house this afternoon. I trust he will make a complete recovery, but you can see that it will be necessary to postpone our dinner party until—"

"Postpone our engagement dinner?" Dismay sounded in Lady Tremayne's voice. "Why on earth should that be necessary? And why is it necessary to have the boy conveyed to your house at all? Surely it is better not to move him if he is dangerously ill." She had her voice under control by the end as she posed this reasonable objection.

"If you had seen the place where they have been living, you wouldn't ask that. It is totally inadequate for nursing an invalid. His sister and Miss Beckworth are worn to the bone already. I am happy to be able to put the resources of my house at their disposal during this critical time, though, as you say, one doesn't like to move a sick person. In this case it is imperative, however. I will be supervising Jean-Paul's removal myself shortly."

"I must of course accept your judgment of the necessity of taking in these children and their guardian temporarily," Lady Tremayne conceded, forming her words carefully, "but I don't understand why it should be necessary to postpone our dinner party. Surely your house is large enough that a few guests won't disturb the sickroom."

Lord Creighton waved this aside, a puzzled expression on his amiable features. "It isn't a question of noise penetrating a sickroom, my dear," he said gently. "I'm sure you will agree that we could not give our engagement announcement the happy atmosphere it deserves while Jean-Paul's condition is so critical."

"I must beg to differ with you," Lady Tremayne retorted coolly. "These children are strangers to you. You are more than doing your duty in providing them with temporary shelter. They have, after all, no claim on your generosity."

Sir Ralph, seeing the blank look of shock on his future brother-in-law's face, shot his sister a quelling glance and said in placating tones, "Well, a few days' delay is of no moment in the long run. Children recover quickly from illness."

Lord Creighton looked at Sir Ralph with gratitude for his intervention. "We must hope so." He turned back to his fiancée. "I am desolated to have to disappoint you, Pamela. I don't like to delay the announcement either, but

I must accept that these children have a legitimate claim on me as my mother's deputy."

"Yes, of course," she agreed, making handsome amends with an intimate smile. "My own disappointment made me less than generous. You wouldn't be the man I chose if your generosity and kindness couldn't be aroused by your mother's request."

The earl's delightful smile rewarded his love. "Thank you, my dear. Naturally I am prepared to do my mother's bidding, but I want to help the children for their own sakes too. You'll understand when you meet them. And now I must rush off, I'm afraid, to set the wheels in motion to receive my guests."

All three rose and left the dining room, Sir Ralph heading back into the salon to allow his sister a moment of privacy in which to bid her betrothed adieu. Lord Creighton promptly took advantage of this tactful gesture by enfolding Lady Tremayne in a warm embrace. She raised her face for his kiss willingly. It was several minutes later that she broke away with a light laugh.

"If you are going to kiss me like that, Dominic, I can only trust that nothing delays our engagement much longer."

"You don't know how I long to make you my own," Lord Creighton muttered a trifle thickly.

Lady Tremayne's smile was edged with triumph. "I think I do," she murmered provocatively, "because it is the same with me. Good-bye for now, dearest."

There was no smile in evidence a moment later when Lady Tremayne entered the drawing room and cast a wary eye on her brother tapping his foot impatiently by the window, where he had been observing Lord Creighton's departure.

"That was not very well done of you, Pamela," he remarked acidly.

The slim, exquisite figure in the rose-colored muslin gown leaned back against the closed door, her chin at a defiant tilt. "Nonsense, he is besotted with me."

"He's thoroughly infatuated, I'll grant you, but he also believes you to be a model of sweetness and light. If you will accept some advice, dear sister, may I respectfully suggest that you refrain from showing your true colors until you have his ring safely on your finger?''

"Well, he surprised me with that lame excuse to postpone the annoucement," she replied defensively. "Any woman might be pardoned for being annoyed. I smoothed it over.''

"Thanks to me, you were able to make a recovery, but Creighton is no fool. You could still lose him.''

"I can handle Dominic. Leave him to me. You concentrate on keeping any whispers of our difficulties from spreading.''

Sir Ralph left the window and advanced slowly toward the middle of the room, eyeing his lovely sister with curiosity. "Do you have any feelings at all for Creighton?''

She shrugged. "I like him well enough. If you must know, I wouldn't consider marrying him or anybody else if Tremayne hadn't left me without a feather to fly with. Widowhood suits me. If the dibs were in tune I'd enjoy the freedom." She sighed resignedly. "Since they aren't, I'll marry Dominic instead.''

"And I'll ride on his coattails. He's not the type to let his relatives languish in debtors' prison, thank God!''

"Are matters very pressing?" she asked anxiously.

He grimaced. "Let's just say I'd like to wring that wretched brat's neck for getting sick at this moment in time.''

"Perhaps I'd better offer to nurse him," laughed Pamela. "That should convince Dominic that my heart is in the right place.''

Sir Ralph's thin-lipped mouth widened into a smiling sneer. "Coming it much too rare and thick, my girl. You just continue to nurse Creighton along. The brat already has a sister and a guardian to coddle him.''

"I had forgotten about the sister," said Lady Tremayne thoughtfully. "I'll check up on her when I see Dominic tonight.''

"Just mind that you don't loose that serpent's tongue of yours again," warned Sir Ralph sharply.

6

A soft knocking roused Adrienne from her rapt
contemplation of the red coals in the fireplace. After a
swift glance at the still figure in the big bed, she made her
way to the door, admitting a diminutive maid bearing a
pitcher and a covered dish on a silver tray.

"The chef thought as how you might like something to
eat later, Mademoiselle Castle," she explained in a whisper
as she advanced to set the tray on a table near the bed, "so
he sent up some of his special fruitcake along with Master
Jean-Paul's lemonade."

"How very thoughtful of him. You must convey my
thanks to him, please, Marie."

"How is he tonight, mademoiselle?" inquired the maid
as she softly collected an empty pitcher and some dirty
glasses and prepared to depart.

"He was very restless earlier this evening, but he's been
sleeping quietly for two hours now."

"Perhaps that is a good sign, mademoiselle."

"We'll hope so, Marie. I'm afraid our coming here has
meant a great deal of extra work for the household. You
should have been in bed hours ago."

"That's all right, Mademoiselle Castle. The master has
arranged that I am free in the mornings so I can sleep late.
It's just gone midnight, and I'll be off to my bed now. Is
there anything else you need before I go?"

"No, thank you, Marie. Good night."

Adrienne stood motionless in the center of the room for
a time after the maid had gone before making her way
back to the chair by the fireplace. They had been installed
in Lord Creighton's house three days ago and had been
treated with every consideration. At the back of her mind

was a nugget of resentment that they should have been compelled to accept charity from her father's family, but the exigencies of their situation prevented giving in to any inclination to dig at it. For Jean-Paul's sake she was prepared to sink her pride completely, and her gratitude toward Lord Creighton was ungrudging at this point. She freely acknowledged that his concern for their plight stemmed from his own kind nature rather than any sense of *noblesse oblige*. It would be up to them to keep their demands on his willing largess to a minimum, but she couldn't think about the future at this stage. Her eyes traveled almost reluctantly over to the small figure of her brother, beginning to move sporadically in his sleep.

If only she could convince herself that there was some real improvement, however slight, in his condition, but sadly, that wasn't the case. The pains in various parts of his body were still severe and the episodes of delirium had not abated. Each time she hoped a period of quiet sleep might have signaled the end to the fever, she was proved wrong within an hour or two. As was the case now, she predicted with a sigh. He would be waking soon, hot and flushed with fever and crying with the pains in his limbs. She must steel herself to deal with it all and not think about the aching tiredness of her own limbs. She recognized this was due more to frustration and the struggle to keep despair at bay than to actual physical fatigue. She and Becky split the nursing chores between them, but Lord Creighton's servants did all the rest. They no longer had to concern themselves with meal preparations, laundry, or fetching supplies. Everything moved on silent greased wheels in their cousin's house.

They had seen very little of Lord Creighton since their arrival at Rue Ducale. He was occupied with his military duties of course, and a sickroom was no place for a man in any case. Becky reported that he inquired for Jean-Paul daily, but Adrienne, having insisted on taking on the tedious task of night nursing, generally spent the daylight hours resting in her room. She hadn't even been all over the house yet, but there was no denying it was an enormous establishment for a lone bachelor—fortunately for the

Castles, she reminded herself quickly. Once she had met him coming in as she was leaving for the short daily walk that Becky insisted she take for exercise and fresh air. Their conversation had consisted of a brief exchange concerning Jean-Paul's condition and Lord Creighton's polite inquiry into her comfort in his house, which she had responded to with equal politeness and even greater brevity.

"Adrienne, my head hurts and my arms ache."

At the first fretful whimpers from the bed Adrienne had risen, and now she glided over to smooth the dark hair back from her brother's damp forehead.

"I'll bathe your face for you, my pet, so you will feel cooler. And Marie has just brought some delicious lemonade that the cook prepared especially for you. Would you like some now?"

"I'm tired of lemonade." Jean-Paul rolled his head away from her ministering hands, but the cool damp cloth felt too good to resist, so he soon quieted his movements without being pressed to do so.

"Would you like a glass of water instead?"

"No. I don't like water."

"Then it will have to be lemonade," she replied with a professional cheeriness that irritated Jean-Paul. The irritability was part of his illness, and Becky and Adrienne had girded themselves to deal with it patiently. When she presented the glass of lemonade, Jean-Paul downed its contents thirstily despite his earlier complaints.

"Does that feel good on your throat?"

"Yes, no . . . I don't know. I wish my head would stop aching."

"It's time for your medicine now, my pet. That will help your head."

"*No*, I don't want it! It's nasty!" Jean-Paul began to cry, and Adrienne feared it was going to be even more difficult than usual to get the bitter-tasting draft down his throat. She was stirring the mixture when a discreet knock sounded, followed by soft masculine tones.

"Might I be of assistance? I heard voices as I passed the door and thought I would just pop in and wish Cousin

Jean-Paul good night." As Lord Creighton approached the bed, coming within range of the candles on the nightstand, the eyes of brother and sister widened in silent tribute to his magnificent appearance in full-dress uniform. The hilt of his dress sword gleamed in the candlelight, as did his fair hair when he sat down by the side of the bed. The fringed sash rippled slightly as he calmly appropriated the glass Adrienne was holding.

"Drink it up, lad. It will help relieve your aches and pains." The words were softly spoken but there was an air about the colonel that discouraged disobedience. The little boy swallowed his medicine without further verbal protest, though his feelings were written clearly on his tearstained face. Adrienne asked their cousin to support the patient's shoulders while she swiftly turned his pillows.

"There, now, that must feel cooler," said Lord Creighton. "You go back to sleep now, lad, and you'll feel better in the morning."

Jean-Paul's eyes were already closing as his large cousin settled him on his pillows again. The two adults watched in silence while the rhythm of his breathing gradually steadied. When Adrienne raised her eyes at last, it was to find Lord Creighton regarding her with compassion. He pointed toward the fireplace, and she led him away from the bed after extinguishing all but one candle.

It was a strange feeling to be sitting around a fire in the middle of the night in a strange house with a stranger who had taken over the ordering of her life. A little shudder passed through Adrienne's slight frame as a sense of unreality plagued her.

"You're cold. Shall I build up the fire or fetch you a shawl?"

Adrienne's hand went out to the stranger's arm when he would have opened the fire screen. "No, please, I'm not cold, I promise you I'm not, my lord."

Again the soft voice and the air of command. "I am your cousin Dominic, nor your lord, my child."

"And I am not a child, Cousin Dominic." Adrienne's voice had regained its customary assurance. If there was also a suspicious tartness, the earl chose not to recognize it as he made her a token bow. "I stand corrected, Cousin Adrienne. Is there any improvement in Jean-Paul tonight?"

The transitory defiance evaporated like morning mist. Her sigh barely reached him across the three feet of space between their chairs. "I don't think so."

"The fever will break soon. I am sure of it." Lord Creighton put all the confidence of which he was capable into his words, in a desire to comfort this courageous child. Something inside him was pressed to the point of pain at the sight of the slight, resolute figure in the limp, faded gown sitting opposite him, her hair glowing in the firelight, sending out sparks that rivaled the flames. There was no other sign of vitality about her tonight. Those remarkable blue-green eyes were shadowed, and he was forcibly reminded of a small woodland creature braced for a life-and-death struggle against a predator. At that moment he knew the frustration of utter helplessness. If any action of his could bring back some of the eager life he had glimpsed at their first meeting, he would gladly perform it without counting the cost. She was too old to be offered the comfort of his physical touch, though it was a torment to keep his arms at his sides, and she was too young to accept the wisdom of the ages if it stressed acceptance of adversity and loss. She was devoting all her young strength of purpose to nursing her brother, but fear was eating away at the core of her strength. No words seemed adequate to comfort her. As a distraction he mentioned idly that he had taken Luc with him to the field marshal's headquarters that day.

Quick alarm darkened the girl's eyes as they flashed to his in protest. "Oh, please, cousin, do not encourage Luc to associate with the military! You do not know how obsessed he has been with joining the army."

"I think I do know," he replied, to surprise her. "Unless I am greatly mistaken, that obsession of Luc's lies behind your somewhat belated decision to return to your own country. Believe me, you are refining too much on a boy's romantic notions of glory. His interest is natural enough at his age, but Luc knows he is too young to enlist. I promise you I will keep a very close eye on him.''

Adrienne watched the firelight play over the face of her new relation as he sat at ease among the shadows of the dimly lighted bedchamber. In full light his fair coloring and charming smile made an immediate impact on an observer, but now with the flickering shadows casting the bones of his head into relief, emphasizing the solid structure of his jaw and the strength of his broad forehead, Adrienne accepted the evidence that his surface amiability was an attractive facade for a character of bedrock strength. He sat quietly under her searching examination, and there was understanding in the partially veiled eyes noting the small signs of relaxation in her taut posture as she mentally shifted some of the burdens she had been carrying onto his broad shoulders.

"I hope you will trust me in this matter?" He held her glance and was pleased when hers did not waver.

"Yes, I trust you, Cousin Dominic."

"Good." Strong white teeth gleamed in the firelight as the earl rose unhurriedly. For a moment his hand closed over Adrienne's shoulder in a friendly clasp on his way to the door. "I'll leave you to your vigil, my dear, with the hope that Jean-Paul will be over the worst very shortly now. I will not suggest alllowing someone else to sit up with him because I know you would not consider it, but try to get some rest on the daybed over there. The night hours seem very long when one is waiting. Good night, Adrienne."

"Good night, D-Dominic."

Lord Creighton headed for his own quarters, thankful for the chance that had brought him past the sickroom when Jean-Paul had been awake and coherent. Tonight he and his prickly female cousin had reached an understanding, and optimism surged through him that this unexpected episode should end happily. He was convinced that the child would recover his health in time. Transferring the youngster to England would have to wait, of course, but there was no reason why the expanded household should not be able to dwell together amicably during the interim. His thoughtful expression dissolved into amusement as he recalled Adrienne's hesitant use of his name in bidding him good night. Funny, he had not noticed before that her English was at all accented, but he had detected the slightest trace of a French intonation in the way she pronounced his name just now. He rather liked it.

He liked it rather less the following afternoon, however, when a somewhat breathless enunciation of his name heralded her untimely entrance into the study.

"*Dominic,* oh, Dominic, the fever has broken at last! Ohhh, I . . . I beg your pardon!"

At the first vibrant words two figures broke apart from a close embrace and Lord Creighton called, "No, Adrienne, don't go!"

As the girl hesitated in the doorway, her cheeks crimson with embarrassment, he led a faintly smiling dark-haired woman across the room toward her, never removing his arm from about the woman's elegant waist. "That's wonderful news about Jean-Paul," he declared warmly. "Pamela, my dear, may I present my cousin Miss Adrienne Castle? Adrienne, this is my fiancée, Lady Tremayne."

"How do you do, ma'am?" When Adrienne dipped a polite curtsy, Lady Tremayne produced a soprano trill of laughter and extended her fingers to the girl.

"Please, Miss Castle, I am not so much older than you as to warrant such a mark of respect."

Adrienne allowed her fingers to be taken for the correct half-second while hotly aware that the color flushing her skin was intensified under the assessing stare of the well-dressed brunette. Lord Creighton, who seemed to notice nothing amiss in his cousin's tongue-tied embarrassment or his betrothed's smiling watchfulness, remarked with engaging smugness, "I had a feeling last night that Jean-Paul would shortly turn the corner. Are the aches and pains gone too?"

"Not entirely, but he is more comfortable and demanding food, which is *such* a relief. I had just gone to check with Becky on arising, and now I must go to the kitchen to order a meal to be prepared for him. If you will excuse me, Lady Tremayne, Cousin Dominic?"

"No, stay a moment, Adrienne, please," begged the earl

as the young girl began to edge backward toward the door. "Lady Tremayne actually came to call on you and Miss Beckworth this afternoon, with no expectation of seeing me. It was just a fortunate accident that brought me back to the house at the same time."

Adrienne had been all too conscious of a cool amber-eyed regard from her cousin's stunningly beautiful fiancée, so she didn't miss the sudden intimate exchange of glances between the engaged pair. Her eyes fell as the uncomfortable feeling of being *de trop* held her awkwardly in place, but the earl was going on cheerfully:

"I regret that I must return directly to headquarters, but perhaps you might offer Pamela tea, my child, so the two of you may have a chance to become acquainted."

"Of course, cousin," she murmured dutifully, keeping her eyes averted for fear he would divine her impulse to slay him where he stood beaming paternal goodwill impartially on both women.

Lady Tremayne came unexpectedly to the rescue. Tucking her hand under the earl's elbow in a consciously proprietary gesture, she looked up at him with a confiding air. "I very much fear, dearest Dominic, that I have chosen an inopportune moment to call on Miss Castle and Miss Beckworth. I am persuaded Miss Castle would prefer to offer me tea at a more convenient time." Her understanding smile played over both members of her audience, and Adrienne's heartbeats increased as she prayed that her reluctance to engage her cousin's fiancée tête-à-tête was not as apparent as she feared. "Besides," Lady Tremayne was explaining brightly, "now that the dear little boy is on the mend at last, Dominic and I must discuss a new date for our betrothal dinner." The smile she focused on Adrienne showed small even white teeth but did not reach those cool alert eyes. "You must know that your brother's illness necessitated a postponement of the official announcement of our engagement," she added in careless explanation before redirecting the smile at Lord Creighton. "So, if you will kindly escort me to my carriage, Dominic, I will beg Miss Castle's indulgence in setting another time for feminine tea-drinking."

Adrienne's shoulders went back in unconscious reaction to the sweetly issued challenge. The earl looked at her expectantly. "Would you be free to take tea with Becky and me tomorrow afternoon, Lady Tremayne?" she invited with unsmiling civility.

"Thank you, Miss Castle, I shall be delighted. I'll look forward to furthering our acquaintance at that time."

Adrienne murmured appropriately and excused herself to go to the kitchen, forcing her feet to a measured tread that would not proclaim her sense of escape.

The kitchen staff was elated to hear of the invalid's improvement and set about with a will to prepare a meal to tempt his returning appetite. Adrienne thanked them before retracing her steps to her bedchamber. She really ought to go straight in to Becky to acquaint her with the fact that they were to entertain Dominic's betrothed at tea on the morrow, but she passed the sickroom without entering, her feet carrying her to her own apartment next along the corridor. She had a few words with Marie, who was just finishing the routine cleaning of the room.

When the maid departed, Adrienne stood before the dressing table staring at her reflection without seeing it, since a vision of Lady Tremayne was superimposed over her own, signaling that the memory of the awkward scene in the study could no longer be kept at bay. *That* ought to teach her to control the impulsiveness so wisely deplored by Becky! If she had waited for permission to enter after her perfunctory tap on the paneled door, she would have been spared this uncomfortable conviction of having blundered tactlessly, but no, her one thought on seeing the blessed improvement in Jean-Paul had been to share it with Dominic, and she had raced down the stairs to inquire from Moulton if his lordship was at home. It was typical of her to have flown to the study immediately on being advised of her cousin's whereabouts, without bothering to check whether it was convenient for him to receive her. This was the second time she had barged in unannounced on Dominic, and on both occasions she had reaped her just deserts in embarrassment.

Tentative fingers crept up to her mouth without

conscious will. She had never before witnessed a passionate embrace between a man and a woman, and she had found herself unaccountably weak in the knees, a rare happening she couldn't attribute to running down only one flight of stairs. In addition to this passing weakness, she had been too stunned initially to effect a quick retreat. Again she regretted that impulsive streak. If she had waited to speak until properly in the room, she might have managed to withdraw unseen. Instead she had been forced to suffer an introduction to the lovely poised woman who was her cousin's betrothed, under circumstances that forcibly brought home to her the Castles' anomalous position in his life. Had she been previously informed of the existence of a fiancée, she would have been prepared for Lady Tremayne's loveliness; at the very least she could have avoided appearing at such a personal disadvantage. Her eyes dwelt in sudden disgust on the outmoded and patently inexpensive gown that covered her slimness. Thanks to Becky's dressmaking talents it fit her well enough, but she could not regard her appearance as anything but dowdy after meeting the elegant Lady Tremayne.

Dominic's intended bride had been absolutely stunning in a pomona-green carriage dress of a lightweight cambric ornamented by rows of self-frills around the hem. Pale yellow silk gloves of openwork had matched a hat of satin straw set at a jaunty angle atop smooth dark hair pulled back from her face and confined in a swirl at the nape of her regally held head. She was tall for a woman and carried her marvelous figure proudly. She and Dominic had made a handsome pair whose combined magnificence had rendered Adrienne insignificant to the point of invisibility.

This was the conclusion she came to after an intent scrutiny of her nondescript features in the mirror. Adrienne had never really considered her physical attributes seriously. There had been little incentive to do so in the past. Her mother had died before she was sixteen and she had slipped into maturity with no one taking much notice. With the exception of two brief periods of affluence when her father's luck had been running strong, their life had been a day-to-day existence for the most part. The boys' futures were much more important than hers. That was the overriding concern that motivated Becky and herself always.

"And nothing has changed," she reminded the downcast girl in the looking glass. "It doesn't signify if you are cast in the shade by Lady Tremayne and every other lady presently in Brussels. All that matters is that you and Becky, with Dominic's assistance, should succeed in transporting the boys safely to England."

With this restatement of her priorities hopefully assimilated, Adrienne left her bedchamber and proceeded to Jean-Paul's room, where she informed Becky of the experience that awaited them on the morrow. She congratulated herself that she had kept her voice uninflected, but since she had her head down, making work by unnecessarily straightening out the patient's bedcovers, she missed the sharp glance Becky sent her way.

"I had no idea Lord Creighton was betrothed," admitted the older woman. "What is she like?"

"Very beautiful and exceedingly fashionable."

"Her title would indicate that she is a widow."

"It had not occurred to me before, but of course that must be the case," conceded Adrienne, looking rather doubtful. "She seems very young to be a widow."

"How young?"

"At a guess, four- or five-and-twenty, but you know I am no good at this sort of thing."

"Perhaps her husband was a military man who was killed during the Peninsular campaign."

No response to Miss Beckworth's speculation was demanded of Adrienne, since a maid arrived at that moment with Jean-Paul's meal, and all attention shifted to the little boy. For the first time in over a sennight his nurses had no need to coax him into taking a little nourishment. To their satisfaction, he wolfed down everything on the tray, even requesting another serving of the chef's special lemon pudding.

While Becky was involved in making the patient comfortable after his meal, Adrienne drifted back to her own room to do some mending, and if the truth were known, to forestall any further discussion of Dominic's fiancée. They were to have the dubious pleasure of entertaining Lady Tremayne at tea tomorrow. That would be soon enough to think about the ravishing brunette. Adrienne's cogitations failed to supply a logical reason why she was so persuaded that knowing Lady Tremayne would not prove to be a pleasure, nor did she succeed in banishing the woman from her thoughts. Her brain was imprinted with a clear image of the lovely brunette's faint smile with its hint of condescension and those strange amber-colored eyes that remained cool and watchful even when she was displaying all of her perfect teeth in an engaging smile. The motions of the needle going in and out of the cloth had lost their even rhythm this afternoon.

Adrienne was grateful for the distraction provided by one of the footmen, who knocked with a message from Lord Creighton which had just been delivered from army headquarters. Evidently the business of setting a new date for this famous betrothal dinner had not occupied a great deal of his time, she mused idly, giving the young footman an absentminded smile that caused him to straighten his shoulders, a reaction completely lost on Adrienne, who was busy perusing the note's contents. It seemed the earl planned on dining at home this evening and desired the company of herself and Miss Beckworth at dinner.

A thoughtful Adrienne nodded dismissal to the silent footman, who had waited to see if an answer would be required. The door had barely closed behind him before she dashed across the room to the mammoth armoire and peered inside. From the gathering frown creasing her smooth forehead, one would have imagined she had expected her meager wardrobe to have increased by some regenerative process in the dark confines of the cupboard. She flicked through the few gowns hanging there with reluctant fingers that seemed to fear contagion. The solid armoire shivered a bit from the force with which its door was shut as Adrienne expressed her disgust with the results of her search. Five minutes' exposure to the exquisitely costumed Lady Tremayne had served to highlight the deplorable state of her own wardrobe. She possessed nothing fit to be worn in the same room with her sartorially perfect cousin.

Adrienne's blue-green eyes reflected bewilderment and a wistfulness that approached unhappiness as she gazed around the large room with its handsome appointments and rich fabrics at windows and bed. A sense of unreality threatened to overwhelm her. The improvident Castles didn't belong in this mileu. What were they doing in a mansion as guests of a relative of whose very existence they had been ignorant less than a fortnight ago? She sighed as her fingers absently assessed the heaviness of the blue brocaded bed draperies, then shook her head to clear it. What a difference twenty-four hours could make on one's perceptions, she marveled. Yesterday she had been too engrossed with Jean-Paul's battle to overcome his frightening illness to give any thought to the incongruity of their present existence, but today the fever had broken and she had met Dominic's beautiful fiancée. Yesterday she would have declared the peak of her earthly happiness to be her brother's complete recovery, but today she had permitted the concomitant relief and exhilaration following on the beginnings of this desired state to be dimmed within minutes by her presentation to a woman who would have little or no impact on her life. Could anything be more nonsensical? Clearly she had been suffering from some form of temporary mental aberration.

The cloud of dissatisfaction disappeared from Adrienne's countenance as the natural buoyancy that characterized the Castles surmounted the strangely oppressive feelings that had tormented her since the brief incident in the study. It would be delightful to have dinner with their splendid new cousin and to hear all the latest social and military news from one in a position to know. Her step was jaunty as she went back to the armoire to take out the first gown her questing fingers contacted. It was certainly beyond question that the Castles were out of their element in Dominic's house, but it would be sheer lunacy not to enjoy the benefits, however temporary, of their stay.

When Marie came in a few minutes later to assist Miss Castle to dress for dinner, her kind heart was pleased to note that her young mistress was humming a lively air as she greeted her with a sunny smile.

7

Saving the unavoidable absence of the youngest Castle, the earl found himself dining with all members of his newly enlarged family for the first time that evening. Abruptly released from the burden of fear, the youngsters' spirits bubbled over, infecting their host and threatening the bounds of decorum on more than one occasion, until restrained by a timely word from Miss Beckworth. The calm good sense and quiet charm of this lady, glimpsed briefly by Lord Creighton at their first meeting, was again in evidence. He noted with satisfaction the absence of tension in the line of her jaw and the softening of her lips in repose, which, with a new sparkle in the clear eyes, took several years from her age. As his smiling glance played between the gentle Miss Beckworth and the vibrant brother and sister, he realized how little he merited the solicitous sympathy Pamela had extended on the misfortune of having his house overrun by strangers. It would not be overstating the case to admit he was in full expectation of deriving considerable enjoyment from the novel experience of having such lively relations in residence.

The youngsters bombarded him for news of the current doings in military and social circles. Luc, displaying a surprising grasp on the situation for one so young, questioned him closely on progress in bringing the available artillery up to a respectable figure.

Lord Creighton smiled lazily at the eager boy before raising his wineglass to his lips. "No commander ever feels his needs are being treated adequately by the War Office. If the Duke get half of what he has demanded he'll consider himself well-served, though I wouldn't bruit that about, young Luc."

"Of course not, cousin." An expression of haughty pride made Luc look older suddenly. It was gone *à l'instant,* but the earl was not sorry Adrienne had been absorbed in conversation with Miss Beckworth at the time. Her present peace of mind concerning her brother, only recently acquired, would be jolted by signs that he was growing up more rapidly than she could wish. By the time her attention returned to the men, Luc's face wore the familiar half-adoring look of boyish eagerness as Lord Creighton mentioned that King William had at long last placed his Dutch-Belgian army under the field marshal's command.

For the first time since their arrival at the earl's mansion Adrienne was eating with enjoyment. She glanced up from the *côtelette d'agneau glacée* she had been demolishing with relish, to encounter Dominic's smiling gaze. There was in his attractive smile an element she would have been hard pressed to put a name to but which caused her to pause involuntarily. Before she could become conscious of embarrassment or curiosity, Dominic was speaking easily:

"Thanks to Moulton I have been most fortunate in securing the services of an adequate cook, do you not agree, cousin?"

"Oh, more than adequate, sir," Miss Beckworth protested before Adrienne could speak, "and most obliging too, considering the increased and varied demands that our precipitate arrival has placed on your kitchen."

"I am happy to hear that my kitchen staff is resourceful," replied the earl, bowing slightly in Miss Beckworth's direction, "since I plan to give a small dinner party next week to formally announce my betrothal. Do you think, ma'am, that you would have time to confer with the chef concerning the menu? I would not dream of asking if it would deprive Jean-Paul of any attention. You must be quite truthful in telling me this, please."

"I would be delighted to assist you in this matter, sir. Now that Jean-Paul is finally on the mend we shall soon get into a more comfortable routine. When is your dinner to be?"

"I thought next Thursday, if that is convenient for you and Cousin Adrienne?"

Adrienne, who had kept her eyes on Becky's serene features during this conversation, glanced up in surprise. "Me?" she echoed blankly. "What does your party have to do with me? I won't be there."

The earl's eyes narrowed but his voice was as pleasant as ever. "Of course you will be there. Why should you imagine otherwise?" He watched the dimpled chin elevate as she girded herself for battle. Wide aquamarine eyes met narrowed blue ones squarely.

"We didn't come here to do the social bit, as you must know, Cousin Dominic. My job is to nurse my brother. Besides," she finished on a strangely triumphant note, "I cannot dine with your friends; I have nothing suitable to wear."

"Adrienne—"

"That's easily remedied," Lord Creighton replied equably, over Miss Beckworth's interjection. "I am persuaded there is ample time to have a gown made by Thursday week."

Adrienne gasped. "You cannot be seriously offering to *buy* me a gown—it would be most improper—nor can you expect me to expend our limited resources on such frivolity."

"Adrienne, you are forgetting—"

"One moment, ma'am," interposed his lordship, raising a hand to stop Miss Beckworth, while he looked pointedly at Moulton, who was standing by the server affecting deafness, his back obligingly to the diners. "Shall we continue this discussion later in the saloon?"

"I must get back to Jean-Paul."

"Yes, of course." Ignoring the girl's flat statement, the older woman rose from the table after a quick glance assured her that Adrienne and Luc had finished eating.

Miss Beckworth wasted no time in rounding upon her female charge once they were established in the saloon, waving her to a seat when Adrienne reiterated her intention of returning to her brother's bedside. "Luc will like to sit with Jean-Paul for an hour or so, will you not, Luc?"

Happy to avoid what he suspected would turn into an uncomfortable discussion, Luc hastily agreed and took himself off.

"Now, what was that little scene all about?" inquired Miss Beckworth, seating herself calmly in a green velvet *bergère* and fixing the young girl with a penetrating eye as she reluctantly subsided onto a matching chair.

"It was certainly not my intention to create a scene," Adrienne muttered defensively before going on the attack. "Can you really expect me to allow Lord Creighton to purchase a gown for me?"

Miss Beckworth continued to gaze calmly at the indignant girl. "You told your cousin that you had nothing suitable to wear," she said in a musing tone, her eyes sharpening as faint color rose in Adrienne's cheeks. "Your blue gown may not be in the first stare of fashion, but it is certainly suitable."

Adrienne bit her lip and directed her eyes to the fireplace for a moment. "There is something I didn't tell you, Becky. Do you recall the gentleman who rescued me on my last visit to a gaming establishment? The one who would have seen me home had I not been able to give him the slip? It was Dominic," she finished baldly. "Oh, he didn't recognize me," she promised, as understanding and consternation flashed across Miss Beckworth's countenance, "but I daren't be seen in that dress, lest it should jog his memory."

"So that is the reason for your incivility just now?"

"I could never allow Dominic to buy me a dress in any case, but I would have handled the situation differently if I'd had any warning. Now that I've had time to consider a little, I believe we can scrape by without raising a dust. I'll go on up to Jean-Paul and you may simply tell Dominic that I was mistaken and do have a gown for the dinner party. That will avoid an argument tonight. On the night of the party I'll develop a headache and send tearful regrets," she declared blithely as she headed for the door. "It should not be too difficult to avoid going into society for the brief time we'll be here," she added, turning back toward the door and nearly colliding with the substantial figure of her quiet-footed cousin, who had entered while she was speaking. His hands shot out to grip her upper arms and restore her balance as the startled girl stumbled.

"I fear you are laboring under a misapprehension, Cousin Adrienne," he said kindly, dropping his hands when she was safely upright once more, "if you think your stay here is going to be short." He extended his hand to the dumbfounded girl, who automatically put hers into it, allowing him to lead her back to the chair she had recently occupied.

"I spoke with Dr. Hume this afternoon after I left here, to inform him of the improvement in Jean-Paul's condition. We had a long talk about the boy's convalescence and what to expect. No," he added in response to the worry that leapt into her face, "there is nothing to fear concerning his eventual recovery, but the period of convalescence is vitally important. He will be on a strict regimen, and travel is out of the question in the immediate future. He cannot be subjected to the rigors of a channel crossing in his present condition."

"How . . . how long?" whispered Adrienne.

Dominic shrugged heavy shoulders. "A month, six weeks perhaps. It depends on his progress."

"Did you know this, Becky?" Adrienne's russet curls swirled about her head as she turned abruptly toward the woman who had sat silent throughout Lord Creighton's explanation.

"I suspected as much," she admitted quietly. "I also have discussed the matter with Dr. Hume."

"So you see," Lord Creighton reminded the still-disturbed girl, "I will be able to enjoy your company for some little time yet."

Adrienne's searching eyes probed his and were convinced of his sincerity. Some slight relaxation in her stiffness manifested itself in the small smile trembling on her soft mouth. "Vastly prettily said, cousin. You are very good and we are most grateful for your hospitality." The man watching her saw the dimples smooth out as those same lips firmed with determination. "Though we are compelled to accept your hospitality—your *kind* hospitality," she added hastily, noting the quick flaring of his nostrils, "the least we can do to repay you is assure you that our presence won't interfere with your own life. There is no reason to include us in any of your social plans, especially this dinner next week. I beg you to believe that I would much prefer to concentrate on my brother."

"Oh, I believe you," he replied cheerfully, "but I beg *you* to believe that this proposed retirement of yours won't do."

"Why not?"

"My dear cousin, you must give a thought to *my* situation."

"Your situation?" Adrienne cast a suspicious look at his bland countenance. "And what might that be?"

"Well, you really cannot expect me to allow all of society to think I am so ashamed of my relations that I have forbidden them to show their faces in public."

"Why should anyone think that, knowing there is illness in the family? You are bamming me, cousin." But Adrienne was looking uneasy as she spoke.

Lord Creighton moved in for the kill. "What else are they to think if you are not present at my table while known to be under my roof?" The irritation on her face told him she had accepted his reasoning. He waited with patience while she scowled absently, her brain scrambling in an unsuccessful effort to come up with a telling argument.

"Very well, Cousin Dominic," she said with immense dignity, "I'll attend your betrothal dinner." A thought occurred which brought the sunniness back in her expression. "It will be the perfect opportunity to explain to anyone with whom I speak that I will be too involved in my brother's convalescence to be able to accept social invitations. Then no one can possibly criticize you."

He shook his head sadly. "I fear you are not well-acquainted with the mentality of subalterns, Cousin Adrienne, if you think they will meekly accept one glimpse of you as their portion. I anticipate a huge upswing in my popularity amongst the younger officers when it becomes known that I am your temporary guardian."

Adrienne had been staring at him in the liveliest astonishment. "Now I know you are joking, cousin," she said accusingly. "Why should anyone pay me any least attention? I am neither beautiful nor eligible."

A fugitive smile flitted across Lord Creighton's lips. "I shall not allow you to be a proper judge of your beauty, and as for your second criterion, what constitutes eligibility?"

"A dowry and feminine accomplishments," she replied promptly. "I have neither."

Lord Creighton passed a thoughtful forefinger slowly up and down one side of his jaw while he considered this. "We cannot dispute the lack of a dowry," he conceded, "but what feminine accomplishments are you lacking?"

"All of them," came the blunt rejoinder. "I neither sing nor play on the pianoforte or harp, I cannot sketch or paint, and have no skill at fancy stitchery. I cannot even dance!"

"This is indeed a formidable litany of imperfections," Lord Creighton agreed gravely, "and yet, do you know I venture to predict that I shall still have to beat a path to my door through a horde of admirers?"

Convinced that he was teasing her, though from the kindest of motives, Adrienne tossed her curls and scowled at the unmistakable twinkle in her large cousin's eyes before turning to Miss Beckworth, who had been a silent but appreciative spectator to their conversation dueling. "If you will excuse me now, Becky, I will go on up to Jean-Paul."

"Just a moment, cousin. It has occurred to me that Pamela . . . Lady Tremayne might be of assistance with the name of a dressmaker when she comes to tea tomorrow. There is a carriage at your disposal, of course. I haven't thought to mention it before because you and Miss Beckworth have been tied to Jean-Paul's bedside."

Adrienne had stopped halfway across the room. She turned with an airy laugh. "That won't be necessary, Cousin Dominic. Becky reminded me that I do possess a suitable gown for your dinner party."

A loud sigh was the only reply from Lord Creighton,

who levered himself out of his chair with discernible reluctance. Adrienne watched his slow approach with increasing wariness that proved justified as he casually positioned himself between her and the door. His smile was rueful, his eyes gentle as he said apologetically:

"We cannot avoid this conversation indefinitely, so with you permission we'll get it behind us tonight, shall we?"

After an instant's charged silence while defiance flared and died in the blue-green eyes, Adrienne shrugged her shoulders in a Gallic gesture and headed back to her chair. Miss Beckworth's hands, clasped in her lap, loosened their grip on each other and she surreptitiously flexed stiff fingers.

Sweet reason colored Adrienne's tones as she settled into the *bergère*. "Surely you realize, Cousin Dominic, that it would be the height of impropriety for you to propose paying for my clothes."

"Of course it would." His quick agreement took the wind out of her sails. As he added nothing to his statement for a second or two, Adrienne lifted one dark brow.

"Then what is the purpose of this discussion, cousin?"

"I am merely acting for my mother, who wishes to aid the children of her favorite relative," Lord Creighton began almost hesitantly, searching for words that would not offend the pride and independence of the girl facing him. "Your brother's illness has delayed your departure by some weeks. My mother desires that you should not be deprived because of a scanty wardrobe of the opportunities for enjoyment that exist for young ladies in Brussels this spring. It will be a real pleasure for her to provide you with the clothes you will need while you are under my roof."

"It is exceedingly kind of Lady Creighton to wish to do this for a complete stranger, but I cannot allow her to be imposed upon by someone with no claim to her charity." Adrienne's voice remained pleasant, but the earl was impressed against his will by the unchildlike expression in her candid eyes.

"I think perhaps you do not perfectly comprehend the strong degree of attachment between our parents throughout their mutual childhood and youth." He glanced at

Miss Beckworth for confirmation, and that lady nodded.

"They were very close."

"To my knowledge my father had practically no contact with any member of his family after his marriage." Adrienne had difficulty keeping her voice free of challenge.

"He wrote to my mother to apprise her of the birth of each of his children, and she did the same."

"A few birth announcements over a thirty-year period scarcely constitute an active correspondence," the girl noted dryly.

Lord Creighton sighed. "I beg you will not think me disloyal to my father if I explain that he was a possessive man and inclined to jealousy where my mother was concerned. Unfortunately, he took your father in dislike from the beginning of their acquaintance and desired my mother to cut the connection. It may have been an unreasonable request, but she loved him, and rightly or wrongly felt that she must accede to his wishes in this matter."

Adrienne made a little moue of distress. "It is not necessary to tell me all this. Believe me, cousin, I bear your mother not the slightest ill will; I am persuaded she is a marvelous person and excessively generous, but the fact remains that my brothers and I have no claim on her generosity."

"That is not the way Mama sees the situation. She feels that you have a very special claim on her, since she considers herself to be your godmother."

In her own surprise Adrienne missed the look of astonishment that crossed Miss Beckworth's face for a fleeting moment. She gaped at Lord Creighton. "I . . . I don't understand, cousin. My godmother was a French lady, long deceased, a friend of my mother's."

"It was always understood between the cousins that my mother would stand godmother to your father's firstborn, and vice versa. The responsibility for the fact that this did not actually come about must be laid at *my* father's door." The earl dropped his eyes as if in the throes of filial guilt and embarrassment.

"I . . . I see." Adrienne turned a troubled gaze to Miss

Beckworth, now expressionless and relaxed in her chair. "I . . . suppose this does somewhat alter the situation, Becky?" Doubt and indecision clouded her vivid face as she plucked nervously at a light-colored thread on her dark skirt.

"It would certainly explain Lady Creighton's ardent desire to be your benefactress," allowed Miss Beckworth, choosing her words with precision.

"Do *you* think it right for me to permit Lady Creighton to pay for my wardrobe?" demanded the forthright girl.

Again Miss Beckworth spoke after careful consideration. "I am persuaded you would not wish to appear careless of her ladyship's sensibilities in this matter or to wound those sensibilities."

"Of course not!" cried Adrienne, aghast at the suggestion that she might be guilty of such a breach of manners toward her elders.

"Then that question is settled." The earl had retired from the discussion during this exchange between the women, and now his casual tones underlined the decision Adrienne could scarcely believe she had made. A faint resentment stirred at the implication that this was a matter of very little moment. "I shan't require more than one or two dresses at most, and perhaps a new hat," she declared, her eyes meeting his straightly.

The earl contrived to remain unaware of the challenge in the firm line of her mouth as he smiled with great charm. "I believe that Lady Tremayne might be of some use in directing you to the most fashionable modistes and hat makers in town."

Adrienne smiled back politely, but held her peace on this subject, having already decided that she had no intention of patronizing the obviously expensive creators of Lady Tremayne's elegant wardrobe. It was one thing to accept the countess's offer to furnish her with the basic necessities for the rest of her stay in Brussels, and quite another to consider the offer as a *carte blanche* to compete with the wealthy women of the upper ranks of British society who populated the city this spring. She barely listened while Dominic and Becky embarked on a discussion of milliners and mantua makers, and at the first opportunity made her excuses, pleading the necessity to relieve Luc at her younger brother's bedside.

Miss Beckworth ended the small silence that followed upon Adrienne's departure. Lord Creighton found her fine hazel eyes fixed rather thoughtfully on him when he turned from the door that he had opened for his cousin.

"It was rather a . . . surprise to me, my lord, to learn of an agreement between Matthew Castle and Lady Creighton to stand godparents to each other's first child," she said in neutral tones.

For a moment the earl met her look; then he gave a rueful laugh and threw up his hands. "It will be a surprise to my mama, also," he admitted, unabashed, "but what else was I to do, ma'am? The girl is so devilishly proud—not that I'd have her any other way! She deserves to have a good time like the others of her age here in Brussels."

"I think you forget, sir, that her situation is not the same as other girls her age."

"No, I assure you I could not forget her situation—it chafes me too much. But there is no reason why she shouldn't receive an acceptable offer eventually. No doubt my mother will see to that. Meanwhile, why not let the lads in Brussels have a look at her? Who knows what might happen? You will see to a *complete* wardrobe for her, ma'am?"

Miss Beckworth's lips twitched. "I will ensure that she has more than a dress or two and one hat, although I can't say that I look forward to the experience of outfitting her against her will. Adrienne has her father's mulish streak in full measure."

Lord Creighton grinned in sympathy. "I don't envy you the chore, ma'am." A stray thought took possession of him. "Did she mean it when she said she could not dance?"

"Where would she have acquired the skill?"

This time the compassion in his face held no touch of amusement. "You have all had a difficult time of it—you most of all, without the shield provided by the natural optimism and ignorance of extreme youth." He shook off the sober mood, and they proceeded to discuss the necessity of employing the services of a dancing master as an equal priority with shopping in the upcoming weeks. By the time he left to keep his evening engagement with his betrothed, the earl and Miss Beckworth were firm allies, having reached a comprehensive though largely unspoken agreement as to how Adrienne's immediate future was to take shape.

8

Adrienne's natural buoyancy, so unaccountably deflated for a time by her first meeting with her cousin's prospective wife, rebounded with customary vigor the next day. As her initial impression of the cool brunette faded, she had difficulty remembering why she had felt instinctively that they would not become friends. It had most likely been her own fault entirely; the humiliation of having to be rescued by relations who were strangers had no doubt left her abnormally sensitive to suspected patronage. It was certainly understandable that Lady Tremayne, having suffered the indignity of having her engagement dinner postponed as a result of the difficulties of a pack of poor relations—and not even her own poor relations at that—would be less than enthusiastic about becoming involved in dutiful relationships with these same persons. In calling on Becky and Adrienne she was making a commendable effort to do the polite thing. Since she was prepared to meet the Castles on terms of civility, it was up to Adrienne to demonstrate that she would not be a social incubus. Lady Tremayne's connection with Dominic suggested that they would all meet fairly frequently. With developing familiarity they would no doubt discover mutual interests. By the time Moulton admitted Lady Tremayne to the main saloon where the two ladies were waiting, Adrienne had almost convinced herself that she and Dominic's lovely fiancée would indeed become friends.

When Moulton ushered their visitor out to her waiting carriage forty minutes later that hopeful piece of self-deception had been permanently laid to rest. Lady Tremayne's appearance was even more startlingly attractive than on the preceding day if such a thing were possible. Becky's softly indrawn breath was evidence that Adrienne had not sufficiently prepared her for the reality of the young widow's dramatic beauty. Today she was clad in a cleverly draped dress of pale champagne cotton trimmed profusely but delicately with burgundy embroidery on bodice and skirt. Her flat-crowned straw hat was swirled in cloudy veils of burgundy gauze anchored by roses of a lighter shade. Adrienne thought she had never seen a hat half so glorious, and promptly said so.

The polite half-smile on Lady Tremayne's lips widened as she acknowledged the impetuous compliment. She extended two fingers to Miss Beckworth when Adrienne made the ladies known to one another. They arranged themselves on chairs around the tea table while Lady Tremayne made polite inquiries concerning Jean-Paul's progress. The meeting proceeded along cordial lines as tea was accepted and tiny frosted cakes declined by their visitor.

Had it not been for Becky's unsuspected expertise at meaningless social chatter Adrienne would have been at a complete loss during the next half-hour. In the past her father's cronies had talked about international politics and the military situation all over Europe; Becky enjoyed discussing the works of the great writers and thinkers of the world, and Luc and Jean-Paul were eager to learn about advances in modern living and science. Lady Tremayne's conversational offerings, which danced lightly over the entire fashion and social scene in Brussels, were as incomprehensible to Adrienne as a Chinese map. She managed an occasional "Really?" and pinned what she hoped was an encouraging smile on her lips to disguise her boredom. For the rest she simply trusted to Becky to keep the talk going if their guest showed signs of flagging. It was during a brief pause following Lady Tremayne's acerbic thumbnail sketch of yet another socialite unknown to either of her hostesses that Becky ventured to inquire the name of a reliable dressmaker.

"Well, Madame Henriette created this dress for me. Of

course she is shockingly expensive, but she understands what best becomes me."

"I should think most anything would become you." Adrienne spoke impulsively, and the sheer surprise in her voice evoked a trill of pleased laughter from her visitor.

"I fear you are flattering me, my dear Miss Castle."

"It's not flattery, it's the simple truth," protested Adrienne, not wishing to be thought a member of a species she abhorred. Evidently Lady Tremayne did not harbor any animus toward flatterers. She again demurred smilingly before going on to give the name of a little dressmaker off the Place du Grand Sablon whom she had heard spoken well of by Mrs. Creevey. "Are you in need of a gown for the dinner party next week?"

"Yes," said Adrienne.

Miss Beckworth enlarged on this. "Actually Adrienne will be requiring a fairly extensive refurbishing of her wardrobe."

A puzzled frown appeared momentarily on Lady Tremayne's smooth brow. "I understood you will be leaving Belgium as soon as your brother is able to travel."

"Yes, that is so, but Jean-Paul's convalescence is likely to be somewhat protracted, according to Dr. Hume, and since Lord Creighton insists that his cousin take an active part in the social life offered in Brussels, she will require a number of additions to her wardrobe."

"I . . . see." The lovely face of their guest had become a careful blank, which might have indicated a lack of pleasure in what she saw. After a visible struggle with herself she suppressed any further sentiments and embarked on those preparations women indulge in when about to take their departure, gathering her reticule closer to her skirts and looking around for the pale gloves she had removed earlier. Her social smile reappeared.

"This has been a delightful interlude, but I must dash. Dominic and I are promised for Lord Betancourt's assembly tonight, and I must try to snatch a few moments' rest before dressing or I shall look like a hag. The constant social round can be hideously fatiguing, do you not agree?"

Miss Beckworth merely smiled in response to this rhetorical question as she pulled the bell cord to summon Moulton. "I trust Lady Betancourt is in good health at present?"

"You are acquainted with Lady Betancourt?"

"If she was Alice Travers before her marriage, I am. We made our come-out the same season."

Lady Tremayne's perfectly arched eyebrows flew up. "But Lady Betancourt has grown children. She cannot be a day less than forty, and looks older."

Miss Beckworth nodded. "I believe she is the same age as I, one-and-forty."

"Well," advised Lady Tremayne with some frankness and less affection than she had so far displayed, "I would not call attention to this if I were you. You look years younger."

As Moulton had appeared by then, the ladies took leave of each other with civil declarations of mutual esteem, and, on Adrienne's part at least, more than a little relief. She turned an expectant face to her companion when the sound of footsteps had faded.

"She is certainly a handsome creature and seems disposed to be fairly affable," conceded Miss Beckworth judiciously.

"Damn with faint praise," murmured Adrienne with a wicked twinkle.

"Nonsense, nothing of the sort." Becky's protest was brisk but she avoided the girl's eyes. "At least she was able to steer us to a fashionable modiste. If Luc will sit with Jean-Paul tomorrow morning, I propose we lose no time in calling on her. The dinner is in less than a sennight."

"Very well. What was her name?"

"Madame Henriette."

"No, that was the expensive modiste, the one who made Lady Tremayne's gown."

"Yes, and the one who will make yours."

Adrienne was appalled. "*No, Becky*! I am uncomfortable enough with the idea of being under such a gigantic obligation to Lady Creighton, even if she does consider herself in some way my godmother. The least I can do is make sure I do not squander her money on exorbitantly priced finery.''

"My dear girl," Becky replied calmly, "Lady Creighton knows exactly what she is about. She wishes that you not fade into the background with a sign over your head labeled 'Poor Relation.' And you must consider Dominic while you are nursing your pride. Do you desire his friends to form the impression that his relatives are a set of dirty dishes he is ashamed to own?''

"We're nothing of the sort!"

"Of course not, but you would not wish to be thought such, or worse yet, to be considered shabby genteel.''

Adrienne glared suspiciously at the bland expression on her companion's face before stalking over to the door. "That is a load of rubbish and you know it, Becky!" she accused, and whisked herself out to avoid the censure such unladylike utterances would surely earn her.

Adrienne's sense of outrage at being manipulated by her new cousin and her oldest friend (however good-naturedly and with only her own benefit in mind) did not disappear overnight. Her pride and independent spirit were smarting at breakfast the next morning and she was still nursing an uncharacteristic resentment which, to her credit, she attempted to conceal. However, since these attempts took the form of a stilted politeness totally alien to her nature, they could scarcely be said to be effective if concealment was indeed her goal on a deeper level. The objects of her unnatural civility rendered her tactics less than useless by refusing to acknowledge them. Becky conversed unconcernedly with Lord Creighton, addressing such occasional remarks to Adrienne as did not require a response, and it is entirely possible that Lord Creighton, secure in his male obtuseness, was actually unaware of any strained atmosphere in the sunny breakfast chamber. His smiling charm and the unfeigned interest he expressed in the ladies' plans for the morning would tend to support this explanation. Adrienne gritted her teeth as her cousin apologized at length for presuming to offer her the platter of meats she had just spurned with the remark that she considered it un-civilized to partake of animal flesh in the morning.

Luc removed his attention from his heaped plate long enough to cast his sister a look of frank disbelief. "What are you playing at, Adrienne? I've never known you to refuse bacon or ham before, whatever the time of day."

"Don't prattle about matters beyond your knowledge," Adrienne retorted, unthinkingly abandoning her punctili-ous manner. Since she avoided looking at Dominic, she missed the little smile he concealed behind his napkin.

"There's no call to get upon your high ropes," Luc replied, offended, "especially when you know I'm right."

"Luc," broke in Miss Beckworth hastily, "you will be sure not to allow Jean-Paul to try to read while we're gone this morning, will you not? I know it's next to impossible to keep him away from his books ordinarily, but the doctor has charged us with keeping him quiet in a dark-ened room for the present."

"I'll read to him if he desires it," Luc promised with cheerful acquiescence, earning a spontaneous smile from his sister, who had forgotten her grievance for the moment.

She remembered it on the way to the dressmaker's, how-ever, and it was a hard-to-please young lady very much on her dignity who greeted the thin middle-aged woman who was the guiding spirit behind the successful dressmaking establishment. Shrewd snapping black eyes made a lightning assessment of her new customer while Adrienne was unselfconsciously looking around the disappointingly bare front room.

No emotion disturbed the wooden facade of the proprietess as she tallied up the client's points. At first glance the *taille* was fairly unprepossessing; the girl was scarcely middle height, not nearly tall enough to display to advantage the more dramatic creations, as well as being too young. Madame Henriette found the generality of young English *demoiselles* insipid and boring in the extreme. Her initial impression began to disintegrate, however, when her gaze left the slightly built figure and rose to the face. *Ah!* This one could never be called colorless, not with that vibrant hair and those remarkable eyes. The elixir of creativity began to flow through the designer as she considered the range of colors that would set off that marvelous hair. And wonder of wonders, the girl had escaped the complexion that usually accompanied red hair. There was not one single freckle to mar the creamy perfection of her skin.

Madame Henriette's eyes brightened with speculation and her ears perked up when the older woman introduced her young companion and explained their situation. Lord Creighton's cousin. Surely she knew that name? But of course—that was the wealthy man the salon's most beautiful but least likable client, the proud and inconsiderate Lady Tremayne, had claimed as her fiancé when she had mentioned the matter of a substantial sum still owing on several gowns delivered over a month ago. Her brain ticked over rapidly as she escorted her customers to comfortable chairs. She bowed in acknowledgment of the introduction, and her clients weren't to know that the sudden delight on her harsh features was less related to any qualities they might possess than to an instinctive realization that a weapon had been put into her hands with which to avenge herself on Lady Tremayne. Intuition told her the latter would not welcome any competition even from a relative of her betrothed. She was of the type who would always be dissatisfied in any setting unless she knew herself to be unrivaled *au fait de beauté*. This unfledged girl might not possess the perfect arrangement of features with which Lady Tremayne had been blessed, but that glorious coloring, complemented by the costumes she would create, and allied with the air of happy anticipation that seemed natural, would certainly draw interested looks from men with the wit to appreciate someone out of the common style. And that voice with its pure Parisian accent despite the English name! Madame was enchanted to find someone of the stolid English race who did not massacre the French tongue. The girl's appeal would not be limited to Englishmen.

Miss Beckworth was more than satisfied with the quality of personal attention the modiste expended on Adrienne

that morning. The girl herself was incapable of sustaining
her attitude of indifference in the midst of such a heady experience. Madame Henriette was inexhaustible in her
desire to enhance her newest client's appearance, even to
the extent of sketching out some of her ideas on the spot.
Adrienne did indeed protest uneasily that they could not
afford to spend any great sum of money on a party dress,
since she would require one or two daytime costumes as
well, but her remarks were ignored by her duenna. When
she repeated them a little later, the expensive modiste
explained that she would naturally be prepared to make a
substantial reduction on the individual items in a large
order. She then ended the discussion by producing a
number of exquisite fabrics for their inspection. In the next
few moments Adrienne lost herself in the rare pleasure of
being able to select from among many beautiful things.
Fashion had played no part in her busy life to date and she
had never before been in a position to pick and choose
what she would like. Her customary decisiveness deserted
her in the presence of so many choices, each lovelier than
the last. For once she was shyly amenable to suggestion
and disposed to accept the judgment of her elders. Though
she gazed wistfully at a bright pink satin she'd unearthed
from a pile of swatches, lightly fingering its shiny surface,
she dropped it obediently, albeit with a gurgle of laughter
at the single gasp of horror uttered by both women.

"Not against that hair!" Madame Henriette shuddered,
thrusting the pink fabric underneath the rest.

"I was only admiring the color." The words were meek,
the mouth was demure, but the spark of mischief in Miss
Castle's eloquent eyes did not escape Madame's narrowed
observation. Ah, but the child was *sympathique!* There
was a youthful *élan tout naturel* that could not fail to
attract. With her rich red hair modishly coiffed, and
exquisitely gowned by the foremost modiste in Brussels
(Madame scorned a show of false modesty), she would
offer an appealing contrast to the overripe charms of the
haughty Lady Tremayne. It just needed the right setting
for those jeweled eyes.

Madame Henriette returned her attention to the fabric samples, her lips pursed in concentration. In the next moment all three ladies made a spontaneous movement forward as a swatch of silk in an intense shade of aquamarine was turned over.

"That is the exact color of Adrienne's eyes!" exclaimed Miss Beckworth.

"*Parfait, absolument parfait* with her hair and skin!" gloated Madame Henriette, holding it up near Adrienne's face. As for the girl herself, she said nothing at all, but her eyes glowed a richer aquamarine as she raised them eagerly to meet the modiste's glance. Obviously all that remained was to decide on a design for the gown.

The euphoria that had enveloped Adrienne in the dressmaker's shop gradually eased its grip as the carriage neared the earl's residence. A puzzled little frown wrinkled her brow as she went over the recent events mentally. She could not call to mind the price of the party dress they had ordered, nor, she realized, biting her lip suddenly, the cost of the three other costumes Becky and Madame had insisted were indispensable items for her temporary lifestyle. Had the modiste ever quoted a price? Adrienne had certainly inquired, that much she clearly recollected, but no numbers came into her head. Her growing uneasiness was reflected in the glance she bent on her companion.

"Becky, how much money did we spend this morning?"

"I don't recall the amount exactly, but Madame's charges were nowhere near so exorbitant as Lady Tremayne led us to believe. I am persuaded Lady Creighton will be pleased with the quality for the price." The serenity of Miss Beckworth's expression might almost be called smugness at that moment, and went some way toward alleviating Adrienne's qualms, though she persisted weakly:

"I really didn't need the ivory carriage dress, you know. The yellow would have been adequate, especially since I'll be too busy with Jean-Paul in the next few weeks to go gallivanting about the town with any of these hypothetical escorts Dominic is predicting will appear out of the air."

"It never hurts to be prepared. You would have required a new wardrobe in any case. Most of your clothes are threadbare as well as being out of fashion."

"Well, I don't like imposing on Lady Creighton's generosity and I never will," sighed Adrienne, "but naturally I do not wish to appear ungrateful or to oppose Dominic in anything. We have caused him enough trouble already."

"A very proper sentiment," approved Miss Beckworth, taking careful note of Adrienne's words in the event it should become necessary to quote them back to her when she learned that today's purchases were just the tip of the iceberg.

9

The rhythm of life in the big house on Rue Ducale quickened over the next few days as the inhabitants and staff embarked on preparations for the earl's engagement dinner. Miss Beckworth and the chef spent hours conferring about the menu while the newly hired assistant cook scoured the local markets for delicacies that were not always readily obtainable. Moulton and the housekeeper, Madame Bonnet, acquainted Miss Beckworth with the household's inventory of linen, china, and silverware so she might decide what additional purchases would be necessary to provide service for eighteen, the final guest list agreed upon by Lord Creighton and Lady Tremayne. The servants were set to polishing silver and washing innumerable lusters from sconces and ornate chandeliers in drawing and dining rooms.

Reports of the unusual activity penetrated even to the sickroom, lately presided over almost exclusively by Miss Castle in order to free her companion to take over the arrangements for the betrothal dinner. Jean-Paul was sleeping through the night at long last, enabling his sister to return to a more normal schedule of living. She spent most of her waking hours with her younger brother, whose convalescence must be carefully monitored to prevent the dreaded complications of rheumatic fever from permanently damaging his heart.

No one could describe Jean-Paul as a docile patient, his loving sister acknowledged to herself as she stoically bore the complaints and recriminations hurled her way when she forestalled his fourth attempt to leave his bed one morning.

"Why *can't* I get up for a while? I'm tired of this stupid

bed and this stupid room. I'm not sick anymore." The boy's eyes glittered and his chin set in a fashion strongly reminiscent of his sister's on occasion.

"Believe me, my pet, I do sympathize with you. It must be a dead bore to be confined to one's room, even such a bright cheery room as this one, but the doctor has decreed that you must remain in bed until your temperature has been normal for two whole days. If you continue to agitate yourself this way, I fear you will make yourself feverish again."

"I am sick to death of doing nothing all day long. I haven't even seen Cousin Dominic's house except for this room, and we have been here for almost a fortnight," Jean-Paul grumbled, but his sister was grateful to detect a lessening in the intensity of his complaint.

"If you will try to close your eyes for a short rest before lunchtime, I will play a game of cribbage with you afterward," she promised.

"Cribbage is for old men!"

"Well, then," amended Adrienne with exemplary patience, "I'll read to you instead. Luc found a copy of *Ivanhoe* on Cousin Dominic's shelves. You will enjoy that, I'll be bound."

Jean-Paul brightened a little at the promised treat but continued to protest against the recommended rest for another few minutes, complaining he was thirsty and that his bedcovers were all lumpy and uncomfortable.

Adrienne accepted the grumbling with unruffled serenity, cheerfully making the tumbled bed and plumping the pillows for the little boy. She handed him a glass of water, which he returned after taking but one sip. She did not comment on this either, but she did bite off an impatient exclamation when a knock sounded at the door just as she had him more or less reconciled to his nap.

It was Antoine, the young footman, with a message that a gentleman wished to see Miss Castle.

"A gentleman to see *me*?" Adrienne took the proffered card, but looked no more enlightened after reading the name thereon. "I'm afraid I do not know any Monsieur Alphonse Daubigny, Antoine. It must be a mistake," she said, handing back the bit of pasteboard and preparing to return to her patient.

"I beg your pardon, miss, but the gentleman said to tell you that his lordship had instructed him to call and that he would take up only a few minutes of your time."

Still somewhat undecided, Adrienne glanced over to the bed, where her young brother was sitting up, avidly taking in the scene. She sighed. "Very well, Antoine. I'll come if you will stay with Master Jean-Paul while I'm gone."

As she entered the small crimson reception room a few minutes later, she was slightly out of breath from taking the staircase in an impatient dash. She paused inside the door to steady her beathing. The man standing by the mantel was of uncertain age, very tall stature, and dark coloring. He set down the convoluted porcelain candlestick he had been examining with delicate precision and turned to face her fully. No trace of self-consciousness appeared on his long sallow face as he met the girl's astonished gaze, which flashed from the candlestick to the long fingers he was fastidiously wiping on a lace-trimmed handkerchief.

"Ah, Mademoiselle Castle, I presume? I am delighted to make your acquaintance." He calmly shook out the handkerchief with a flourish before tucking it into an inner pocket of his coat.

And what a coat! Accustomed to the neat military appearance of most of the male population of Brussels, Adrienne was hard put to refrain from staring rudely at the odd figure facing her with complete *sangfroid*. Even the exaggeratedly padded shoulders of the puce-colored garment could not disguise its wearer's extreme thinness, since it was styled with a wasp waist. Pantaloons might have helped, but he had elected to wear tight knee breeches of a cinnamon hue that warred with the puce. Yellow silk stockings that matched his striped waistcoat contributed to the spindle-shanks impression.

Adrienne blinked and elevated her fascinated gaze from the intricate arrangement of a monstrously wide neckcloth that seemed to raise his ears, to encounter smiling dark eyes that belied the lugubrious arrangement of features that nature had bestowed on her visitor. "H-how do you do, Monsieur Daubigny?'' she stammered, consulting the name on the calling card. "How can I help you?''

"But it is I who have come to help you, mademoiselle!'' exclaimed the disconcerting individual, sweeping her a bow that was a masterpiece of fluidity and grace, though decidedly overdone.

It was the bow that supplied Adrienne with a clue to the identity of her caller. Her own eyes began to twinkle in response to the amused gleam in his. "The footman said my cousin had sent you to me. Can it be that you are a dancing master, sir?''

"Ah, you have twigged me, as they say in your country. Your cousin, then, is Colonel Lord Creighton, who strongly pressed me to instruct you in the art of social dancing. I can come to you every morning at ten if that is agreeable, mademoiselle?''

"Every day!'' exclaimed Adrienne, widening her eyes. "Is that not a bit excessive? Would not one or two mornings a week be sufficient?''

"Your cousin was most insistent that you become proficient as quickly as possible. He has even asked me to arrange for someone to play for the lessons at an additional charge." Monsieur Daubigny pressed his point with expressive gestures miming piano playing.

"Then I suppose I had better make myself available." Adrienne was beginning to recognize the steely determination behind Dominic's unruffled courtesy and to reassess his apparently easygoing nature as their acquaintance progressed. Really, the man was a despot beneath the surface charm! In the short time they had known him he seemed to have taken over every aspect of their lives.

It was a somewhat subdued and thoughtful girl who quietly reentered the sick-chamber after completing arrangements with the dancing master. Deep in her bones Adrienne felt a compulsion to resist being taken over by her new cousin. There was a nagging fear, not quite articulated, that her strength would be permanently undermined when the temporary support was withdrawn, as it must be in a few short weeks.

The sight of Antoine perched on the side of her brother's bed playing cards with the invalid brought Adrienne's uneasy ramblings to a halt. Both the therapeutic rest and his earlier fit of the sullens had evidently been dispensed with in favor of the stimulation of a new presence. Jean-Paul was gleefully totaling up the score after having trounced the young footman at casino. His incipient protests at losing his victim on his sister's return were dealt with firmly, and in truth he was happy enough to settle back for a nap almost immediately, having little understanding of the general debility caused by his illness. Still, the change had probably been beneficial, his sister considered as she warmly thanked the accommodating footman. Perhaps it was time to increase Jean-Paul's contacts beyond his immediate family. If a satisfactory balance of stimulation and rest could be achieved, they might yet avoid the trial of wills she had anticipated during the necessarily lengthy convalescence from such a serious illness.

Over the next few days relations between the reluctant invalid and his watchful attendants did improve significantly. Moulton was willing to release Antoine or Marie for regular duties to keep Jean-Paul company during Adrienne's daily session with Monsieur Daubigny, and the Castles were sincerely touched to see that other members of the household staff extended themselves to dream up diversions and treats to make the time pass more pleasantly for their little brother. The formidable Moulton himself unbent enough to give the lad some rudimentary instruction in the art of whittling, a skill at which he was, unexpectedly, more than proficient. Adrienne had to repress an undignified impulse to throw her arms about the butler's neck when she reported that Jean-Paul's enthusiasm for the craft was such that he was currently employed in carving a set of chess pieces for Luc's birthday.

"Miss Beckworth and I are so very grateful to you, Moulton. We had nearly despaired of finding some quiet activity that would keep him happily occupied."

Looking down into the beaming face, the butler permitted an infinitesimal smile to crack the habitual set of his lips. "I am pleased to have been of some help in Master Jean-Paul's convalescence, Miss Castle."

Adrienne laughed ruefully. "The only problem with his present obsession with whittling is that he is always half-buried in wood shavings. It makes extra work for the maids, but they have been so good, never a complaint from any of them."

"Naturally not, miss." Moulton's features returned to their permanently rigid set, and Adrienne, recognizing that she had been put in her place, hastily retreated to the sickroom, bemoaning her congenital lack of diplomacy. Of course Moulton would resent any slightest hint that his staff might not be firmly under control at all times.

She would have been relieved and pleased to overhear the butler agreeing with Madame Bonnet in the privacy of the Room when that lady ventured her opinion that the earl's young relatives were appreciative of the service rendered to them and knew how to conduct themselves in a gentleman's house despite having lived most recently in reduced circumstances.

Moulton, who had risen through the ranks to the coveted position of butler in the late Lord Creighton's town house, was not about to allow a newly hired foreigner to presume to pass judgment, even favorable judgment, on the family he had served for thirty-five years. He proceeded to inform Madame Bonnet in measured terms that his lordship's family was long distinguished in England for its unexceptionable breeding and comportment. It didn't occur to him to explain that the Castles were related only by marriage. All those who entered the Norcross orbit were gilded by association. It would have eased Adrienne's mind a great deal to learn that the caste-conscious Moulton had revised his earliest unfavorable impressions of the earl's poor relatives because, unlike her brothers, she was unable to forget their true status in this great house. Their dependence on Dominic's charity continued to chafe her proud spirit, though with no other course open to her, faced with Jean-Paul's need, she was sensible enough to banish such feelings to a back corner of her mind.

Excitement continued to build in the earl's house as the date of the betrothal party finally arrived. Her involvement with her little brother had kept Adrienne aloof from most of the preparations, but she was pressed into service on the day of the party to assist Miss Beckworth with the flower arrangements. Great masses of blooms had been delivered that morning, ordered by Becky, who rather prided herself on her creative way with flowers. She had preferred to design the arrangements herself rather than leave the task to professional florists.

The house the earl had hired was overfurnished with rather ponderous pieces of carved dark wood and the color schemes in the various rooms also favored intense dark shades. The ladies had agreed that it was imperative to lighten the effect for the festive occasion. To this end three or four tables and candlestands had been removed temporarily from the large drawing room to create more space. Miss Beckworth had conceived the bold stroke of filling one corner of the room with masses of graceful blossoms and feathery greenery from floor to ceiling level. Dark green predominated in draperies and upholstery coverings here and the walls were painted a particularly virulent shade of green also. Against this unpromising background Miss Beckworth and Adrienne labored to create large light floral arrangements, limiting themselves to yellow and white blossoms only.

In the dining room a huge Persian rug with a dark red background set the tone for a crimson-and-gold color scheme. Here the ladies chose to display flowers ranging from pure white through the pink tones to red, combining late tulips with peonies, roses, and branches of white apple blossom. It took hours to accomplish, but neither woman grudged the effort and both felt more than repaid by the sheer beauty of the final result.

"Isn't it amazing what can be achieved when cost is no object?" gloated Miss Beckworth, sighing with satisfaction as she lingered in the dining-room doorway to admire their handiwork.

Adrienne qualified her agreement. "All the money in the world, unless it is at the service of good taste, would not serve to create this marvelous effect. You have a positive genius with flowers, Becky. Dominic can't help but be pleased with your work."

"I hope Lady Tremayne approves of the result."

"What could she think except that you've designed a fitting setting for her beauty?"

Miss Beckworth did not comment on the somewhat dry tone in which this remark was delivered, but she shot a quick look at her charge, whose color deepened slightly as she declared that she must run upstairs to check on Jean-Paul and release Luc from his duties as sickroom attendant.

Adrienne's finished gown was not delivered until late in the afternoon, by which time the anxious girl had worked herself into a rare state of nerves. No more had been said about her original intention of developing a headache on the evening of the party. Though Miss Beckworth was much too kind to tease her on her *volte-face,* the situation did provide her duenna with some secret amusement. This was subordinate of course to the very real pleasure she took in seeing Adrienne about to enjoy for the first time some of the pleasures that most girls of her age and class took for granted. Miss Beckworth raced through her own toilette so that she might supervise the final stage of Adrienne's. She leveled a swift glance at her image in the glass to ensure that no strand of hair escaped from her neat bun before hurrying down the corridor to tap on Adrienne's door. The pearls she hadn't waited to fasten about her neck dangled from her fingers as she approached the dressing table where the girl was seated while Marie arranged her hair.

"Don't you look nice, Becky," said Adrienne admiringly. "That Brussels lace we bought really does give a new life to your gray silk." Catching sight of the necklace, she jumped up from the bench. "Here, I'll fasten your pearls."

Poor Marie did a juggling act with the hairbrush that Adrienne's sudden movement had jostled out of her hands. Miss Beckworth turned her back obediently but scolded gently:

"I beg of you, dearest, to remember to think before you act or speak tonight. A lady does not act with intemperate haste."

"Yes, Mama," said her unrepentant charge, dimpling.

"Mademoiselle Adrienne, there is not a great deal of time left for me to dress your hair," reminded the maid.

"I'm sorry, Marie. The interruption is my fault. I just wanted to see Miss Adrienne's gown before she descended. It is exquisite, my dear," she added as Adrienne pivoted slowly. "Madame Henriette is truly an artist. This fabric drifts and floats when you move, and of course the color is just right for you. It needs no more enhancement than your mother's gold locket. I'll leave her in your hands, Marie, while I go down to check the table one last time. Try not to be too long, Adrienne."

"I'll be down directly, Becky, but first I must pop in to show Jean-Paul my finery. I promised."

"Very well, but the guests are expected in fifteen minutes."

Miss Beckworth cast a sideways glance at the clock on the mantelshelf from her position by the fireplace, where she was engaged in conversation with General Forrester and his daughter. The last of the guests had arrived a few minutes earlier, and still Adrienne had not come down. It was unlike the girl to be late. For all her impetuosity, Adrienne was never guilty of inconsiderate behavior. Miss Beckworth smiled in vague encouragement at the general, though she had heard nothing of his last remark. His gaze intensified with quickened interest, but this went unnoticed since hers had drifted away toward the doorway by then. Perhaps she ought to slip out and speak to Moulton about sending someone to fetch Adrienne. As she turned her head slightly with the intention of excusing herself to her companions, her line of vision changed to include Lady Tremayne.

The beautiful brunette, looking stunningly regal in a gown of heavy white silk lavishly trimmed with gold lace, and wearing a magnificent ruby-and-diamond betrothal ring, had inquired pointedly for Miss Castle on her arrival with her brother. Dominic, his eyes filled with the glorious picture made by his fiancée, had shrugged a disclaimer, leaving Miss Beckworth to explain that Adrienne had promised to check on the invalid. Lady Tremayne had been immediately engulfed by admirers and was still in the midst of a crowd of young officers vying for her attention, but her eyes were fixed unwaveringly on the empty doorway, though she smiled and flirted her fan at members of her court.

At that moment Miss Beckworth caught a glimpse of aquamarine out of the corner of her eye and sighed with relief. Finally Adrienne had arrived! Miss Beckworth's relief was short-lived however. Her gaze, still turned partly toward Lady Tremayne, was transfixed by a series of expressions that flashed across the younger woman's face as she caught sight of her fiancé's cousin. Shock, disbelief, and cold rage followed in quick succession before long dark lashes swept down to veil her emotions. Miss Beckworth, shaken by what she had seen, involuntarily sought Dominic's eyes and knew by the stunned question there that he had also been a witness to a parade of emotions that had crossed those perfect features. Automatically he turned in the direction of Lady Tremayne's glance, to discover Adrienne trying to slide unobtrusively into the room. His cheerful voice rose above the buzz of conversation as he started forward.

"There you are at last, cousin!"

Nothing could have been more efficacious in highlighting Adrienne's late entrance. Embarrased color flew to her cheeks and her lips parted soundlessly as all eyes in the room gravitated toward her.

With one part of her mind Miss Beckworth proudly acknowledged that her charge had never looked lovelier. The potential that had been smothered by the constant struggle against poverty had come to blazing life tonight. Madame Henriette's exquisite creation flattered the slim perfection of Adrienne's small-boned figure, and Marie had succeeded beyond expectation in bringing order to her mistress's unruly tresses. She had swept the girl's hair back from her face and anchored it on top of her head, where gleaming russet ringlets had been allowed to fall where they might. A ribbon of the same color as her dress confined the curls. The simple style was superbly effective in exposing the delicate planes of her small face and the pointed charm of the dimpled chin. Huge jewel-bright eyes dominated her face beneath surprisingly dark brows and were made more dramatic by a forest of thick lashes. Miss Beckworth was fleetingly conscious of a spasm of regret that neither Matthew nor Juliette had lived to see their daughter's debut, for such this dinner party must be considered, but just then the main force of her intelligence was concentrated on dealing with the consequences.

Dominic had reached Adrienne now and was leading her into the room, wearing a proud avuncular smile. Miss Beckworth, however, had not missed the involuntary hesitation in his progress as the full impact of the girl's loveliness had hit him. He had recovered quickly and continued his leisurely approach, but at that moment the attention of everyone in the room had been riveted on the pair. Lady Tremayne was not going to appreciate having another woman take center stage for even so short a time as it took to perform the necessary introductions. It was no pleasure to Miss Beckworth to see confirmation of her theory written clearly in the careful rigidity of the beauty's jaw, which hinted at clenched teeth within, and the glitter of her light brown eyes as she watched her fiancé lead his cousin up to her.

Miss Beckworth held her breath, but she need not have entertained any worries on that head. Lady Tremayne was too socially adept to create a scene. Her greeting to Adrienne was correct, if cool, and her only reaction when the girl apologized for her tardiness was a slight inclination of her dark head, accompanied by a half-smile.

The next few minutes were so crammed with introductions to what seemed a literal army of strangers that Adrienne had no thought to spare for Lady Tremayne. In the ordinary way she did not suffer from shyness, but it was a bit daunting to be paraded in front of numerous staring faces before her embarrassment at being the unwitting cynosure of all eyes had even died down. Consequently she acknowledged the introductions in a shy little voice, making no attempt to prolong the moment, though several of the younger gentlemen gave her every opportunity to do so.

As soon as the earl had completed the round of presentations he was claimed by Lady Tremayne, who laid a proprietary hand on his sleeve. Adrienne seized the opportunity thus afforded to attach herself to Becky, who had resumed her conversation with General Forrester. In truth she needed time to catch her breath and recover her equilibrium, which she was able to do in the undemanding company of Miss Forrester, a quiet-faced young woman a year or two senior to Adrienne. They were still politely discussing the scenic parks of Brussels when dinner was announced.

A military gentleman, whose name Adrienne must have heard just moments ago but which now escaped her, presented himself at her elbow and announced that it was his privilege to lead her in to dinner.

"Delighted, sir," she replied with what she hoped was an airy smile, but evidently she had not fooled her unknown partner, who heaved a heavy sigh.

"That's twice you've forgotten me, you know, Miss Castle. It is a very lowering thought that one is completely forgettable."

"Twice?" queried a startled Adrienne. "Good Lord, sir, can you mean that we have been introduced on two occasions? I confess that I do not recall the other and must sincerely beg your pardon for my deplorable lapse."

At her look of real distress, the quizzing smile on the officer's lips disappeared. "I say, now, Miss Castle, it is I who should apologize for teasing you, although it is true that we *almost* met before." At her puzzled look he explained, "I was present at your initial meeting with Dominic in the room across the hall from here."

"Ohhhh!" The soft exclamation was drawn out, and the major frankly enjoyed the faint rise of color that accompanied it. However, Miss Castle surprised him by rounding on him suddenly. "I think I must concur that it is for *you* to apologize, sir, for being so ungentlemanly as to remind a lady of an occasion when her conduct fell short of that standard. For shame, sir!"

The words were serious, but twin imps danced in the sea-blue eyes. Major Peters raised his hand in a fencer's gesture. "I cry *pax,* Miss Castle. I mounted an unworthy attack and you have sent me to the rightabout. But for the moment, unless we wish to draw speculation to ourselves, I suggest that we follow the others into the dining room."

Adrienne enjoyed herself mightily at her first dinner party. Having more the appetite of a healthy young animal than a young lady of fashion, she did full justice to the delectable meal set before the guests. In addition to superb food, she was kept in a state of high entertainment for the next hour by the dry wit of Major Peters and the determined flirtation carried on by the junior officer on her other side. Lieutenant Markham directed a stream of flowery compliments at her with such an exaggerated air of earnestness that his sincerity would have been suspect even in the eyes of a lady considerably more gullible than Adrienne, who was well aware that staff officers were, practically without exception, young men of good families, well-versed in the niceties of social conduct. He began innocuously enough with a compliment on her dress that was received by Adrienne with a smiling thank-you. Thus emboldened, Lieutenant Markham went on to produce encomiums on her hair, which he likened to autumn leaves, and her eyes, which he labeled (erroneously) the color of lapis lazuli. After this she was more than ready to allow Major Peters to recall her attention. Her heated cheeks had time to cool while she listened to an amusing tale of an ill-fated trip to the opera. Eventually civility would compel her to converse again with her other dinner partner, but she trusted he would have settled on some unexceptionable topic by then.

In actuality, Lieutenant Markham appeared to have used the interval to restock his store of compliments. She ignored his confession that he was enchanted by the bloom on her cheeks and ravished by her dimples, exhorting him instead, as a footman came between them, "Do try some of the *vol-au-vent de quenelles,* sir, and I can recommend the chef's *sauté de merlans aux fines herbes*. He has a real flair with fish.''

"Pouring the butter boat over your head, is he?'' queried a low amused voice from her left as the business of serving took up the lieutenant's attention momentarily.

Adrienne quickly choked back the laugh rising in her throat and whispered indignantly, ''He cannot believe any female could be so simple as to swallow all that flummery.''

"I don't know about that. Believe Markham's had reasonable success with that line of his a time or two.''

Adrienne directed a disbelieving look at the major's bland countenance before returning her eyes to her plate.

"Has anyone ever told you your eyes are the most incredible color?'' came the unceasing voice at her right.

"Yes, Lieutenant,'' Adrienne replied, dazzling a smile at him, ''dozens of people, including yourself just a few moments ago. You are beginning to repeat yourself.''

The faintest quiver disturbed the young officer's mouth, but he came back smoothly, ''Ah, beauty allied to quickness of wit is above all things the most desirable in a woman. There is not another lady in the room, indeed in the whole of Brussels, who can hold a candle to you, Miss Castle.''

Adrienne's eyebrows flew up. ''Oh, you *poor* man! I had no idea you suffered from impaired vision. It must be a great handicap in your profession.'' She derived great satisfaction from the look of consternation that crossed the handsome features of her antagonist as he stammered:

"I . . . I beg your pardon?''

A soft chuckle reached her from the left, but Adrienne managed to preserve her countenance as she explained gravely: ''Well, you have just declared me to outshine all the beauties of Brussels, and here is Lady Tremayne sitting no more than ten feet away. Obviously you suffer from advanced myopia.''

The lieutenant's ready tongue deserted him for an instant as he stared into her politely sympathetic face. ''Well . . . uh . . . naturally I would agree with the consensus that holds Lady Tremayne to be a very beautiful woman.'' Gaining confidence from the sound of his voice, he went on, "But my own taste runs to redheads, so I stand by everything I said before.''

Adrienne grinned saucily at the irrepressible young man, but was prevented from continuing the contest when Dominic rose to his feet to make the announcement of his betrothal. In concert with the other guests, his cousin smiled, applauded, raised her glass in a toast to Lady Tremayne, and then drank to the couple's future happiness. As she turned her eyes from the smiling faces of the engaged pair, she discovered herself to be the object of intense study on the part of a gentleman seated across the table. She had the instantaneous impression that he was trying to fathom the deepest secrets of her heart and soul, which left her a trifle discomposed, as she could not help wondering how long she had been under such a pointed scrutiny. Had he witnessed the nonsensical passage-at-arms with Lieutenant Markham? What was he making of her, and why should she be of particular interest to a perfect stanger? She had no recollection of his name, but there was something familiar about his cast of countenance.

Puzzled and a bit intrigued, Adrienne regarded from beneath her lashes the man sitting opposite. A disinterested observer would have to call him well-favored, although she had reacted to his stare with an instinctive shrinking, which, to be fair, might have been caused entirely by the natural disinclination anyone would experience at being so minutely observed when unaware. The man's evening attire, what she could see of it, was faultless, his dark hair was painstakingly styled in the popular windswept fashion, and his thin features were of classic proportions and regularity. It was the light shining on amber-colored eyes as he turned his head to reply to his neighbor that settled the question of his identity for Adrienne. This was Sir Ralph Morrison, and it was the resemblance to his sister that accounted for the sense of familiarity. His interest in herself remained a mystery, however. Offhand, she would set his age at several years older than Dominic, whom she knew to be nine-and-twenty, and from something in his expression which recalled her father's friends, she would judge him to be very much a man of the world. No reason for more than a passing interest in an anonymous and unfledged young woman suggested itself to her intellect.

It would never have occurred to Adrienne that Sir Ralph, privy to all his sister's moods, was studying this unexpected addition to Lord Creighton's life in the light of a possible stumbling block to the very desirable marriage that was going to retrieve the family fortunes. Lord, Pamela had been livid tonight when the red-haired chit had made her big entrance! For a minute he'd feared that temper of hers would explode, but she'd had the wit to keep her tongue between her teeth, thank heaven. Granted, the girl was a long cry from the little mouse his sister had described, but she was still no threat to Pamela. Creighton wasn't a youngster to be captivated by all that wide-eyed innocence. If unopened buds appealed to him, he never would have fallen for Pamela despite her beautiful face. No, it wasn't Miss Castle who might yet threaten the consummation of their hopes, but that abominable temper of Pamela's. She thought she had Creighton wrapped around her little finger, but he was nobody's fool, not the man to be led by the nose or to live under the cat's paw. If Pamela couldn't see that, for all his easygoing manner, Creighton was unmovable as rock in his principles, she wanted her head examined.

Nor would her fiancé stand still while she played fast and loose with other men. They could breathe a sigh of relief now the engagement was official, but if he knew his sister, it would be his unenviable task to keep her on the straight and narrow until she got the earl to the altar, an event that couldn't happen soon enough to suit Sir Ralph. His own affairs were pressing enough, but acting duenna to Pamela held all the appeal of minding a keg of explosives during an enemy attack. Sir Ralph sighed soundlessly as he cast an assessing eye over his sister's animated countenance as she sat in rapt conversation with her fiancé. Before the ladies left the room he must try to catch her ear for a second to warn her to leave the little cousin alone.

Unfortunately for Adrienne, Sir Ralph did not manage to drop a hint in his sister's ear before the ladies withdrew, and by the time the gentlemen had rejoined them, all her earlier pleasure in the party had gone into complete eclipse. Had she been less conscientious, she might have avoided the reversal altogether, but she was persuaded she owed Lady Tremayne an explanation for her late entrance. There had been time for no more than a quick apology before dinner. She would have spoken immediately and gotten the matter off her chest had not Lady Staveley sought her out to present her two daughters once again. It seemed the Staveleys were old friends of the Norcross family, and Lady Creighton had written to Lady Staveley requesting her good offices for her young relative while she was in Brussels.

"Which I am most pleased to offer, my dear child, for Arabella Norcross has always given my girls the run of Harmony Hall, even though they are several years younger than her own daughters. I hope you and Miss Beckworth will call on Marjorie and Eleanor whenever you feel you can leave your young brother for a time."

The Staveley ladies were of a gregarious nature, and Adrienne spent the next few moments trying to listen equally to all three, who chatted nonstop in unison, continually interrupting one another. At one point, seeing the bewilderment on Miss Castle's face, Lady Staveley laughed and promised she would soon get the hang of deciphering their jumbled conversations, all their friends soon acquired the knack. Their genuine friendliness was warmly welcome to Adrienne, who vastly enjoyed the interlude, but when Colonel Lacey's lady approached to speak to Lady Staveley, she excused herself to seek out Lady Tremayne, who had just moved away from Miss Beckworth to sit in one corner of a long sofa.

Adrienne seated herself beside the lovely brunette, who had watched her approach with an unsmiling mien. "Lady Tremayne, I must apologize again for my deplorable lateness this evening and explain how it came about. I—"

"Oh really, Miss Castle, do not trouble yourself. No explanation is necessary, believe me," replied Lady

Tremayne with a tinkling laugh. "I am not so advanced in years that I have forgotten how very important it is to contrive to be noticed when one is—forgive me—young and somewhat negligible in society."

Adrienne gasped, and the healthy color drained from her cheeks. "It was not like that at all . . . I never intended . . . I pray you to believe that my tardiness was totally unintentional. Jean-Paul accidently spilled some lemonade on my gown and it became necessary for my maid to remove the stain. She worked on my gown as quickly as possible, but of course it took time to dry the area. We placed the gown close to the fire and fanned it to circulate the air and—"

"You are looking most distraught, Adrienne. What is wrong?" asked Lord Creighton, who had come up soft-footed behind the sofa where the two women were sitting, so intently absorbed in each other they had failed to notice that the gentlemen had joined the ladies in the drawing room.

Adrienne jumped up. "I . . . I didn't see you, cousin. N-nothing is wrong! I . . . I was just explaining to Lady Tremayne that my lateness this evening was due to a stupid accident to my gown. I had to wait while it dried."

Lady Tremayne rose gracefully and wrapped both hands around her fiancé's arm. She glanced up at him provocatively and laughed. "And I have been assuring Miss Castle that explanations are unnecessary. We all understand that very young ladies like to make an entrance." She shrugged smooth shoulders and directed a brilliant smile at Adrienne. "No offense taken."

A pale Adrienne faced her cousin's betrothed squarely. "I'm sorry that you believe I would behave in such a manner, Lady Tremayne," she replied stiffly. "There is nothing more I can say except to repeat that my tardiness was unintentional. If you will excuse me now, I believe Becky wishes to speak to me." There was a blind look in the aquamarine eyes that passed briefly over the engaged couple before she turned away.

A short silence thrummed between the pair standing by

the sofa; then Lord Creighton said gravely, "Could you not have pretended to believe her, Pamela?"

"Of course I will, darling, if you wish it," Lady Tremayne responded cordially, slanting a seductive smile up at him. For once the earl seemed unmoved by the charming picture she made with her regal dark head thrown back and her perfect profile emphasized. He sprang almost eagerly to obey a summons from one of the footmen who suddenly appeared at his side, though his apology to his fiancée was courteously spoken.

Lady Tremayne stood quite still, staring after Lord Creighton until her brother, who had been hovering a pace away, said in an undertone, "That was not very wise of you, Pamela. This is your night of triumph. You could afford to be generous to the girl. She is Creighton's cousin, after all."

Lady Tremayne's sculptured nostrils flared as she whirled to face Sir Ralph. "Are you suggesting I should have allowed her deliberate attempt to steal the limelight to go unmentioned? You don't know me very well, Ralph."

"I know you all too well, my dear," came the weary retort. "What I am suggesting is that you curb your jealousy. Creighton won't thank you for showing up his cousin."

"*Jealousy*!" She almost spat out the word, and her brother raised a warning eyebrow. Lady Tremayne moderated her tone to a soft hiss, but the venom came through clearly. "How dare you accuse me of being jealous of that little nobody!"

"Now, now, Sir Ralph, can't have you monopolizing the guest of honor, you know, even if she is your sister. Must give the rest of us a chance." A jovial gentleman sent his booming voice ahead of him to break up the tête-à-tête.

Lady Tremayne made a graceful play with her gold lace fan and her gold-toned eyes. "How sweet of you to rescue me from my dreary brother, Lord Staveley," she purred, turning her back squarely on the former.

Miss Beckworth had had the foresight to have the pianoforte in the drawing room tuned that week in the event the company should prefer music to conversation or cards. When several of the gentlemen requested the pleasure of hearing Lady Tremayne sing, Lord Creighton opened the instrument and led the fair performer to it, seating her with a smile.

Lady Tremayne was possessed of a husky soprano voice that she used to great advantage, and she was a competent performer on the piano. She sang a ballad of her own choice and then accepted several requests before turning resolutely away with a little crash of chords. "My throat is becoming dry and it is time we had a little variety. Perhaps Miss Castle will favor us with a song or two?" She flashed her famous smile at Adrienne, who sternly willed herself not to blush or stammer.

"I am so sorry but I don't sing."

"Well, play for us, then. I am persuaded everyone is tired of feminine trilling and would welcome an instrumental work," said Lady Tremayne in an encouraging voice.

"I'm afraid I don't play either. Perhaps another lady will oblige?"

"My cousin insists that she has no accomplishments," said Lord Creighton before an awkward silence could develop. "She does not regard the acquisition of five languages as worthy to be deemed an accomplishment, but I believe those of us who struggle daily with the intricacies of the French tongue would beg leave to differ with her."

"By Jove, wouldn't we just!" Major Peters concurred feelingly.

Lord Creighton allowed the little ripple of laughter that followed this remark to die before adding, "Meanwhile, though I am aware that Miss Forrester is no less modest about her skill on the pianoforte than Adrienne is about hers with languages, I hope we may persuade her to give us the great pleasure of hearing her play." He directed his delightful smile at the young lady in question, who flushed faintly.

There was a prompt chorus of requests to Miss Forrester, who quietly took Lady Tremayne's place at the piano. For the next half-hour the company was treated to a performance of exquisite talent and sensitivity from the general's self-effacing daughter. She was familiar with the works of all the prominent composers and played selections from several.

During the two or three periods of relative affluence when the Castles had possessed a pianoforte in their lodgings, Miss Beckworth had given Adrienne some elementary tuition on the instrument. The opportunity to hear a gifted performer had been at the top of her list of special treats ever since, but tonight Adrienne's expression of rapt interest was difficult to maintain because her mind was in a turmoil that music could not soothe. The confrontation with Lady Tremayne in which the beautiful brunette had made it plain that she did not choose to believe Adrienne's explanation for her tardy entrance had robbed the evening of all its pleasure and left the inexperienced girl thoroughly shaken. To be accused of putting herself forward, to be thought capable of trying to steal the attention away from the guest of honor, was so shaming to a gently reared girl that she would have welcomed it if the floor beneath her feet had opened and swallowed her up. And to have her humiliation witnessed by Dominic, who had been their kind and generous benefactor, had put the seal on her misery. That he should think she would repay his kindness in such a manner! Physical escape was denied her; to make her excuses would be to draw more attention to herself, but it took every ounce of moral courage she possessed to sit quietly by Becky and produce the occasional smile or response required by civility, all the while avoiding a meeting of glances with her cousin's fiancée. It had been a relief when the musical portion of the evening began, but her respite had been cruelly brought to a halt by Lady Tremayne's gay challenge to her to perform.

As Miss Forrester moved into a Beethoven sonata, Adrienne cast about in her mind to recall whether she might have mentioned her lack of musical talent to Lady Tremayne during that abysmal tea party. Not that it really signified. There could be no question after the earlier incident that it was Lady Tremayne's intention to humiliate her fiancé's cousin in retaliation for what she perceived as an affront. The lovely notes of the musical selection washed over her unheeded as Adrienne endeavored to cope with the appalling discovery that she had made an enemy. Her hands twisted uneasily in her lap while she continued to direct an unfocused gaze at Miss Forrester. She had been loath to admit even to herself that she might have taken Dominic's betrothed in dislike, and, guilt-ridden at her inability to like the woman wholeheartedly, had striven mightily with herself to disguise this disloyalty from everyone, even Becky. Perhaps she had been unsuccessful at hiding her distaste? Perhaps Lady Tremayne had sensed an unadmitted animosity and had been hurt by it? Perhaps she had seen confirmation of it in Adrienne's tardiness tonight and had reacted in anger and chagrin? Adrienne was miserably conscious that she was very much at fault, and the worst of it was that she could see no avenue of reparation ahead.

Through the rest of the interminable evening Adrienne was withdrawn in spirit from the other guests, trying mentally to assess her future position *vis-à-vis* her cousin's fiancée. The best she could come up with after much unhappy ratiocination was simply to avoid being in company with Lady Tremayne and Dominic as much as possible. She felt Becky's eyes on her once or twice as she evaded being singled out by one or another of the young officers while tea was being served. Perhaps if she told her friend the whole story tomorrow, Becky would be able to advise her as to her future conduct. She had religiously avoided meeting Lady Tremayne's glance from the moment she had declined to perform, but she had been uncomfortably aware of an inimical regard directed at her on several occasions when she had chanced to raise her eyes to reply to some conversational overture. This awareness of latent hostility produced a sensation not unlike a chill on the back of one's neck and was not something she would care to experience with any degree of frequency.

It was surprising, therefore, when the guests had finally departed, to find herself being profusely thanked by Lady Tremayne for her efforts toward making the announcement party such a success. Surprising and rather disconcerting, for when Adrienne looked up hopefully, it was to discover that no trace of the cordiality in Lady Tremayne's voice was reflected in the amber eyes. They were as cold as if carved from the stone they resembled. She had at first directed her gratitude solely to Miss Beckworth, who had mentioned Adrienne's part in creating the flower arrangements that had evoked expressions of admiration from a number of the guests. There had been no hesitation as Lady Tremayne graciously included Adrienne in her thanks while Dominic tenderly wrapped her evening cloak about her shoulders, but those implacable eyes told Adrienne she was unforgiven. Despite the warmth of the May evening, she shivered a little as her troubled gaze followed the betrothed couple from the room. It was with a feeling akin to release that she said good night to Becky and sought the peace of her own chamber.

10

Colonel Lord Creighton of the field marshal's staff nodded to a passing neighbor and climbed the steps to his house, his expression abstracted. It was unusual to be coming home in the middle of the morning, but he'd just received orders to go to Ghent to the French king's court in exile. He needed to instruct his batman about packing and he intended to write to Pamela before he left. She would have to make his excuses for a number of upcoming social events in the next few days. His mind busy with last-minute details, he didn't hear the front door open and nearly collided with Luc running down the stairs. He put out a hand to steady the boy.

"Whoa, lad. Where are you off to?"

"I . . . I thought I'd go down to the canal and watch the fishing boats come in near the Quai aux Briques."

Dominic's eyes narrowed slightly but he refrained from mentioning that the fishing boats would have come in earlier than midmorning if they hoped to do any business. "Are you finished with your studies for the moment?"

"Yes. That is, I have some more Latin translation to do, but I'll get to it after lunch."

Luc's eyes slid from his, and Dominic sighed silently. Something was going to have to be done about Luc in the near future. He needed to have his time more occupied. With the women so involved with Jean-Paul, the earl suspected he was taking advantage of the resultant freedom to haunt the barracks. It was time to find him a tutor.

"Luc, I'll be away for a few days. You'll keep an eye on the ladies for me?"

The boy straightened up immediately and his eyes held

the man's. "Yes, of course, Cousin Dominic. Where are you going, or must I not ask?"

"Nothing secret about it. I have to go to Ghent with messages. I should be home in three or four days."

Dominic looked even more thoughtful as he went quietly up the stairs a moment later. It was rather inconvenient having to leave Brussels right now, and not just because of Luc. Pamela wouldn't be pleased to lose his escort services, and he preferred to be on hand to look over the young men who were sure to come calling on Adrienne since her official appearance at the betrothal dinner. He had so looked forward to that evening, to making his claim on Pamela official, as it were, but it had been oddly disappointing. He didn't think it was just in his imagination that his relations with both young women had subtly altered since the dinner, though he was hard pressed to say how or why. No, he corrected himself, that was only partly true. He knew that Adrienne was avoiding him and he supposed he knew why. She had been distressed at Pamela's intimation that she had deliberately staged a late entrance at the party to make herself the center of attention. Pamela was mistaken, of course; artifice wasn't a part of Adrienne's makeup, and she had no ambitions to cut a dash in society. He had been at pains to explain this to his love when he had escorted her home that night. She had been sweetly penitent, had even admitted with a catch in that seductive voice that she might not have behaved with generosity when Adrienne had apologized, though she had tried to make amends by inviting his cousin to sing for their guests. He had been struck almost dumb with surprise to hear Pamela confess to a tiny spurt of jealousy at seeing Adrienne so radiant and making such a hit with the young officers. Dominic had laughed at such nonsense, of course, and had taken her in his arms to assure her in the most convincing manner he could think of that there wasn't a woman on the face of the earth who could be compared with his beautiful fiancée. It had taken all of his resolution to let her go inside that night. Her beauty and charm went straight to his head and inflamed his senses, but he had reluctantly had to deny her suggestion that they marry immediately. There was simply too much on his plate at present, what with his house full of relatives and the military situation growing daily more intense. Much as he longed to make her his, prudence dictated restraint.

Pamela hadn't been pleased to find him beyond the reach of her cajolery on this subject, and had been treating him with a deliberate coolness ever since. She had allotted him only one dance the other night and had accepted the invitation of a Dutch officer to lead her in to supper. When they were alone her conversation was of the most trivial, as she ignored the relationship between them and treated him like the merest acquaintance.

Engagements were an invention of the devil, he decided, giving his bedchamber door a savage shove. They tried a man's patience, frustrated his senses, and ruined his disposition. When he had tried to kiss Pamela last night she had pulled out of his arms with some damn fool excuse of its being better to remain at arm's length, since their betrothal was likely to be prolonged. She was punishing him, of course; he wasn't such a green youngster as to be taken in by her simulated regret, but he'd made the mistake of telling her so instead of accepting his dismissal and allowing her time for reflection. Naturally she had resented being challenged and had held to her story, buckle and thong—like all women, he editorialized sourly as he gave orders to his batman and sat down to write to his fiancée. The error of confronting a woman with her real motive had been driven home to him, and he had bowed in acquiescence as he bade her a polite good night. But he hated like the devil to be at odds with the people he cared about!

He should be pleased as punch that Pamela was no less eager than he to consummate their union—and he was! It was inevitable that a woman as admired and courted as she would become accustomed to getting her own way. It was really a wonder she wasn't more spoiled by all the adulation. He could make allowances for some slight willfulness. And the truly ridiculous aspect of the entire situation was that they wanted the same thing! A momentary trace of bitterness at the irony distorted his mouth; then he banished it and set out to write warmly to his beloved, aware of how much he would miss her, though it was no penance to forgo the hectic round of social activities that women seemed to find necessary to their well-being. Sealing the note, he gave it to his batman to deliver and went down the hall in search of Adrienne. He'd not pressured her to explain her avoidance up till now, but he didn't like to go away without making a push to right matters. His cousin was a delightful girl and he wanted no awkwardness to spoil the rapport that had grown up between them.

He didn't have far to look. As he descended the stairs, Adrienne stuck her head out of the music-room door. "Is that you, Luc? Oh . . . Dominic! I . . . I beg your pardon. I was expecting Luc to come partner me in the dancing lesson."

A knowing laugh escaped the earl. "So that explains why I met Luc sneaking out the door as I arrived."

Adrienne's dimples came into play as she grinned in response. "That boy is as slippery as an eel. I fear it was a mistake to tell him last night that the accompanist could not come today."

"I'd say he shows a remarkable ability to take evasive action in the face of a suspected ambush. Will I do as a substitute?"

"Oh, no!" Adrienne backed away.

"Why the horror? I will have you to understand, Miss Castle, that I am generally accorded a more-than-adequate practitioner in the terpsichorean art."

"You know I didn't mean that!" Indignation chased away embarrassment. "I wouldn't dream of taking up your time with something so unimportant. And what are you doing home at this hour, anyway?"

"I protest, cousin. I consider your introduction to the pleasures of dancing as a very important aspect of your education as a young lady of fashion." Dominic cursed his hamhandedness as a remote look entered the aquamarine eyes.

"Yes," she replied evenly, "it will be nice to be able to claim at least one feminine accomplishment."

"Now, look, my dear cousin,"—he didn't pretend to misunderstand, but spoke sternly—"you would be foolish beyond permission to refine too much on what happened the other evening. A female need not be a performing monkey to be a success in society. Some of the most charming women I know neither sing nor play, my own mother among them, and yet they continue to be sought after for the qualities of their minds or the sweetness of their natures long after the performers have lost their audience. Now that you know you have only to decline if invited to play, you will not again be flustered. Pamela felt very badly that she was the cause of your embarrassment the other night, especially since she was trying to make amends for . . . the earlier misunderstanding."

"Was she?" Adrienne asked in neutral tones. "How kind of her."

"Yes, of course. If you and she had been better acquainted she would have known you aren't the sort of female who needs to be the center of attention. Now," he added, giving her no chance to ponder his words, "to answer your second question, I came home to see to some packing, as I'll have to be away for a few days. Ah, Monsieur Daubigny!" as the dancing master appeared in the open doorway. "How do you do? I have offered my support to my cousin for her lesson, since her brother has absconded."

"But, Dominic, you cannot spare the time, surely," protested Adrienne.

"Ten minutes more or less won't change the course of history. What are you working on at present, Monsieur Daubigny?" The earl possessed himself of his cousin's hand and drew her into the music room.

For the next few minutes while the dancing master played for them, Dominic guided Adrienne through some of the complicated figures of the new quadrille. They had to imagine the movements of the other three couples, of course, but at least she was able to step out of the *tour de deux mains* and the *pas de zéphyr* and approximate the *chain des dames*, with Dominic switching roles to assist her.

"And now, Monsieur Daubigny, if you will play a waltz, I shall claim my reward," the earl requested of the smiling teacher, who obligingly shifted to a waltz melody.

"May I have the honor, Miss Castle?"

Adrienne dropped a low curtsy in response to Dominic's courtly bow and glided into his arms. The furniture in the music room had been pushed against the walls to create a very respectable ballroom. The earl took advantage of every foot of space, whirling her expertly around the room. Adrienne, abandoning herself to a heady sense of exhilaration like nothing she had ever known, followed him instinctively.

"May I say, Miss Castle, that the dress you are wearing, the color of the new leaves on the chestnut trees, makes your fascinating eyes appear more green than blue today?"

Adrienne continued to gaze dreamily over his shoulder, a half-smile on her lips.

The earl drew back slightly and reminded her, "A lady is expected to do more than dance on a dance floor, Miss Castle. She is not playing her part if she neglects to acknowledge the flowery compliments paid her by her partner."

Adrienne's delightful chuckle fluted between them and her wide-eyed gaze met his amused eyes innocently. "Do you not mean *leafy* compliments, my lord? I was too busy minding my steps. I hope," she added with unflattering directness, "that my partners, if I am ever present at a ball, will not ruin a dance by uttering inane compliments. I just love dancing and I thank you most sincerely for arranging with Monsieur Daubigny to teach me."

Dominic drew her a little closer and gave himself up to enjoying the moment. Let someone else instruct her in the art of receiving compliments. He had a hunch Adrienne was not going to adapt readily to being molded into a typical debutante, but she was a natural dancer. They finished the waltz without another word being exchanged. As the music ended, Dominic glided to a stop and smiled down into the vivid little face sparkling up at him, lips parted and cheeks glowing with a faint tinge of peach. She was adorable! His teasing prediction that she would draw the young officers like a magnet was certain to be fulfilled, he realized with a little pang. It would be up to him to see that she didn't get hurt. She was so very young, not in years, true, but in experience, although there were times when she appeared oddly wise and practical beyond her years. Not in this area, though. In the arena of male-female dalliance she was naught but a babe. And likely to be a great responsibility. A small frown creased his brow.

"Why are you frowning? I merely thanked you for the waltz. It was wonderful," Adrienne said happily. "Is not a lady allowed to thank her partner then?"

"Of course. If I was frowning, it was because I hate to call a halt to such a delightful episode, but I really must be on my way. My compliments, Monsieur Daubigny, you have done wonders in a very short time."

"I have been blessed with a talented pupil, milord," countered the Frenchman smoothly, "who will do you great credit as soon as she overcomes a lamentable tendency to brush aside the gallantries of her partners."

Dominic laughed at the guilty blush that swept up over his cousin's throat, and pinched her chin lightly on his way out. He was still smiling a few minutes later as he climbed up on Trooper, his huge bay gelding. The prospect of a courier trip that would entail the constant exercise of diplomatic language still did not appeal, but his spirits had certainly risen as a result of the impromptu dancing lesson. The slight estrangement from his cousin had been mended, and he trusted his note to Pamela would do the same in that quarter.

Lord Creighton would have been a good deal dismayed had he been present when Lady Tremayne read his apologetic letter. It had been delivered before noon, but she had been out for lunch before driving in the park, and found herself entering the house at the same time as her brother in late afternoon. Sir Ralph flipped through the visiting cards and post and extracted one envelope which he held up in front of his sister's eyes. One smooth, perfectly arched brow elevated. She accepted the missive with discernible reluctance and went into the saloon. Sir Ralph strolled in after her and closed the door. He leaned against it, arms akimbo, silently watching while his sister mastered the contents of the note.

Lady Tremayne uttered an angry exclamation and tossed the single sheet of paper onto the table beside her chair. "He must imagine I have more hair than wit if he hopes to put this across." Her fingers drummed an impatient rhythm on the tabletop. When her brother picked up the note without a by-your-leave, she made an instinctive gesture of protest, then shrugged, resuming the annoyed finger motions.

Sir Ralph looked up over the paper in his hand and said mildly: "The man has to go out of town for a few days and, very properly, if somewhat sentimentally, expresses his regret at having to leave his loving fiancée behind. What is there in that to make you switch your tail like an angry cat?"

"He's doing this deliberately to get back at me! He knows I have counted on his escort for several affairs in the next few days."

Sir Ralph dropped the offending note back onto the table and pinned his sister with an acute stare. "The colonel is not a free agent, you know. He does have to execute the commands of his superiors. And why should he wish to get back at you? Have you two been quarreling, with the betrothal announcement scarcely yesterday's news?"

"That's my business!" snapped his sister.

"Don't be a fool, Pamela! I know you think you have Creighton completely under your spell, but I tell you you could still lose him if you try to play off any of your tricks on him."

"It's you who are foolish! Dominic would never cry off from a public engagement. It would go against his code of honor." Lady Tremayne gathered up her reticule and the note and prepared to leave the room. "You will have to take me about this week, Ralph."

"I already have plans for tomorrow night. It wouldn't hurt you to stay home for once."

Lady Tremayne paused with her hand on the door and smiled at her brother. "If you are unable to act as my escort, I'm sure I'll have no difficulty in finding a substitute,'' she said sweetly before closing the door behind her.

Sir Ralph scowled in impotent fury at his sister's Parthian arrow. She had him in a cleft stick, damn her! He was not so sanguine as Pamela that Creighton would go through with the marriage if his betrothed's behavior became totally outrageous. The earl might be a man of honor, but in Sir Ralph's considered opinion, his sister's uncertain temper nullified this advantage. He could envision a situation where a violent enough quarrel might result in Pamela's flinging the ring in her fiancé's face. This chilling thought sent him over to the desk to write a note expressing his regrets to his proposed host for declining tomorrow night's engagement.

The next few days sped by for Adrienne who was experiencing for the first time an exciting taste of the social whirl that constituted the daily life of the upper class. Since the dinner party, visitors had begun to leave cards at the big house in Rue Ducale. Lady Staveley called one morning with her daughters and kindly brought the earl's relatives up-to-date on the *on-dits* floating around Brussels that spring. Dominic tried to satisfy his ladies' curiosity as to Lord Wellington's social appearances, but it was from the Staveley girls that they learned that Lady Frances Webster, whose name had once been scandalously coupled with that of the notorious Lord Byron, was being pronounced Wellington's latest flirt. Another of Lord Byron's former conquests, Lady Caroline Lamb, was seen everywhere about the town in her revealing dampened muslins which through repetition had ceased to have the same shock value. Adrienne grew big-eyed while Miss Staveley and Miss Eleanor revealed the inner workings of society as observed from the discreet distance permitted by their watchful mama.

Lieutenant Markham dropped in almost every day to pay his respects. Once he abandoned his line of extravagant compliments, the young officer proved to be a reasonably conversable individual, and he and Adrienne quickly got upon terms of easy friendship. Adrienne and Miss Beckworth appreciated that his good nature extended to Luc and Jean-Paul, who was permitted to rest on the daybed in the small saloon for a period each day. The whole family was gradually widening its social circle.

Miss Beckworth and Adrienne called on Miss Forrester, who had left her card one morning while the ladies had been out shopping. As luck would have it, the general also chanced to be at home for tea that afternoon. Though his manners were polished, it was readily apparent to Adrienne that he was more than a little taken with Miss Beckworth's quiet charm and ready wit and had every intention of remaining by her side, however many people came to call. This left Adrienne and the general's daughter to entertain each other.

Sarah Forrester was a young woman whom it was easy to overlook in a crowd. She was of moderate height and slightly plump figure, and there was nothing especially eye-catching about her gentle features or mid-brown coloring. Her principal asset was a pair of large hazel eyes that reflected both her quiet nature and her good understanding. Adrienne had liked her at their first meeting and fully expected that future meetings would only confirm her first impressions. In the course of becoming acquainted, Miss Forrester revealed that she had acted as her father's hostess since her mother's death four years peviously. She had accompanied the army to Spain to try to maintain a home whenever possible, and she made light of the dangers and hardships such a course entailed, the fact that her father had needed her making all other considerations irrelevant. In reply to Adrienne's interested questions she had described her life in Spain before the defeat of the French and contrasted it to the way she and her father spent their time in Vienna the past winter at the Congress. The young women made considerable strides along the route to friendship that afternoon.

It was a new experience in Adrienne's life. Never before had she possessed a female friend of her own generation. Hers had been a gypsy existence, traipsing along in the train of a man with a wanderlust. The family had clung

together out of love and necessity and had supplied all th
companionship she had ever known. She had never minde
not having a settled home and a stable circle of friends—
after all, one can't miss what one has never had, but as sh
and Miss Beckworth walked back from the Forresters
lodgings, she was in a pensive mood.

"I like Sarah Forrester very much, Becky. The Stavele
girls are perfectly pleasant and likable too, but they ar
essentially hen-witted, though I don't mean that in
critical sense. I enjoy their company, but I feel that Sara
is someone from whom it will be a wrench to part when w
leave Brussels. I've never felt this way about anyon
before. I've never had a real friend before, except you, o
course."

Miss Beckworth smiled at the earnest girl beside her
though her eyes were sober. "You have missed a lot
dearest, but there have been compensations, too. Mos
girls your age lead a very circumscribed life, sheltered bu
narrow. It is small wonder they haven't as much to offer a
you. You have seen a good deal of the world and the wa
others live. You will never be afraid to be helpful whe
needed. I'm glad you and Miss Forrester find yourselves *e
rapport*. There is no reason why you shouldn't correspon
when we get to England. She will be returning there event
ually. I am quite taken with her too. She has a fine under
standing and a pleasant nature, and she is a very devote
daughter."

"Yes. I like the general too, although I have so far re
ceived a minimal share of his attention," Adrienne replied
slanting a teasing glance at her companion, who smile
faintly but refused the bait. "I imagine he will be beref
when Sarah marries."

"Actually, General Forrester is quite concerned tha
Sarah should have a life of her own. He is aware that sh
has devoted years of her youth to him already, and that—
and you will not repeat this, I know—she has refused a
least two offers because she would not leave him. She con
vinced him in both instances that her affections had bee
untouched, but I believe now that his own grief has abate

somewhat, he is feeling guilty and anxious over Sarah's future.''

Adrienne murmured something noncommittal. In truth she had all she could do to keep from her displaying her surprise at the rapid development of a rapport between Becky and General Forrester that had him divulging his deepest family concerns at their second meeting. In comparison, her own and Sarah's approach to friendship struck her as scarcely tentative.

Over the next few days Adrienne observed her oldest friend with eyes from which the veils of familiarity had been snatched. Becky had been as much a part of her life as her parents, and for as long, someone to be taken for granted. Now Adrienne was shaken out of her complacency. Her eyes, following her companion's movements, and her ears, listening to the familiar voice, had an acuteness put there by the sight of General Forrester and Becky ostensibly engaged in conversation but, to Adrienne's alerted fancy, actually enclosed in a world that contained only two. She was forced to admit there was nothing different about her friend's behavior to support this theory, nor did Becky make her the recipient of any of her thoughts, supposing they existed, about the general; in fact, she did not once mention his name. Far from supposing that this was an accurate indication of his importance, Adrienne was inclined to consider her friend's reticence as evidence that he was indeed in her thoughts, and, furthermore, that these were too precious to share.

As for evidence that would convince a jury, there was none. A note had been delivered to Becky one day which struck Adrienne as being written in a masculine hand, but her friend had not spoken of the matter. Adrienne's speculations were based solely on intuition and the recollection of how right and complete the picture of Miss Beckworth and General Forrester sitting in close conversation had seemed. It had not impressed her as anything of moment at the time, but distance and reflection lent it increasing significance.

Her first reaction to this prickling awareness had been

negative, a denial based, she soon realized, on an instinctive fear of change in their lives. Immediately swamping this selfish shrinking had been a burgeoning hope that Becky might yet find a personal happiness, if not with the general, then with someone else whose affection would repay her in part for the long years of selfless devotion to children not her own. On the heels of this hope came the iron conviction that Becky would deny herself her chance of happiness for the sake of Adrienne and her brothers unless she believed that their future was assured.

And there was the rub, for the optimistic Adrienne, who had never faced, let alone feared, the future, was suddenly tremblingly conscious of the precariousness of their situation. They had, literally, almost no money behind them and no close family ties. To be sure, Lady Creighton had extended a generous hand to enable them to return to England, but they could not *live* off her charity. It was strange, she mused, but before Dominic had come to their rescue she had looked no further than getting the family to England, as if once there their problems would miraculously be solved. She shook her head in wonder at the naiveté—no, the abysmal ignorance—that could have supported such a rationalization.

Looking back, it struck her that she must have been existing in something bordering on a comatose state before Dominic had drawn them into his orbit. For the most part the awakening had been enjoyable beyond her imaginings and not just in the ease and comfort of improved circumstances and widened social contacts. Perhaps the greatest benefit was in becoming closely involved with Dominic himself. After years of taking care of her much younger brothers she was finding it a delightful experience to acquire a surrogate elder brother, especially one as charming as Dominic, who considered it his province to look after *her*. She had been amazed these last few days to discover how much she missed her cousin's cheerful presence in the house after such a short acquaintance. It would not do, however, to become dependent on the kindness of her cousin, any more than on the generosity of his mother. *Au fond,* the Castles had no right to depend on anyone save themselves, and she must keep this circumstance squarely in view at all times.

For the next two nights Adrienne's sleep was interrupted by confused dreams and sudden awakenings. She would come instantly awake, driven by the need to take some action. On one occasion her legs were already over the side of the bed before she recollected where she was and that there was no positive action that could alleviate the basic situation. She fell back onto the pillows, and half-formed plans began squirrelling around in her mind once again. The boys would have to be self-supporting, of course. They must have professions, but how to set them on the path of attaining the capability of entering a profession completely defeated her intelligence at present.

Her own future she dismissed with little thought. She assumed she could always find a place as a governess in some genteel family, forgetting, in her absorption with her brothers' probable careers, her own lamentable lack of any qualifications considered necessary to instruct the young.

11

"No, no, Adrienne, not like that! I keep telling you, don't *chop* at it! *Shave* lightly around the center. You want to get the feeling of roundness in the duck. Yours is going to look emaciated if you continue hacking at it like that."

The man on the stairs paused as the impatient young voice reached him from the small sitting room. A feminine murmur in reply was too indistinct to decipher, but the tired lines vanished from his face as he smiled and changed his course.

Adrienne glanced up as the sitting-room door opened. *"Dominic!"* she cried, jumping up and dropping her tools in her haste. "Have you just returned from Ghent? Welcome home!"

The man striding into the room could not mistake the warmth of the greeting in his cousin's voice and eyes. He seized her hands and squeezed them smilingly. "After such a welcome, I'm glad I did not brother to change first. All three dimples present and accounted for, I see." The earl turned to the other occupant of the room and smiled at the boy watching them. "It was Jean-Paul's voice that brought me in here in all my dirt. You sound and look a great deal stronger than when I left, lad. What is that you are working on?" he asked, releasing Adrienne's hands.

"I am carving a set of chess pieces for Luc," replied the boy, holding up a bishop for his cousin's inspection.

This was done thoroughly and in total silence. The earl turned the almost completed piece around in his hands, examining it from all sides; then he said with gratifying sincerity, "This is a fine piece of work, lad. You've the knack of carving, all right."

Jean-Paul visibly swelled with pride at this encomium,

and Adrienne rewarded her cousin with her sunny smile.

"Is this your work, cousin?" Dominic inquired, bending down to retrieve the fallen object at her feet. This too he turned over in his hands and subjected to a scrutiny, while Adrienne, by dint of stern discipline, remained expressionless, awaiting the verdict.

"I feel you have not progressed to quite the same point as Jean-Paul," the earl began tactfully, before he was interrupted as his cousins went into whoops of laughter.

"One more nonaccomplishment to add to my formidable list," Adrienne said when she had mastered her giggles. "Will you be home for dinner, cousin?"

"Well, no. I haven't seen Pamela yet, so I thought I would change and take her somewhere for dinner."

"Oh, of course, I didn't think." Adrienne looked a trifle embarrassed. Seeing that he was still turning her unfinished carving absently in his hands, she reached out and relieved him of it. "I hope you have a pleasant evening," she finished politely.

"Yes, well, thank you." Dominic seemed to hesitate briefly before heading to the door. "I'll see you at breakfast." He shook off the slight sense of constraint that had arisen inexplicably and went upstairs whistling to bathe away the dirt from his long ride.

An hour later, freshly groomed and relaxed, Lord Creighton headed for the Place St. Catherine, where Sir Ralph's rented lodgings were situated. His first disappointment came when the servant reported that his employers were out for the evening but disclaimed any knowledge of their destinations. Unable to recall any specific plans for this evening, Dominic could do nothing except return home and consult his calendar—as anyone but an eager fool would have done before leaving the house, he berated himself.

His mood was lightened by finding Major Peters almost on his doorstep. It required little effort to persuade his friend to stay and dine *en famille*. Fortunately the earl was kept in ignorance of his chef's reaction when Moulton informed that individual that there would be two more for dinner, to be served almost immediately.

Adrienne was taken aback when she walked into the drawing room and discovered Major Peters comfortably ensconced in a wing chair near the fireplace, sipping sherry with every evidence of enjoyment. Her initial surprise mastered, a little rush of pleasure warmed her smile, and she was thankful she had obeyed an impulse to wear her new buttercup-yellow muslin to lift her spirits. Marie had confined her riotous curls behind a matching riband, allowing two to fall over her ears. Conscious of looking her best, Adrienne accepted the major's offer to pour her a glass of sherry. Dominic, returning to his guest after checking his social engagements, found his friend and his female cousin engaged in cheerful conversation with the ease of old friends.

"You two look very cozy. Where is Becky?" The earl had adopted his cousins' name for Miss Beckworth in private, though he had referred to her as Cousin Anthea the other evening for the purpose of establishing her eligibility to act as his hostess.

"She meant to look in on Jean-Paul before coming down," replied Adrienne. "I think I hear her and Luc now. We didn't expect you for dinner, cousin."

"Lady Tremayne and Sir Ralph were dining out," Dominic said, getting to his feet as the rest of the family came in together.

They lingered over dinner, which became a congenial occasion with the numbers small enough for general conversation. Moulton was subsequently able to soothe the sensibilities of the temperamental chef by reporting that his culinary offerings, though nowhere near as elaborate as for the dinner party, were very well-received, and that their guest had praised his *escallopes de volaille aux truffes*. Miss Beckworth and Luc, who had not encountered the earl on his initial return that afternoon, were eager to hear about the Bourbon court. Dominic good-naturedly answered all their questions, and the time passed so agreeably that the party lingered until at last Miss Beckworth signaled to Adrienne, interrupting a lively discussion the girl was having with Major Peters, and the ladies left the table.

When Luc strolled into the small drawing room a half-hour later he passed on the men's apologies to Miss Beckworth. It seemed they had evening engagements of long standing. Both ladies accepted the explanation with aplomb, but each privately regretted the loss of that stimulation that a masculine viewpoint brings to conversation.

The earl and his old friend, having discovered they were bound for the small ball, wended their way in company, passing the time in idle discussion of their current assignments. At one point Major Peters revealed his disappointment that Miss Castle would not be among the guests at the Hatherleighs' do that evening. Dominic explained that so far his cousin had met no one save those persons who had been present at the betrothal party. Though disappointed, the major consoled himself with a tentative plan to invite his comrade's cousin to go riding with him when next he could arrange free time in Brussels. He complained that being stationed in Ninove, where Lord Uxbridge had set up his headquarters, rather cramped his style, but received no sympathy from his friend, who had just come back from a four-day mission.

Tonight's ball was on a larger scale than Lord Creighton had anticipated. Mr. and Mrs. Hatherleigh were still receiving their guests in the narrow gallery outside the ballroom when the officers arrived, and it took more than a half-hour to make their way through the line. By this time Dominic was beginning to fear the world was conspiring to keep him away from his beloved, but Mrs. Hatherleigh put him out of his misery when she remarked with an arch smile that there was someone in the ballroom she knew he would be anxious to see.

"Just so, ma'am," he replied, giving her his best smile before moving on.

He was detained just inside the ballroom by Lady Georgiana Lennox, the Duke of Richmond's lively daughter, who had been presented to him recently by Lord Wellington. No one would have guessed from his attentive manner and pleasant chitchat that he was champing at the bit, though his eyes were inclined to roam every now and then. He obtained his release after a few minutes by presenting his comrade to Lady Georgiana and leaving Major Peters to secure her interest with his ready conversation. Dominic carefully quartered the ballroom with his eyes, his commanding height an advantage in this activity. Even so, he did not immediately spot his betrothed's lovely form. Undaunted, the earl started to make his steady way toward a corner where a number of blue and green uniforms denoting members of the Dutch and Belgian military forces were clustered. Longtime knowledge of his fellow officers told him he would always find the reigning belles in their midst. In a few minutes the colonel had bowed his way through the press of people surrounding the dance floor, tossing off a greeting now and then, but refusing to be intercepted by importuning friends. His persistence was rewarded with a glimpse of a shining dark head and a slim figure clad in a rose-colored gown within a crowd of foreign officers. He stood quietly outside the circle for a few seconds until he caught Pamela's eye. Her famous smile flashed briefly in his direction before she returned her attention to the members of her court.

Dominic's pleasant expression did not alter by a hair, but appalled chagrin flooded through him. They had been apart for five long days. Could she still be intent on carrying on that ridiculous campaign of retribution? It seemed she could, incredible though it must be thought. In the next ten minutes there were none of those speaking glances exchanged between lovers; indeed, the earl might have been invisible or absent for all the notice taken of him by his betrothed. He stood there patiently, his countenance calm, and when one of Pamela's admirers bowed and left the inner circle, moved into his place by her side. At that point she allocated him another of her smiles.

"Dominic, are you acquainted with these gentlemen? May I make you known to Captain van Dorn, Major van Schuyler, Graf Doelsma, Captain Count Henri Levèque, and Major Rasmussen. Gentlemen, my fiancé, Colonel Lord Creighton."

Everyone acknowledged the introductions with punctilious form, and the bantering talk continued, though now the earl was included. He played his part perfectly, his breeding such that he automatically controlled a rising impatience to be private with his fiancée, which was all to the good, since she apparently felt no similar longing. When the musicians struck up for the first number, a young British officer in the dress of a hussar appeared at Lady Tremayne's side to claim his dance. Dominic laid a finger on his fiancée's arm and said with a smile, "I trust you have saved me some waltzes?"

Lady Tremayne widened her eyes at him. "Why, darling, how could I? I didn't know you would be returning today. My card is filled, I'm afraid, but," she added with a provocative flick of long lashes at one of the officers surrounding her, "Captain Count Levèque has written his name in for two waltzes. I am persuaded he will be gracious enough to turn one of them over to Colonel Creighton, will you not, Captain?"

The Belgian officer fingered the end of his dashing mustache and bowed. "Since you ask it, fair lady, I will, with extreme reluctance but a latent sense of justice, relinquish the pleasure of a waltz to your fiancé. But only one, mind!"

The earl gravely thanked the handsome dark-haired officer whose polite words were belied by the wicked white smile beneath the waxed mustache.

It was a long evening, made longer by frequent glimpses of Lady Tremayne that convinced Dominic his betrothed was not sharing his longing for a few moments of privacy. She whirled past him, laughing gaily up at her numerous partners. She was seen flirting with her fan in quiet corners between dances and sparkling in the center of all-male groups. He wasn't even permitted to take her in to supper, although it was his dubious privilege to be sitting near enough to witness the impartial scattering of her favors. He did his duty by a number of young ladies presented to him by Mrs. Hatherleigh, who tempered her gratitude at providing the wallflowers with such a personable partner with words of commiseration on his fiancée's popularity. After a half-dozen duty dances, he escaped to the card room, where the time passed more agreeably among a congenial band of fellow officers.

His own waltz with Pamela, which was scheduled near the end of the evening, did not turn out to be a period of unalloyed joy either.

"Alone at last!" he exclaimed theatrically, directing a warm smile at his beloved as he whirled her onto the floor. "I thought my turn would never come."

"It has certainly turned into a hectic evening," she agreed.

"Do you realize it has been almost five days since we last saw each other? I've missed you terribly."

"Then why did you go?" inquired Lady Tremayne, her expression unsoftened by his warmth.

"Why did I go?" the earl repeated blankly, pulling back slightly to examine the flawless face raised to his. "Surely you do not imagine I had any choice in the matter?"

"Did you not?" Lady Tremayne managed a graceful shrug while being swept down the floor to the fast German music.

"Of course not! A day without seeing you is like a year!"

"Vastly prettily said, Dominic." A faint smile appeared on Lady Tremayne's lips, but Lord Creighton detected nothing in the steady amber gaze to dispel the cloud that her reception had cast over his homecoming.

"We can't talk here. I'll see you home later."

"I came with Ralph," Lady Tremayne demurred. "He expects to escort me home."

"I've ordered my carriage. Tell your brother I'll be taking you."

Lady Tremayne hesitated, but a glance at her fiancé's determined face decided the issue. "Very well . . . although . . . Wait! Should you not escort your cousin home?"

"My cousin? Adrienne? Adrienne isn't here tonight."

"Oh. I would have expected her to be included in all your social invitations now that she is launched, so to speak." Lady Tremayne's tones were casual.

"Adrienne has never met the Hatherleighs. She has very little acquaintances in Brussels as yet. Her social engagements will be limited while she is here."

"I see."

Since the music had been winding down during this

exchange, the earl and Lady Tremayne were separated once more by a number of persons wishing to speak to one or the other, and did not meet again until he sought her out when his carriage was announced at the end of the ball.

The first part of the ride home was accomplished in complete silence. Lady Tremayne, glancing sideways at her companion's rigid jaw, finally broke it to ask:

"Was your mission, whatever it was, successful?"

The earl turned a serious face to her. "Are you really interested?"

"Why, of course, darling, since it was important enough to take you away for days."

He ignored her comment. "Pamela, I fell deeply in love with you months ago. Was I wrong in hoping my feelings were reciprocated? Are you regretting our betrothal?"

Surprise and consternation flashed across the perfect features and her mouth dropped open. "Of . . . of course not! How can you think it?"

"How can I *not* think it after this evening?" he countered, the gravity of his expression unaltered. "We have been apart for five days, but my return roused in you none of that sense of joy that lovers feel when reunited. In its place was either a real indifference or a determination to bring me to heel, neither of which sentiments is compatible with love."

Lady Tremayne had had time to recover her startled wits during this lengthy speech. Now she caught her bottom lip with her teeth and slowly released it while the brightness of unshed tears glistened in her eyes. She laid a hand over his on his knee. "I'm sorry, Dominic. You are quite right, I *was* trying to force you around to my way of thinking and it was wrong of me. But indifference—*never*!"

The earl had been studying the lovely face intently during this confession, and now he gathered her swiftly into his embrace, ending all discussion. Her lips were warm and eager under his until, with a laughing sigh, he released her. "The carriage has stopped, my love. Pamela, you must know that I would do anything for you, give you anything you could ever desire, but the next few weeks could bring all sorts of trouble. I'd feel easier in my mind if you were safely out of Brussels entirely, except that I cannot bear to see you go."

"Do you really believe Napoleon will attack?"

"The army has remained faithful to him. Our intelligence is often contradictory, but somewhere, sometime soon, he must act. There is no other course open to him. He cannot allow the allies time to join forces against him."

"Oh, Dominic, I feel the uncertainty about the future makes it imperative that we seize what happiness we may!"

"No."

The word was softly spoken, but Lady Tremayne recognized the finality and subsided in her arguments. She bade her fiancé a fond good night shortly thereafter, went into the house, and mounted the stairs. She wasn't aware that the saloon door had opened until her brother's voice arrested her step.

"You are looking very thoughtful. What plot are you hatching now?"

"I didn't see you tonight, Ralph," she said, her tones indifferent. "When did you get home?"

"A few minutes ago. I saw your worthy staff officer helping you on with your cloak and made myself scarce so as not to disturb love's young dream."

Lady Tremayne paid no more attention to this sarcasm then she had to his earlier remarks, except that her lips tightened. She'd have passed him and gone into her room without even the courtesy of a good night had he not laid a detaining hand on her arm.

"Did you succeed in patching up your differences?" he inquired with a straight look.

"Yes, but you were right. Dominic can't be manipulated, at least not by me. He's not that besotted," she finished with a tinge of bitterness.

"Oh, he's in love with you, Pamela, but he isn't the man to be driven by a woman. It's actually a mark in his favor, though damned inconvenient just at present," said Sir Ralph dryly. A rueful light gleamed in the light brown eyes so like his sister's. "I take it the only course left to us is to hope Bonaparte attacks soon and Creighton survives the battle."

His sister tossed her head, a determined set to her mouth. "I don't propose to stake my future solely on that chance. He is not the only fish in the sea."

"What do you mean?" When she didn't answer, Sir Ralph's sharp features registered faint alarm. "I'm warning you, Pamela, you will lose Creighton if you make a play for other men!"

"He won't know anything about it. Naturally I'll be discreet. Was there ever the slightest breath of scandal while Tremayne was alive?"

"Do you mean to tell me you played Tremayne false?"

"Why the surprise? The man was more than thirty years older than I. You certainly couldn't have thought it a love match. Have you forgotten that you and my father sold me to him? Why should *I* not get something out of the exchange?"

"I see," said her brother slowly. "Then I must commend you on your accomplished performance as a devoted wife. I never knew Tremayne had cause for complaint in his bargain. He treated you like a queen, even to the extent of beggaring himself to pay for your extravagances."

"The old lecher didn't have anything to complain of," she retorted caustically. "He made sure he got what he paid for."

Sir Ralph's thin nostrils flared as he regarded his beautiful sister with distaste. "I never before realized how very vulgar you are, Pamela. Spare me a recital of your sufferings in the marriage bed, I beg of you. The fact remains that Creighton is not a doddering old fool to have the wool pulled over his eyes. And he has a large number of friends who would be only too happy to whisper any scandal broth in his ears. You must be aware that you are not overly popular among the tabbies who rule society."

"Pah, do you think I fear a pack of jealous women?"

"It is too dangerous, I tell you. You overestimate your powers, Pamela."

"I think not," riposted his sister, and this time she did brush past, leaving Sir Ralph standing in the hall glowering at the closed door to her bedchamber.

12

"Good morning, cousin. May I say you look like a ray of sunshine today?"

Adrienne, again attired in her buttercup muslin, responded cheerfully to her cousin's smiling gallantry and allowed him to seat her at the breakfast table. Luc, the only other person present, grunted a reply to her greeting before returning his eyes to his filled plate. Nothing was permitted to interfere with the daily replenishing of the growing boy's strength, least of all meaningless social chatter.

Adrienne expressed the polite hope that Dominic had enjoyed his evening, upon which he felt obliged to regale her with a few details of the affair while she was being served from the platter of kippers presented by Moulton. She enjoyed his word sketch, though it did not escape her notice that he made no mention of his fiancée while describing the splendors of the Hatherleigh ball. The talk was desultory while all present did full justice to the chef's offerings. Then Dominic, accepting a second cup of coffee, said, to surprise her:

"It is such a perfect morning. What do you say to a ride in the park, cousin? Have you a habit yet?"

Adrienne halted the cup she was raising to her lips and sent a hooded glance toward the smiling earl. "A habit? Do you mean a riding habit?" she asked.

"Of course."

"I'm afraid I don't have one," she replied, tossing a quelling look at her brother, who had emitted a bark of laughter.

Dominic looked disappointed. "The trees are almost completely in leaf now, the chestnuts and the limes are especially lovely. Brussels is looking its best. You have scarcely left this house in weeks. It is time you were getting out and about. Will it be ready soon?"

"Will what be ready soon?"

"Your habit."

This time Adrienne lowered her cup to the saucer, placing it exactly in the center before she spoke. "Actually, Dominic, there is no point in owning a habit when one doesn't ride."

"You can't ride a horse?"

"Or a donkey or a camel or an elephant or any other four-legged creature," put in Luc, grinning wickedly.

Adrienne's dimpled chin was significantly elevated as she leveled a blue-green gaze at her cousin. "That is one more item on my impressive list of nonaccomplishments," she said with a touch of defiance. "I never learned to ride."

"Well, that's not so terrible," replied the earl soothingly. "We will have you riding in a week or two. I'll arrange for lessons today."

"If it is all the same to you, Dominic, I would just as lief not bother. There is so much to do in the house, what with Jean-Paul to care for and the dancing lessons, and we shan't be here a great deal longer in any case. There is too little time."

The earl frowned. "It will be weeks yet before Jean-Paul is able to travel. There is ample time to learn, unless you do not wish it for some reason?"

"Well, I . . . that is, riding habits are so expensive, after all. I mean . . ." She faltered, and Luc rushed into the breach.

"What Adrienne is trying not to admit, Cousin Dominic, is that she has never learned to ride because she is afraid of any animal larger than a lapdog."

"That's not true!" Adrienne denied hotly. "There never seemed to be a need to learn. We have always lived in town, after all."

Dominic looked from the teasing gleam in the boy's near-black eyes to his sister's flushed cheeks, and a wave of pity washed over him. She had missed so much, this uncomplaining girl. He wanted to make it all up to her, to give her, in the few weeks remaining to him, all the things she had never had, but her pride was a formidable barrier. Aloud he said gently, "If you will allow me to teach you, Adrienne, I promise that you will quickly overcome any nervousness you may feel around horses. They are, unarguably, large, but horses have more placid natures than most of the lapdogs it has been my misfortune to encounter. Riding is a skill you will always be happy to possess."

Adrienne still looked unconvinced, but before she could refuse outright, a distraction was created by the entrance into the breakfast parlor of Miss Beckworth, who smiled a general greeting to those assembled.

"Becky, Adrienne needs a riding habit," announced Dominic, attempting a *fait accompli.*

"No, I don't. I—"

"It will be ready this afternoon." Miss Beckworth, in the process of pouring herself a cup of coffee, didn't look up from her chore.

Adrienne was scandalized. "I didn't order a habit!"

"No, I know you did not, but Dominic said you would need one, so I had Madame Henriette make one up in celestial-blue gabardine. I am persuaded you will find it quite to your taste."

"Capital! Then we will merely postpone your first lesson until tomorrow."

Dominic beamed impartially at Miss Beckworth, who was buttering toast fingers, and Adrienne, who appeared to be struggling to regain her powers of speech. He rose from the table to bring the discussion to a close, saying casually, "By the way, I thought you ladies might like to go to the opera tonight, so I have rented a box. Pamela and Sir Ralph will be coming, as well as Major Peters and General and Miss Forrester."

Adrienne let out an undignified squeal, then clasped her hands together as if to keep her delight confined within the bounds of propriety. "Oh, Dominic, you wonderful, marvelous man! Becky, did you hear that? Oh, I vow I am so thrilled I could burst! *Thank* you, Dominic!"

"Seems to me you're making an awful lot of fuss about a bunch of people in tights standing around on a stage screeching at each other," said Luc dampeningly. "I wouldn't regard that as a high treat!"

Dominic had been enjoying Adrienne's uninhibited delight. Now he rested a thoughtful glance at his younger cousin. "When you have finished here, Luc, come into the study. There is something I wish to tell you."

"I'm finished now." Luc pushed back his chair and scurried to join his large cousin at the door.

The breakfast room was quiet for a few seconds after the masculine contingent had withdrawn. Miss Beckworth was going about the business of ingesting her food, and Adrienne was gazing raptly into space, still lost in a pleasant dream of anticipation, until the click of a cup on a saucer brought her back to the present.

"What shall I wear tonight, Becky?" she asked abruptly.

"The aquamarine will do nicely. It is really the only suitable gown until the others arrive."

"*Others*! *What* others?" Adrienne fairly shrieked.

Miss Beckworth winced. "Please, dearest, do moderate your tones, I beg. Remember, a soft voice is an excellent thing in a woman."

"Becky, what have you done?" Adrienne's voice had sunk to a hoarse whisper. "First a riding habit and now more dresses! How many more?"

"Only four, two for daytime wear and two for evening."

"*Only* four? I don't *need* four more dresses!"

"Yes you do. None of your old gowns are at all acceptable. You'll also require gloves and sandals and hats to go with them, not to mention shifts and petticoats." Miss Beckworth spoke matter-of-factly as she liberally added sugar to her second cup of coffee, but Adrienne moaned:

"Becky, how *could* you? I'll never be able to look Lady Creighton in the eye. Perhaps the things can be returned or even canceled if Madame Henriette has not yet begun them. I'll get my bonnet and go to see her now and beg—"

"It's too late for that. The dresses have already been cut

and fitted to your pattern. The first walking dress will be arriving with your habit this afternoon.'' As Adrienne continued to shake her head and wring her hands in distress, Miss Beckworth pushed back from the table and came around behind her charge, placing her hands comfortingly on her shoulders. ''Please, dearest, there is not the slightest occasion to fly into a pelter. Lady Creighton knows all about the purchases; indeed, everything has been done to her order from the beginning. I was privileged to read the letter she sent Dominic in which she charged him with outfitting you in the first style of elegance.''

''It's too much,'' the girl protested wretchedly, slewing around in her chair to look at her companion. ''How will I ever be able to repay her?''

''By allowing her the pleasure of doing something for the daughter of her favorite cousin. This means a lot to her, Adrienne, more than you can be expected to understand, but pray believe that Lady Creighton is sincerely looking forward to having you and the boys visit with her this summer.''

''Suppose she takes us in dislike after all this?'' Adrienne waved an all-encompassing hand at her luxurious surroundings and her charming new dress. ''Oh, it is all too horrible to contemplate!''

''Now you are being nonsensical, my dear—idiotish, in fact.'' Miss Beckworth administered an admonitory little shake to the shoulder she still held before returning to her chair and her interrupted breakfast.

Adrienne said no more on the subject but she could not be easy in her mind under such a weight of obligation. She went about her duties in a subdued fashion that morning, earning several speculative looks from Monsieur Daubigny as she performed her part in the dances meticulously but without her customary sparkle. Despite her high-flown principles, however, she was still a very young woman and not proof against temptation in the form of lovely clothes. A despised squiggle of excitement rose in her breast at sight of the bandbox delivered from the modiste's, and she could not resist trying on both the riding habit and the cool-looking dress of lavender and white striped cotton, fashioned high to the throat with the most entrancing little ruff of pleated white lawn under her chin. She had to concede that Madame Henriette certainly knew her business, for both costumes fit perfectly, and it was difficult to say which was more flattering to her skin and hair. She fancied the dress might have a slight edge since its vertical stripes seemed to lend her a little much-welcomed height. Adrienne was barely of moderate height and built along delicate lines like her mother. She always felt dwarfed and insigificant when in the presence of Lady Tremayne, who carried her additional inches and pounds with such queenly assurance.

Not that Adrienne wasted many minutes regretting that her looks paled beside Lady Tremayne's. Until very recently she had never been in the habit of thinking about her looks at all, and she was much too excited about her first visit to the opera even to be daunted at the prospect of an evening spent in company with her cousin's fiancée.

They dined early to be in good time for the performance, though Adrienne was so deep in the grip of nervous anticipation she could not have listed the dishes that had comprised her meal five minutes after consuming them. The only thing of significance that occurred was Dominic's announcement that he had secured a temporary tutor for Luc, a young line officer whose military duties had been suspended while a broken arm healed. Adrienne cast an anxious eye on her brother, but Luc appeared to have accepted the curtailment of his freedom with a better grace than his female relatives could have anticipated.

To Adrienne's distorted fancy the meal seemed to stretch out interminably, her companions being bitten with a bug of garrulity that caused each to become uncommonly chatty that evening. She answered at random, squirming and seething with the effort required not to shoo them on their way like so many chickens.

The opera was certainly worth waiting for. For sheer spectacle it outshone Adrienne's wildest imaginings, and she sat enthralled throughout the production, only gradually becoming aware that she was decidedly in the minority. Sarah Forrester was equally engrossed in the performance, and so, somewhat surprisingly, was Sir Ralph Morrison. Most of the well-dressed people in the boxes, however, obviously came to be seen by their friends. There was a constant stream of visitors to their box during the intermissions, something she had not anticipated. In a way this proved quite helpful, in that Adrienne was relieved from the self-imposed chore of guarding her tongue in the presence of Lady Tremayne. There was actually very little conversation between the two after an initial exchange of insincere compliments on either side.

Lady Tremayne looked stunning as usual in a diaphanous creation of red muslin that Adrienne suspected had been dampened *à la* Caroline Lamb, so faithfully did it cling to her spectacular figure. Though suspecting there was very little beneath the dress except perhaps an invisible petticoat, the younger girl consciously averted her eyes to keep from staring. She was intent on remaining in the background, not wishing to give her cousin's betrothed the least cause to complain about her behavior. Her attitude toward Lady Tremayne could best be described as one of nervous deference, and she only relaxed when the beautiful brunette's attention was totally taken up with others. Fortunately for Adrienne's enjoyment of the evening, her innocence protected her from discovering that Lady Tremayne was well aware of her placatory attitude, and more annoyed than gratified by it.

The steady stream of visitors, almost exclusively male, gave the earl's box the distinction of being the most popular in the theater that night. That Lady Tremayne was the main attraction was readily apparent, for she gathered admirers like flowers gather bees. Adrienne herself received a great deal of flattering attention from a number of aristocratic sprigs of fashion as well as the ubiquitous military officers, who sought introductions to Lord Creighton's attractive cousin. It would be idle indeed for a newly launched bud to deny all pleasure in such a gratifying state of affairs, not did Adrienne, a naturally friendly soul, make the attempt. She did feel, however, that she owed the members of her party the lion's share of attention and civility. During the course of the evening she had ample opportunity to observe that Lady Tremayne did not share this belief, if her behavior was any indication. Certainly she had begun the evening at her fiancé's side, but Dominic's duties as host demanded that he make introductions and cater to the needs of all his guests. By the time the first interval was over he was displaced at her side, and thereafter changed seats frequently to accommodate a number of persons in the course of the production. Lady Tremayne appeared perfectly content to do without his attentions; indeed it would have taken a far ruder person than Lord Creighton to insinuate himself between her and the more pressing members of her court. This was only gradually assimilated by Adrienne in the gaps in her own conversations. She noted that Dominic unobtrusively saw to the comfort of his guests, stepping into the breach should Miss Forrester or Becky be stranded conversationally at odd moments, and good-naturedly but effectively clearing the box of excess humanity when the temperature and the curtain began to rise.

Adrienne was besieged by young men begging permission to call. Unprepared for such an event at first, she looked beseechingly at Becky and Dominic, who calmly stated their pleasure at the prospect. By the second interval she felt herself equal to granting the requests herself. Initially she was a bit surprised that none of their callers appeared to be interested in discussing the program, though their opening remarks were generally questions as to how she was enjoying the performance. She never managed to get beyond a general statement of her favorable reaction before the subject was abandoned by its perpetrator in favor of compliments or personal questions.

There was only one bad moment during an evening that lived up to its promise of enchantment. Major Peters had, with quiet persistence, managed to regain a seat beside Adrienne after each interval. Toward the end of the performance he promoted a moment of comparative privacy in which to invite her to go riding in the park with him the following morning.

Adrienne bestowed an apologetic smile on the dark-eyed

officer. "I'm so sorry to be obliged to refuse, sir, but I'm afraid I don't ride."

"Well, that is easily remedied," Major Peters said, returning her smile. "I shall be most happy to give you some tutelage. It won't take long to attain enough competence to enjoy a quiet ride in the park."

Dominic, from his place on the other side of his cousin, entered an objection. "Sorry, old chap, but I have already promised to teach Adrienne to ride myself. I'm taking her out in the morning now that her habit is ready."

"I'll come along too so she'll learn twice as fast," returned his old friend imperturbably.

Lady Tremayne then demonstrated her ability to monitor other conversations while conducting her own by breaking off a bantering flirtation with two Belgian officers to propose gaily: "And if I come along too, Miss Castle will learn *three* times as fast. We shall make her an expert rider in a week."

Before she could disguise the alarm that spiraled through her being at the thought of Lady Tremayne witnessing her initial efforts on horseback, Adrienne's eyes had sought her cousin's in mute supplication and her lips had parted involuntarily. This panic lasted no longer than a fraction of a second before she dropped her eyes to her tightly clasped hands and pressed her lips together, but Dominic must have understood because his amused voice glided into the hiatus.

"Haven't you ever heard the maxim 'Too many cooks spoil the broth'? I shudder to contemplate Adrienne's confusion, not to mention that of the horse, if she had to try to follow the instructions of three teachers at once. Thank you all for your kind offers of assistance, but since my cousin is my responsibility, I shall engage to be her instructor until she is competent enough to go out with others."

"Well, since Creighton has elected to put aside our standing engagement to ride together in the mornings in favor of instructing the young, I expect I shall be needing another escort," said Lady Tremayne with a dazzling smile directed at the Belgian officers.

In chorus these gentlemen responded instantly and gallantly with the expected invitations to Lady Tremayne. At the same time Adrienne summuned up a small voice to implore her cousin not to change any of his plans for her sake. Before their voices had quite ceased, the earl smiled at his fiancée and said in his quiet, calm manner, "My dear Pamela, I plan to take Adrienne out before breakfast. I shall be available for our usual ride at ten."

Lady Tremayne's smile was firmly in place as she said sweetly, "Thank you, Dominic, but now that the weather is growing so warm, I have decided to ride earlier in the day."

"As you wish, of course, my love," replied the earl, bowing slightly.

Adrienne's eyes made a quick circuit of the box. Was she the only person suffering from a distinct feeling of embarrassment, as if she had blundered into a private discussion? Becky and General Forrester were speaking quietly together, giving no indication of having heard any part of the recent exchange. Sarah was searching (or pretending to search) in her reticule for something, and Major Peters was staring over the rail of the box at some undefined point of interest. Sir Ralph's gaze was directed at his sister with the same intensity that had unnerved Adrienne at the betrothal dinner when she had been the target. Lady Tremayne seemed impervious to it, however. She had resumed her laughing conversation with her two admirers, excluding the others.

The incipient rising of the curtain for the final act of the opera signaled the end of the little drama that had been played out in the earl's box. Adrienne sat staring unseeingly at the stage, utterly appalled that, once again, she seemed to be the unwitting cause of dissension between Dominic and his promised wife. Perhaps she was mistaken, though. She stole a glance at her cousin, but his face revealed nothing save polite interest in what was occurring onstage.

Lady Tremayne's expression just before the opera had recommenced had been, oddly enough, one of satisfaction. Adrienne sighed silently. Her experience of lovers was almost nonexistent, but it was being borne in upon her gradually that her cousin and his fiancée behaved like no lovers she had ever read or heard of. A stranger would certainly not have been able to pick out the betrothed pair on the evidence of tonight's events. The disinterested observer would have noticed that Lady Tremayne had accorded the earl less of her favor than almost any man who had visited their box, and that in his turn, the earl had made no effort whatsoever to secure her undivided attention. Had Adrienne not witnessed that passionate embrace in the library she would never have believed their mutual regard was sufficient to produce an engagement. To the forthright girl this contradiction between feeling and demeanor was strange and unnatural.

It was with relief that she was able to turn her attention back to the characters on the stage. Their emotions might perhaps be judged a bit excessive, but at least they were comprehensible to the ordinary person. The performers emoted and sang their way to their appointed ends. Adrienne allowed herself to be carried along on a tidal wave of melody, pleased to be able to defer thinking about her cousin's betrothal, which, she acknowledged, was all to the good, since it was absolutely none of her affair in the first place.

13

Adrienne opened her eyes to sunshine and anxiety. She lay perfectly still for a few moments, trying to account for a feeling of oppression, and all too soon recalled that the hour of her first riding lesson had arrived. She groaned and rolled over, burying her face in the pillow in a vain attempt to block it out of her mind. Never in her life had she experienced the slightest desire to see the world from the top of a horse, and after the scene at the opera last night, she was even less inclined to participate in the activity today.

In the carriage on their way home from the theater she had labored to make an opportunity to convince Dominic that she really would prefer to cancel any plans for riding lessons. Her cousin had engaged Becky in a long discussion of the merits of the performance, courteously inviting her own contributions but diverting each hesitant attempt on her part to introduce the subject of riding lessons. Not until he bade them good night at the foot of the stairs had she, in desperation, blurted out her dismay at the idea of depriving Lady Tremayne of her fiancé's company on her daily ride. Dominic had followed Becky's retreating back up the stairs with his eyes before making any response to her words at all. Then he had taken the gloved hand she had in her agitation laid on his forearm and raised it to his mouth for a brief salute while his fingers pressed lightly on her parted lips. His eyes were gentle yet compelling as he told her to banish any thought of Lady Tremayne from her mind.

"I'll take care of Pamela; you just see to it that you are ready at half-after seven tomorrow morning."

When her lips had moved in protest under his finger, he

153

had increased the pressure slightly. "Shh, not another word. Good night, Adrienne, pleasant dreams."

At the time she had been bemused enough to accept her dismissal meekly, but now it was morning and the cloud of enchantment spun by last night's exciting performance had dissipated. She swung her legs over the side of the bed, determined to make one last push to escape the dreaded encounter with a huge equine specimen of suspect docility. Even the undeniable attraction of the stylish blue habit failed to reconcile her to her fate. She considered sending a message to the earl pleading an indisposition that would cancel the outing, but even if Dominic believed her it would only postpone the ordeal, and in the light of her previous efforts to avoid the lessons, it was doubtful that he would accept any excuse as genuine. He would label her a pudding heart; in fact, thanks to Luc's mischievous tongue, that was most likely his opinion at this very moment. The resentment she was experiencing at being coerced was transmitted through the vicious strokes of the hairbrush she wielded like a weapon, until her eyes watered in pain.

At this point the girl glaring at her image in the mirror over the washstand took herself in hand and resolved that no one was going to guess from her conduct that she was a craven coward. Her motions with the brush became more deliberate as she smoothed down the wild halo of curls she had created. She donned the blue habit with its navy frogging and epaulettes *à la militaire* and gave the crisp lace of her shirt ruffle a twitch to set it more evenly between the lapels of the jacket. A faint hope that the boots Becky had ordered might prove too small was strangled at birth when her foot slid inside easily. She had to concede that she presented a very professional picture in her high-fashion habit and dashing high-crowned hat with its military visor worn tilted daringly toward one eye, but her satisfaction was quickly quashed by the conviction that she would make a greater fool of herself falling off a horse in this costume than in more conventional garb. As a final gesture of bravado she doused herself liberally with the perfume Dominic had brought back to her from Ghent before it occurred to her that horses might object to perfume. She frowned in concentration as she headed for the stairs, pulling on her navy gloves as she went. *Did* horses have a keen sense of smell? Her knowledge of that noble beast could be written on an eyepatch, with room to spare.

"In spite of that ferocious scowl, you are a sight to quicken the heartbeat of any man under seventy in that costume, cousin. I trust I am not the cause of your annoyance?" The teasing gleam in Dominic's merry blue eyes as he gazed up at her from the bottom of the stairs brought Adrienne's dimples flashing into play, and she spoke her thoughts without censure.

"Dominic, do horses dislike perfume?"

He controlled his twitching lips and replied gravely, "I have never known a horse to refuse to carry a young lady because he objected to her perfume."

It required all of Adrienne's courage to stand her ground at first sight of Trooper, her cousin's huge bay gelding awaiting them outside the front door in the care of a groom. By contrast, the dainty chestnut mare standing quietly beside him seemed no more intimidating than a child's pony.

"Oh, isn't she beautiful!" Adrienne exclaimed unprompted.

"Yes, a lovely little lady." Dominic gave the mare's neck a pat. "Small but with beautiful conformation and a mild disposition."

Adrienne laughed as the chestnut nuzzled against the earl's hand. "She knows you are praising her."

"She knows I have sugar for her. Here, you give it to her." Dominic instructed his cousin in the technique of hand-feeding horses and she gingerly offered the mare the treat, which was lipped instantly. Adrienne snatched back her hand with a slight loss of confidence.

"She tickles," she explained lamely, stretching out her hand again to pet the chestnut's soft nose. "What is her name?"

"Bijou, which is just what she is, a little gem of a lady's mount."

Just then the door opened and Luc came ambling down the steps to inspect his sister's mount.

"Isn't she a beauty? Look at those soft brown eyes," urged Adrienne when Luc seemed more interested in the mare's knees.

"She's good-looking all right," the boy conceded, "but not up to carrying much weight, I'd say. For my money Trooper here is a real horse. Look at the strength of those flanks and that powerful chest. He's built for endurance and speed."

"That he is," concurred the earl, pardonably proud of his favorite. "He has carried me over all kinds of terrain in all kinds of weather for hour after weary hour, and Lord knows, I'm no lightweight. But your sister scarcely weighs a feather. Bijou won't even know she's on her."

Luc grinned impishly. "Probably because she won't *be* on her after the first five minutes."

"Thank you, we can do without your brand of encouragement, young man," Lord Creighton said sternly. "Here, make yourself useful by holding Bijou while I assist Adrienne to mount."

Actually, Luc's teasing had served to stiffen Adrienne's backbone so that she concentrated on following Dominic's directions. He helped her to arrange her skirt and adjusted the stirrup when she was as comfortably settled as was possible, considering the state of her nerves. Bijou cooperated by standing perfectly still during the process, allowing Adrienne time to accustom herself to this new view of the world.

At a signal from his large cousin, Luc took himself and his critical eye back inside the house after expressing a casual wish that his sister would enjoy her ride. The anxious look on Adrienne's face deepened as the mare took a sidling step or two in response to Trooper's sudden nudge. Dominic smiled reassuringly into dilated aquamarine eyes.

"There is nothing to worry about, cousin, and nothing to think about either. Until you feel comfortable with the motion, I shall put Bijou on a lead rein and we'll just walk to the park. Nelson here," indicating the smiling groom, "will hold your reins while I mount."

Dominic was as good as his word. By the time they reached the park, Adrienne had relaxed enough to look around her at the splendors of spring, and, after a few more minutes, to actually respond in a sensible fashion to her companion's conversational overtures. She found the slow, steady motion of the horse strange but not at all alarming, and experienced no reluctance when at last Dominic suggested she might like to take the reins into her own hands. In due course she became accustomed to the feel of the reins, though she would be the first to admit that so far Bijou had not required any control from her rider at all.

There was scarecely a person to be seen in the park at that hour of the morning save a few riders like themselves, and those few seemed intent on their own business. Adrienne quickly lost all self-consciousness and eventually the suggestion that they increase their pace came from her. Concealing a smile of triumph, Dominic readily acquiesced. In another fifteen minutes he was able to compliment his cousin on her seat without reservation, having watched her adjust easily to the trotting motion of her mount. Knowing, as Adrienne did not, the probable effect on her untrained muscles of this new form of exercise, the earl called a halt at this point to her first lesson. He was pleased to see that an instinctive protest rose to Adrienne's lips before she remembered her manners and concurred politely.

As they turned their horses toward the entrance to the park, Dominic was startled to witness a sudden stiffening of Adrienne's body and a resumption of the anxious expression she had shed after the first five minutes. Glancing around quickly, he caught sight of a familiar figure in a black habit entering the park between two Belgian officers. He put out an instinctive hand to Bijou's bridle and headed the mare down another path, putting as much distance as possible between themselves and Pamela and her escorts. They circled around and left the park by another exit, making their way back to Rue Ducale through the still-quiet streets. Neither Dominic nor Adrienne mentioned having seen Lady Tremayne, but the conversation on the return trip was less spontaneous and tended to be punctuated by sudden silences as the cousins pursued their individual trains of thought.

Adrienne was surprised to find herself a trifle stiff when Dominic lifted her down from the mare, but after an involuntary little grimace she summoned up a genuine smile and thanked him most sincerely for her lesson.

Bright blue eyes laughed into hers as, with his hands still spanning her waist, he coaxed, "Admit it, little cousin, that was not nearly the hideous ordeal you had envisioned, was it?"

"Oh no, it was wonderful!" Adrienne dimpled adorably. "And for once my natural clumsiness did not lead me into disaster."

"What is this idiotish notion?" Dominic asked with a little frown.

"It's not idiotish at all, unfortunately. Luc was quite right when he told you I was prone to accidents. I am forever knocking things over or tripping over something. You cannot have failed to notice."

"You are often impetuous in your movements, I will grant. However, I shall not allow anyone to call you clumsy, my girl, and that includes your charming self. Have I not danced with you? Your natural grace is certainly evident on the dance floor, and I'll have no more of this imputed clumsiness—is that understood?"

"Yes, sir, Colonel, *sir!*"

The alien sternness vanished from Dominic's face at Adrienne's mock humility. He grinned and pinched her chin. "Minx! Let's go in to breakfast; I'm starving. You go inside. I'll be along as soon as I've had a word with Nelson."

At the mention of breakfast Adrienne discovered that the unaccustomed exercise in the early-morning air had provided her with a healthy appetite also. She stayed just long enough to give Bijou a valedictory pat before obeying her cousin's command.

That first ride marked the beginning of a period of carefree enjoyment for Adrienne. Unless it rained, Dominic made himself available for a riding session before breakfast each day. Once having overcome her unreasoning fear of horses, she proved a quick and able pupil. If her teacher had any complaint to make at all, it was that she tended to push herself faster than he thought advisable, but he certainly was impressed with the rapid development of confidence in the saddle that she displayed. The awareness that her cousin was proud of her progress was a source of continuing pleasure to Adrienne. She glowed at his praise and looked forward eagerly to each morning's ride. The acquisition of what she privately considered her first actual accomplishment meant more to the inexperienced girl than she wished her relatives to guess, but one would have had to be devoid of all sensibility to miss the aura of happiness surrounding Miss Castle during those early June days.

The prebreakfast ride was incontrovertibly the high point of her day as Adrienne rapidly mastered the rudiments of horsemanship. After a few lessons Dominic was able to relax his vigilance enough to make it possible to extend their territory to include rides along the *Allée Verte* beyond the city gates. The beautiful lime trees were in full bloom now and there was always activity along the canal. Sometimes Luc would join his sister and cousin, but their ambling progress was not best suited to his own style of riding, which Dominic indulgently described as "neck or nothing." An uneasy conscience had prompted Adrienne to suggest that Lady Tremayne might like to accompany them on occasion. She had not been able to suppress a guilty feeling that she had usurped the right of an affianced wife to first consideration, and this niggling little worm of conscience prevented her contentment from being absolute. To her secret relief, Dominic vetoed this suggestion with the casual explanation that Lady Tremayne had not after all preferred the earlier hour for her ride. A delighted Adrienne was left to the undiluted enjoyment of her teacher's company for that first hour of the morning.

If he rode later in the day with his fiancée, the earl never mentioned the fact to his cousin. For her part, Adrienne was prevented by some unadmitted but instinctive reluctance from introducing the person of her cousin's betrothed into any conversation. She would have been happy to be able to banish Lady Tremayne from her thoughts too, but since she was thrust into occasional contact with the beautiful brunette, this desirable state was impossible of achievement. At least thoughts of Lady Tremayne were not permitted to intrude on those idyllic morning rides.

Just as Adrienne was enjoying for the first time a ripening friendship with a female of her own generation in the person of Sarah Forrester, so too was the concomitant development of a satisfying companionship with a male not too removed from her in age a novel and agreeable experience. She and Dominic talked unrestrainedly about everything under the sun on their daily rides. Had she thought about it she would have marveled at how closely attuned they were in their minds, but Adrienne was too caught up in pleasure to have time for introspection. She simply accepted the presence of this splendid new cousin in their lives as a gift of the fates.

The earl's ladies found their social engagements increasing during this period also. Lady Betancourt, having discovered that one of Lord Creighton's cousins was known to her from her youth, called one morning and renewed her acquaintance with Miss Beckworth. Subsequently, Adrienne and Becky received an invitation to a dance given in honor of Miss Elvira Betancourt, her ladyship's eldest daughter. Thanks to Monsier Daubigny's efforts, Adrienne was able to look forward to her first ball with no qualms about her ability to perform the dances correctly. Her own gregarious nature ensured that she would enjoy the company.

And so it turned out. Midway through the evening Lord Creighton was waltzing with his betrothed when his cousin whirled by in the arms of a dashing lieutenant of hussars.

"Adrienne seems to be enjoying herself mightily at her first dance," he remarked with a tolerant smile.

Lady Tremayne's eyes came back from following the

couple and met his coolly. "Yes, I've noticed a number of callow youths buzzing around her like flies."

Some of the animation of Dominic's features was replaced by impersonal courtesy as he held her gaze, but all he said, and that mildly, was, "We all go through that stage along the way."

"I don't believe you were ever callow even in your youth," Lady Tremayne said consideringly. "You have such complete self-possession, I think you must always have been sure from your cradle that your way was the right way."

The earl's eyebrows rose in comical dismay, but before he could question this strange utterance the music wound down and they were immediately surrounded by members of Pamela's court, which, Dominic noted, ran heavily in favor of so-called men of the world. No callow youths there, but one or two of dubious odor. He would have dispatched them speedily had they made Adrienne the object of their gallantry, but Pamela was no innocent debutante and would not welcome his interference. He bowed and effaced himself.

The next dance was his waltz with his cousin, who greeted him with a radiant smile before excusing herself from a chattering group of young people. It took only a few measures to convince Dominic that Adrienne had acquired confidence on the dance floor. Though a trifle short for him, she was a perfect partner, very responsive to his every move. For a time they danced in silence; then he looked down into the vidid little face raised to his and said with a twinkle:

"Allow me to compliment you on your choice of gown tonight, Miss Castle. It is supremely becoming."

"Now, don't you start," she began in impatient tones, then colored guiltily. "I mean," she amended, "I thank you, sir."

He examined her quizzically. "Do you have some rooted objection to compliments? It has always been my impression that young ladies found nothing to object to in a well-turned compliment; indeed, I would have said they welcomed them."

"An honest compliment, yes, but it is *my* impression that most young men tell every girl she is the most beautiful in the room, and that is *not* honest!"

"Is that what all the young men are telling you tonight?" he asked with an odd little smile.

"Yes, and it is all fustian of course!"

Dominic made no answer but pulled her closer to avoid a collision with a couple whose enthusiasm was not matched by an equal degree of skill. He executed a couple of impromptu turns and they were safely on their way again.

"That was very smoothly done," Adrienne said admiringly. "I thought my dress was about to be stepped on back there. You must be the most skillful dancer in the room, or the best waltzer at least."

Dominic drew back and looked at her in sorrow. "You disappoint me, Miss Castle. I never thought to find you offering Spanish coin."

Adrienne's mouth dropped open. "Of course I'm not!" she sputtered indignantly. "You *know* you are a wonderful dancer. Why, you as good as told me so that day you helped Monsieur Daubigny with my lessons!"

"Ah, but how do I know you haven't told every partner the exact same thing tonight?" The more-in-sorrow-than-in-anger look remained.

"Of course I haven't!" Adrienne scowled at him suspiciously; then a reluctant smile trembled at her lips. "Dominic, you *beast*! It was not the same thing at all. I *meant* what *I* said!"

One eyebrow escalated. "And yet you cannot bring yourself to accept that your partners were equally sincere?"

The pointed chin elevated dangerously. "The cases are not the same," she insisted. "I am *not* the most beautiful girl here. There are *dozens* of prettier girls!" She removed her left hand from his shoulder and gestured comprehensively about her.

"In my opinion there are two, possibly three, ladies present who outshine you *au fait de beauté,* but that is only *my* opinion. Perhaps Lieutenant Markham, for example, would not agree with me."

"Oh, Lieutenant Markham!" Adrienne cried dismissively.

"He has a singular penchant for red hair, or so he claims."

"You are proving my point, my dear little unbelieving cousin. The sincerely of the compliment does not depend on whether *you* agree with the content."

Adrienne digested this for a minute. "I can't dispute what you have just said, that's true, but I certainly can and do dispute the sincerity of most of what passes for gallantry on the dance floor." She eyed him challengingly. Dominic grinned and said with saintly smugness:

"If I have caused you to question your suspicions at all, I am satisfied." So saying, he pulled her closer for no better reason than to administer a friendly hug, an action which, had it been witnessed, would have served to confirm the fears of careful mothers who had predicted that the scandalous waltz would inevitably lead to a lapse in public morals.

Fortunately the new German dance was so fast that on-lookers would have to train their eyes on a particular couple to note any aberrant behavior. In this instance, however, two pairs of eyes had been idly watching the earl and his partner glide over the floor for several minutes.

"Creighton and his young cousin certainly dance well together," General Forrester remarked to Miss Beckworth in the alcove where they were enjoying a few quiet moments off their feet.

"Yes. I was a bit concerned for Adrienne at her first dance, but she has made rapid strides with her dancing lessons and already performs with the best of them, though that may be my natural partiality speaking."

"Not at all. Miss Castle is a singularly graceful dancer. The cousins get along well together too, do they not? One can almost sense the closeness—in spirit, I mean," the general added hastily as the earl chose that instant for his impulsive embrace.

The comfortable cadence of Miss Beckworth's voice took on a thoughtful shade as she agreed. "Yes, all the children adore Dominic. He has been wonderful to us all." She drew her companion's attention to another waltzing couple with a comment on their style, and he obligingly followed her lead.

If the general found Miss Beckworth a trifle absentminded

for the remainder of the evening, he was too much the gentleman to appear to notice. The truth was that just lately Miss Beckworth's complaisance at the friendly relationship existing between Lord Creighton and his cousins had become a bit frayed around the edges in Adrienne's case by an unwelcome but persistent suspicion that a deeper element than cousinly affection was creeping into the girl's feelings for Dominic. She would take her oath that Adrienne was unaware that she stood in danger of tumbling into love with her handsome cousin. The girl was very inexperienced, and she had displayed no signs of partiality for any of those who had recently sought her company.

Life would be a lot simpler if Adrienne remained a stranger to the pangs of love, at least until their future became clearer. This heady interval of gaiety was just that —an episode taken out of the context of their lives and not to be taken seriously. Adrienne had recognized this once, but she was young and it would be unreasonable to expect that she could come through unscathed. Even Miss Beckworth, a severely practical woman, had not been able to prevent herself from considering each young man who entered their orbit in the light of a possible suitor, despite Adrienne's patent ineligibility. There was no way she would be able to shield the girl from disappointment should she form an attachment for one of the well-connected officers who surrounded her. A girl would have to be unnaturally cool indeed to remain unaffected by such flattering attentions. Her dependence had been entirely on the shortness of their projected stay in the earl's house as a deterrent to the formation of any serious attachment.

Just lately, however, she'd have almost welcomed a preference on Adrienne's part for one or other of the soldiers who showered attentions on her. Better, infinitely better to succumb to a sudden romantic infatuation with a dashing uniform that was almost guaranteed to wither with absence than to drift unknowingly from cousinly affection to undying love for Dominic. Every feminine and maternal instinct warned Miss Beckworth that this was the real danger, and that her beloved girl was headed straight for heartache.

14

Adrienne sat relaxed in her corner, humming one of the dance melodies the orchestra had played that evening. There was enough light from the lamps outside the carriage to highlight the dreamy expression on her face. The flickering light also danced over her companion's hands clasped tightly together in her lap, but Adrienne wasn't looking at Miss Beckworth, and she started a little when that lady's voice interrupted the humming to ask if she had enjoyed her evening.

"Oh yes, Becky! I don't wish to brag, but that time you pinned the tear in my flounce was the only dance I missed all night." The dreamy expression had been replaced by a teasing gleam as the girl looked at the other woman from under her lashes. "I don't believe you sat out many dances either."

Miss Beckworth chuckled low in her throat. "It's been years since I've danced at all. Tomorrow I shall probably ache in every joint as a reminder that I am not so young as I pretended tonight."

"General Forrester puts many a younger man to shame on the dance floor, doesn't he?" Adrienne asked with studied innocence.

"Most of the Duke's officers are splendid performers in the ballroom."

"Ah, but not as good as General Forrester, do not you agree?"

"From my observation," said Miss Beckworth, refusing to be drawn, "I would have to award the palm to Dominic tonight, though Major Peters was rather impressive in the quadrille."

"Yes," Adrienne agreed, "but not quite so easy to

follow as Dominic, to my way of thinking. I would rather dance with Dominic than anyone else."

"Isn't he a bit too tall for you?" asked Miss Beckworth with assumed carelessness. "I am persuaded he and Lady Tremayne were the handsomest couple in the room tonight. They are so well-matched, both tall, one fair and the other dark."

"I would agree that they were the handsomest *young* couple there, but you and the general were by far the best-looking *mature* couple."

"That's very kind of you," Miss Beckworth replied politely. Only the dry note in her voice betrayed that Adrienne's teasing had not gone unnoted. She sighed and abandoned temporarily any further attempt to reinforce the situation *vis-à-vis* Dominic and Lady Tremayne in the young girl's mind. Given the funning humor Adrienne was in at present, she could not even be sure she had made a beginning. It was something that must be done, however. From now on she would not neglect a single opportunity to impress upon Adrienne that her cousin and Lady Tremayne were committed to each other. She only wished she dared indulge optimism that her words would have the intended effect. She settled back and allowed the girl's cheerful prattle to wash over her almost unheeded.

Disappointment flooded through Adrienne the next morning when she arose to see a light rain falling from leaden skies. There would be no early ride today. Disconsolately she padded back to her bed and sat on the edge. No call to hurry through her morning toilette; breakfast wouldn't be served for an age yet. She yawned hugely and eyed her warm pillow. It had been nearly two by the time she had retired to bed last night.

When she opened her eyes again the morning was much advanced. She scrambled into her clothes with no thought expended on her appearance.

Miss Beckworth looked over at the slightly breathless girl in the doorway to the breakfast room and smiled a greeting. "Did you oversleep?"

"Yes, I . . ." Adrienne's eyes left the crumpled serviette at the place at the end of the table and dwelt on the sole occupant of the room. "Has Dominic already left for headquarters?"

Miss Beckworth nodded. "A few minutes ago. He said to tell you he was sorry to miss your morning ride." She followed the girl's movements as she seated herself at the table, noting the slight droop to her posture and the downcast eyes. "According to Dominic, you are making splendid progress," she continued brightly. "Soon the lessons will be unnecessary."

The aquamarine gaze lifted from the steaming liquid in Adrienne's cup to her duenna's face. "Did Dominic say that?"

"Not in so many words," Miss Beckworth denied after a barely perceptible pause. "I know he has been pleased to oversee the lessons and is quite proud of your prowess, but it must be a bit of an inconvenience to him, so busy as he has been lately." Not a lie, certainly, though her conscience protested that such a free interpretation of Dominic's thoughts was unjustified. She gave her conscience a metaphorical kick with the rationalization that desperate situations called for desperate measures. It was her duty to do all in her power to protect one who stood in the position of a daughter to her from the consequences of bestowing her heart on an unattainable object.

It would be unjust to say that Adrienne moped about the house that morning. She spent an hour or so playing cards with Jean-Paul before joining Miss Beckworth in the parlor the ladies used when they were alone. She willingly followed Becky's lead in conversation and remained politely attentive, but the older woman felt the effort that was expended to maintain a cheerful air. There were no callers that morning to provide a diversion, but a note was delivered while they were at luncheon inviting Adrienne to watch the scheduled review that afternoon of the English, Scottish, and Hanoverian troups stationed in Brussels and its environs. The girl brightened considerably at the request, which was from Major Peters, and looked to Miss Beckworth in hopeful anticipation.

"Major Peters says we could see it better on horseback, and he has included Luc in his invitation too. May we go please, Becky? You would like that, would you not, Luc?''

At that moment Miss Beckworth was experiencing all the discomfort of one who has been hoist with her own petard. Not four hours ago she had been hinting that Adrienne's riding lessons would soon be unneeded, but the girl had never ridden except with her cousin, and she was somewhat loath to grant permission without seeking Dominic's opinion. On the other hand, here was a perfect opportunity to widen Adrienne's experience with a person-able young man, and perhaps, hopefully, give her thoughts another direction. She could not think that Major Peters would be other than solicitous for his guest's safety, and Luc would be there for additional protection. She smiled at the expectant young faces regarding her and voiced her approval of the plan, since the sun had come out and promised to dry out the ground.

Adrienne's spirits rebounded with true Castle volatility as she dashed upstairs to change into her habit after lunch. While Marie's clever fingers tamed the glowing mass of russet curls into a neat setting for the flattering visored hat, her mistress hummed a march tune, pausing once to ask after the condition of Marie's mother, who had been feeling poorly of late. She listened intelligently to the symptoms the maid listed and recommended a special elixir she and Becky had found soothing in the past. Before leaving the room, she slipped some money into Marie's hand and promised to ask Madame Bonnet to allow the maid an hour off from her duties to go to the apothe-cary to make the purchase.

Adrienne joined Miss Beckworth in the small drawing room, where each worked on a piece of stitchery in a com-panionable silence punctuated by short exchanges of famil-ial observations. The girl's smile of welcome when Major Peters was eventually ushered in by Moulton caused that gentleman's step to falter momentarily while his own polite smile warmed in response.

Adrienne was uncannily like her father, Miss Beckworth marveled, observing the scene. Matthew too had drawn people like a magnet to the core of his human warmth. And neither of them recognized it for the rare gift it was. Miss Beckworth dissembled her amusement when their guest recollected his manners suddenly and turned to greet her first, looking slightly self-conscious despite his fluency. She extended her hand with a friendly air, approving his correct address to a young lady and her chaperone. Nevertheless, when the social preliminaries were over, she voiced her concern that Adrienne was still an inexperienced rider.

Major Peters nodded reassuringly. "I am aware, ma'am, and I promise you very little in the way of actual riding skill will be required of Miss Castle today. It just seemed that horseback offered a better vantage point for watching the review, but if you would be easier in your mind, we could drive to the area and join the crowds on foot."

Before Miss Beckworth could reply, Luc stuck his head in the door and announced that Nelson had brought the horses around. Mindful of the depths of disappointment the boy would plumb at being obliged to ride tamely in a carriage when he might be on horseback, Miss Beckworth swallowed her reservations, saying all that was proper in seeing the small party off at the front door.

"Where are we heading? Where is the review?" Adrienne demanded as soon as they were mounted and their escort had dismissed the groom and given a coin to the enterprising adolescent who had walked his black charger while he was inside.

Major Peters smiled down into the eager face with its jewel-bright eyes. "The review is in the Allée Verte."

"Will the hussars be parading? I should love to see all those beautiful horses and their magnificent riders."

"Don't you read the papers?" snorted Luc. "There won't be any cavalry at all. This is a review of the troops that will make up Wellington's Reserve Corps."

"Never mind, Miss Castle," Major Peters said in response to the disappointment his guest could not quite conceal, "Sir Denis Pack will be parading his Highland brigade, and where there are Highlanders there are sure to be pipes. Between the plumed hats and the kilts and the pipes there should be color and magnificence enough to satisfy even the tastes of a gypsy.''

And so it turned out. The Scots brigades may have been favorites of the cheering, waving crowd of Bruxellois, but as Major Peters pointed out, the British Fifth Division, which would be commanded by Sir Thomas Picton, included some of the most experienced regiments in the army, and the Hanoverian troops commanded by Colonel von Vincke were also seasoned men.

Luc was searching among the green-coated ranks of the Ninety-fifth Riflemen for a soldier he had met somewhere in the town and Major Peters was quietly enjoying the vidid picture Miss Castle made in her blue habit with the sea-green eyes sparkling and cheeks flying flags of color when the object of his admiration gave a squeal and tugged at his arm.

"Look over there, practically next to the Duke. Isn't that Dominic?"

"I believe it is. When the last of the troops have passed, shall we drift over there to say hello if the crowd permits?"

"Oh yes," breathed Adrienne ecstatically. "I may never come this close to the Duke again. Wait till I tell Becky!"

Major Peters sighed dramatically. "Alas, the rest of us hardworking fellows don't stand a chance to keep the ladies' attention when Old Hookey is around."

"Don't be nonsensical," scolded Miss Castle. "Of course everyone desires the honor of seeing England's savior at close range. There is nothing personal in it."

"You greatly relieve my mind, Miss Castle," said her escort meekly, accepting along with the set-down the knowledge that his naively charming companion had little taste for flirtation.

The trio was spotted by Lord Creighton before the field marshal's party left the reviewing area. Surprise and a quickly suppressed flash of some emotion more difficult to identify showed in his face before he turned and said something to his commander. Fortunately for an inexperienced young lady's shaky composure, they were almost upon the scene before a pair of keen blue eyes under heavily marked brows were directed her way. At the same instant she became aware that Lady Tremayne was also present. She was too intent on subduing the automatic *frisson* of aversion that accompanied any meeting with her cousin's betrothed to have leisure to develop any nervousness at the honor that was about to be hers.

Dominic came and lifted her down from Bijou, tucking her hand under his arm as he brought her up to the Duke. "Sir, may I present my cousin, Miss Adrienne Castle?"

"So you are the reason all the subalterns wish to run errands to Creighton's house lately," the Duke said, to widen Adrienne's eyes as she rose from her curtsy. "Can't say that I blame them. Delighted to meet you, Miss Castle."

When Adrienne had said how-do-you-do in a soft voice tinged with shyness, it was Luc's turn to receive the great man's benevolent attention. His bow was a credit to his upbringing, but he was too tongue-tied to do more than utter, "Sir!" in a reverent croak.

His Grace of Wellington laughed good-naturedly and clapped the boy on the shoulder. "You'd soon lose that awe if you were a foot soldier under my command. I shudder to think what they call me when I'm out of earshot."

"I w-wish I *were* a soldier under your command, sir," Luc declared fervently, finding his tongue in a rush.

"Come see me in a couple of years," said the field marshal kindly.

"You remember Major Peters, sir," Colonel Creighton interrupted before Luc could recover enough to beg the Duke to accept his enlistment on the spot.

"Of course. General Uxbridge was telling me last week that you were settling in well. Glad to hear it, Major."

"Thank you, sir."

The Duke expressed the hope that everyone had enjoyed the review. He was listening to the Castles' enthusiastic comments with a tolerant smile when an aide approached to remind him of an appointment.

There was an appreciable void after the field marshal had excused himself. Wellington wasn't a large man, not physically imposing except for that formidable Roman nose, nor did he conduct himself with any degree of consciousness, but his electric presence was always felt by well-wishers and foes alike. At his request the colonel had accompanied him to speak with several other officers. Lady Tremayne, who had taken no part in the brief meeting of the Duke with her fiancé's cousins, beyond an initial greeting, was pulling her gloves back and forth through her fingers, not troubling to conceal her boredom as Adrienne and Luc relived the thrill of the last few minutes, both bubbling over with excitement. Major Peters answered their questions with smiling good nature until Dominic came striding back.

"We left our horses quite close by. Shall we ride back together?" he suggested pleasantly.

By the time the enlarged party had reassembled, the crowds had dispersed somewhat from the area. They rode at the leisurely pace demanded by the clogged conditions of the Allée.

"Had I known that you wished to see the review, I'd have made arrangements for you to come with Pamela and me," Lord Creighton remarked to Adrienne when Lady Tremayne had engaged Major Peters' attention for the moment. "You should have told me."

Adrienne produced her infectious chuckle. "Well, I could not very well tell you when I was not even aware there was going to be a review until I received Major Peters' invitation today."

There was a short silence; then Lord Creighton said, "I am a bit . . . surprised that Becky allowed you to go riding on your own."

A puzzled aquamarine gaze swung to his. "But you told her you were very pleased with my progress. And as Major Peters pointed out, there is very little skill required to amble along as we have done today."

Overhearing this observation, the major addressed his old friend. "You are to be congratulated, Dominic. Your pupil does you great credit in the saddle."

"She is not yet ready to go jauntering off all over town with every young redcoat who fancies himself a devil to go on horseback," the earl replied rather shortly for one of his equable nature.

"I could not agree more, old chap." The major's voice was a smooth contrast.

Lady Tremayne angled her large gray closer to Adrienne, and the earl obligingly fell back to make room. "You have made wonderful progess with your riding, Miss Castle. You look quite at home in the saddle and are no doubt ready to move up to a more suitable mount."

Adrienne thanked her but laughingly denied any intention of changing horses as she leaned over to pat the chestnut's neck. "Bijou is my friend. We understand each other. I could never serve her such a backhanded trick."

It was unclear precisely what happened next, but the nervous gray that Lady Tremayne handled so superbly apparently took exception to something along the way and lunged sideways. While his rider struggled to bring him under control, Bijou suddenly bolted across the avenue. *Her* rider was too stunned and alarmed to put forth any constructive efforts at all. To the contrary, she dropped the reins, closed her eyes, and clung to the chestnut's mane while half-formed prayers whirled through her mind. Above the drumming of her own heartbeat in her ears she was dimly aware of thundering hooves and a voice calling her name. It almost sounded like someone was yelling for her to jump, which was absurd of course. She was having all she could do to avoid being thrown; in fact, she was losing her grip and sliding farther and farther . . .

"Adrienne, speak to me! Please, love, open your eyes. *Adrienne*!"

The voice was very far away but quite insistent, and she did her best to comply—there was a note of urgency that compelled her—but the effort was too great. The darkness was pleasant, though the bed was decidedly uncomfortable, and something was sticking into her hip. Strange, her hand was being raised and held and . . . surely, *kissed*! Who would do such a thing? Her lids lifted reluctantly. At first nothing was clear; she blinked and the blur resolved itself into two burning blue eyes in a white face set in a grim expression she had never seen before. It frightened her.

"D-Dominic?"

"Thank heavens!" His jaw softened a bit and she felt her fear dissolve. How foolish to be afraid of Dominic!

"Did I fall off?" she asked in such surprise that her cousin's lips twitched.

"You did indeed."

"Someone told me to *jump*! Was that you?" Surprise had given way to indignation.

"Bijou was heading straight for the canal," he explained. "She veered away at the last minute. That's when you were thrown."

"Oh!" She became aware that her hand, stripped of its glove, was being held in his, and at the same instant, that the world consisted of more than the two of them. The concerned face of Major Peters came into view above her.

"Are you all right, Miss Castle?"

She gave him what she hoped was a reassuring smile. "I think so." She registered Lady Tremayne's black-habited figure at the periphery of her vision but avoided looking that way. "Where is Luc?"

"He went after Bijou," said Dominic. "Do you think you can sit up now, Adrienne? There are no bones broken, but if anything hurts when I lift you, sing out."

Dominic was kneeling at her side. He slipped an arm under her shoulders and bent toward her. As she came up off the ground, there was a second when his face was so close she could feel his breath on her cheek. His mouth was only a fraction from hers. A gasp escaped Adrienne's lips and pure horror stared out of her eyes.

"Are you in pain?" demanded Dominic, halting his movement.

She closed her eyes and shook her head numbly, her lips pressed tightly together.

"Are you sure?"

"Yes."

After that, everything went well. Adrienne sat up, and when her cousin was convinced that she was not feeling giddy, she was assisted to her feet. She accepted her hat, slightly dented from its contact with the ground, from Lady Tremayne with a brief murmur of thanks, and spent the few seconds before Luc came up with Bijou in tow brushing the dirt from her skirts. The men were discussing how to convey her home, but her attention was directed on the purposeful movements of her hands. When the mention of a carriage reached her ears, she looked up finally, her face composed.

"I am perfectly capable of riding home."

"You've had a shaking-up," Dominic began.

"True, but I am unhurt, everything works, and I have always understood that one should get right back on after a spill."

"That's the dandy, Adrienne," approved Luc. "Everyone takes a tumble now and then."

Dominic's eyes roamed assessingly over her calm face. "Very well, I'll take you home."

"*No,* Dominic!" She forced a laugh to cover the urgency that had rung out. "Major Peters and Luc are quite sufficient as an escort, and you must see Lady Tremayne home."

He bowed, accepting her decision. Major Peters lifted her into the saddle as if she were made of glass. The earl helped his fiancée to mount the gray, and the party rode back toward the lime trees that lined the avenue, scattering the few onlookers who had collected after the accident.

Except that she initiated no conversation on the return trip, Adrienne seemed fully recovered from her fall, sitting her horse easily and managing the ride with almost automatic competence. The rest of the party conversed in spurts, all in the most amicable fashion possible, until the earl and Lady Tremayne parted from the others.

Lord Creighton fell silent when they were alone, and when his fiancée glanced his way a few minutes later, he wore a look of frowning abstraction as he stared straight ahead. Her tinkling laugh broke the silence.

"Little did I guess when I allowed you to drag me to that excessively boring review what an eventful afternoon it would turn out to be."

"You certainly contributed your bit to the excitement," replied Lord Creighton, his eyes still focused in front of him.

"*I* did? Whatever can you mean, darling? I was the veriest supernumerary this afternoon. It was all a Castle show."

At this blithe comment, the earl trained a grave, searching look on his betrothed's beautiful face. "Is that why you did it, because for once you were not the center of attention?"

"Did what? Really, my dear Dominic, you are not making any sense."

The earl made a weary gesture with his free hand. "I know that you caused that accident just now," he replied with quiet conviction. "What I don't know is *why* you—"

"How *dare* you, Dominic!" Two spots of color flared in Lady Tremayne's cheeks and her eyes flashed with fury. She looked magnificent in her rage, he thought with detachment.

"I saw you spur the gray. He didn't start lunging about on his own. While you were pretending to try to bring him under control, you angled him close to Bijou, and it worked. The gray kicked the mare and set her off. Bijou is a beautifully mannered horse. She would never bolt for no reason. Don't think to deny it."

"Of course I deny it!" hissed Lady Tremayne through clenched teeth. "Gray Ghost may have kicked the mare, but you have no right to say I intended it so, and I very much resent it! It was an accident, pure and simple!"

"It was neither pure, simple, nor accidental. Oh, I'm not accusing you of wishing to seriously injure Adrienne, but you did hope to show up her lack of equestrian skill by creating an emergency situation. *Why*?" As Lady Tremayne shook her head adamantly, he went on as if musing to himself:

"I have been aware, of course, that you and Adrienne have not become friends as I had hoped, but there is no reason for such dislike. My poor little cousin is not an adversary worthy of your attention, Pamela. You've never had cause to doubt my affection, nor do you care enough to be roused to jealousy on my account. The fact that we never spend any time alone together and that I cannot command more of your attention in public than any one of a dozen of your favorite admirers is testimony to that. So why do you go out of your way to embarrass Adrienne?"

They had slowed their pace almost to a crawl during this last observation, but now Lady Tremayne, her eyes glittering with anger, pulled her horse up short and faced her fiancé with heaving bosom and pinched nostrils. "I do not intend to waste my time denying your insulting accusations, nor do I intend to stay and listen to any more of these ridiculous ramblings." With that she kicked the big gray and rode swiftly down the street, leaving the earl to follow at his own speed.

As they had dispensed with the services of a groom that afternoon, Lady Tremayne's parting gesture lost some of its dramatic impact, since she was obliged to wait until her fiancé drew up in front of the house to collect her horse. She had dismounted unaided and was pacing in a tight little circle when the earl arrived. That the intervening moments had not had a calming effect on her temper was apparent as she thrust the gray's reins into his hands and glared up into his impassive countenance.

"You claim your 'poor little cousin' is no threat to me? Well, ask yourself this, Dominic. Would you have devoted all those hours to teaching your *cousin* to ride had she been plain, or muffin-faced, or possessed of a squint?" As his lips parted, she laughed harshly.

"Do not trouble to reply. I already know the answer." A challenging look, a whirl of skirts, and she disappeared into the house.

15

At the same time that Lord Creighton and Lady Tremayne were embroiled in their acrimonious confrontation on horseback, the unwitting author of their troubles was engaged in an activity with which she was previously unacquainted—the art of dissimulation. Evidently this initial attempt was successful, for neither Luc nor Major Peters found anything in her pleasant though subdued manner that could not be attributed to her recent fall and the aftereffects of shock.

Major Peters made his adieux at the front door while Luc rode around to the stables with the horses. A little sigh of relief escaped Adrienne as she entered the house, but her ordeal was by no means over; she still had to face Becky, who knew her better than anyone else in the world. She squared her shoulders and took a calming breath. It was absolutely vital that she be convincing in the role of a girl without a care in the world, and one, moreover, who has just had the signal honor of meeting and being complimented by the Duke of Wellington. She wondered fleetingly if actresses experienced this strange fluttering feeling in the pit of the stomach before an important performance, and concluded, with a wry twist to her lips, that they very likely did if the audience was as exacting as hers was going to prove. She pinned a bright smile on her lips and burst through the door to the small saloon, entirely determined to accomplish her objective.

A half-hour later, slumped in a chair in her bedchamber, her hands limp in her lap, she acknowledged the minor comfort of having succeeded in pulling the wool over her best friend's eyes. It hadn't been easy; her expurgated account of this afternoon's events had omitted any reference to her tumble, and there had been one bad moment when she had felt the dreaded heat invade her cheeks at Becky's sharp look when she had mentioned Lady Tremayne's presence at the review. Blushing was such a cursed handicap! She had quickly introduced the person of the field marshal at that juncture, and her genuine delight in that part of the day's happenings had colored the rest of her tale.

So, mission accomplished, she thought drearily, rising from the chair and heading toward the washstand, unfastening her habit as she went. She tossed the coat in the general direction of the bed and proceeded to bathe her face in the cool water with meticulous care. At last she could avoid the truth no longer. Patting her cheeks dry with the linen towel, she peered fearfully into the mirror and saw in her shadowed eyes the pain she had been attempting to deny since that terrible moment on the banks of the canal when she had realized that she was in love with Dominic. The knowledge had hit her like a *coup de foudre* as he had bent over to help her to her feet. His mouth had been a hairbreadth from her own for an instant, and the distance had been too great! She'd experienced an aching desire to know the touch of his lips on hers, a feeling that had horrified her as soon as she identified it, and left her gasping with shock and self-recrimination until her brain began to function again with the necessity for concealment. Dominic had attributed her reaction to pain. She could only pray that Lady Tremayne had not been in a position to see her face at that moment.

She closed her eyes briefly and turned away from the mirror to begin an aimless wandering about the room. Thus far her guilty secret was safe, but the prospect of maintaining an eternal vigilance over her expression and her tongue was truly appalling to one of her open disposition. Heavens, here she was less than two hours after making the discovery that her feelings for Dominic were anything but cousinly, and she was as drained and weary as during the worst days of Jean-Paul's illness, perhaps more so because then she had been fighting with all her strength. This situation was and must remain hopeless. Her energies would be expended in the essential but unrewarding chore of maintaining a decent silence and denying her heart the relief of expressing her love. No, that wasn't exactly true. She could best express her love by ensuring that Dominic was spared the embarrassment and distress that the discovery of it would mean for him.

She turned away from the dressing table where she had been idly fingering the brushes on top, reluctant to carry her line of thinking to its logical conclusion. Her fingers crept up to massage her throbbing temples as she plodded over to sink down on the edge of the bed and confront the stark reality. They would have to leave here immediately— strange how the fact of their ultimate departure had gotten lost in the excitement of their lives since arriving at Rue Ducale. Jean-Paul had been gaining steadily these past weeks. She must put a flea in Becky's ear and trust the older woman to approach Dominic. Until they could arrange their travel plans, she must simply avoid her cousin as much as possible.

Which meant giving up their morning ride. She clenched her fists against the protest of her heart and sat staring forlornly at one of the bedposts. How had matters come to such a pass? she wondered in honest bewilderment. The entrance of Dominic into their lives at such a low point had seemed providential. It had been so delightful having a relative who enjoyed their company and was pleased to make himself responsible for them. She absently traced the pattern of carving on the bedpost. This dependence on others was insidious and weakening. She had grasped that intuitively from the beginning, but somehow amid the pleasures of the past few weeks she had lost sight of her native caution. There was no one to blame but herself. Dominic had treated her in the same kind, brotherly fashion as he had Luc and Jean-Paul. His affection for his young relatives was quite genuine and it could have been hers forever if she had not been so stupid as to fall in love with him. But who could have failed to love him, the kindness of his heart and the sweetness of his temper, not to mention the endearing smile that started in his eyes and warmed and attracted one even against one's will?

Small even teeth sank into her bottom lip as she expelled a ragged breath. At least today's revelation had solved one small mystery—her instinctive dislike of Lady Tremayne, which had caused her some pangs of guilt in the past. It was pure jealousy, of course. Not very admirable, admittedly, but understandable enough in the circumstances. Adrienne's delicately pointed chin firmed, then quivered as her eyes filled with scalding tears. Lady Tremayne wasn't good enough for Dominic! That sense of superiority over the ordinary run of females that she did not trouble to conceal, and the tenaciously held assumption that her beauty entitled her to the attention of every gentleman who took her eye, were characteristics unlikely to endear her to the majority of her own sex. Apart from the unrestrained exercise of a talent for exciting envy and dislike in other female bosoms, she was vain and selfish and delighted in flaunting the power her beauty gave her over all men. Adrienne was utterly convinced that she did not really love her fiancé.

But Dominic loved her! Into Adrienne's mind flashed a picture of her cousin and Lady Tremayne locked in a passionate embrace in the study as she had seen them together on that first occasion. Though she had been barely acquainted with Dominic at the time, something inside her had ached and protested against the reality her eyes had witnessed. Her own love for Dominic must have been growing even then. Her cup overflowing with misery, the slight figure on the bed crumpled and gave way to the tears that had been threatening since the accident. She wept until, for the moment, she was drained of all emotion. Her mind felt depleted too, but she didn't shirk the decision. At the first opportunity she must begin the process of detaching her family from Rue Ducale and Brussels, and in the meantime it was imperative, for Dominic's sake, that she keep herself at a distance. She would send a message to him tomorrow canceling their morning ride. The bruise coming out on her hip would provide a plausible excuse.

Adrienne wasn't the only female intimately connected

with Lord Creighton who was doing some painful soul-searching that afternoon. A glittering-eyed, tight-lipped Lady Tremayne had stormed into her apartment after the quarrel with her betrothed. If there was room for any other emotion than pure rage in her seething consciousness, it could only be a passing sense of relief at having attained the privacy of her boudoir without encountering her watchful brother. Like Adrienne, she spent some time pacing about, though in her case it would be more accurate to describe her movements as striding, or even stalking. That Dominic had persisted in accusing her of arranging his cousin's accident in the face of repeated denials had badly shaken her confidence. Anger that he had not accepted her explanation, at least for form's sake, rapidly followed shock. It mattered little that she *had* in fact caused Gray Ghost to leap about, hoping some discomfort might result for his precious Adrienne. Dominic was *her* intended husband and he owed her his first loyalty. No more than most people did Lady Tremayne relish being put in the wrong.

It afforded her some slight satisfaction to recall that Dominic hadn't had it all his own way. She had given him something to think about at the end of that trying scene. When he came up to collect Gray Ghost he had been wearing that polite calm look that never failed to irritate her, the mask he habitually donned to hide his reactions. For once she had managed to penetrate that facade. She had been too angry to wish to hear one more word from him at that point, but her last glimpse before she entered the house had revealed a man dazed enough to have just been struck by lightning. Or a verbal thunderbolt at least, she amended, her mood veering from anger to sardonic humor.

Lady Tremayne had rung for her maid on first entering the room, and now she drifted over to stare at herself in the mirror while she waited. Fury had lent her complexion heightened color and her eyes added sparkle, she noted as she surveyed her smoothly coiffed head and the severely tailored black habit that suited her fine figure so admirably. She might as well have been wearing rags for all the effect her appearance had had on Dominic just now. His eyes had held all the warmth of blue ice as he had raked her over the coals in defense of his insipid little cousin. Her own eyes narrowed and her mouth thinned as she ripped off the masculine-styled stock about her throat just as her maid entered the room upon a soft knock.

"It took you long enough to get here. I suppose you've been trysting with some tradesman or underservant in the neighborhood the minute I turn my back."

"I beg your pardon, my lady. I was below stairs ironing the dress you said you planned to wear tonight. I thought it better to take a minute to finish than to leave it where an accident might occur." The maid had been hanging the dress in the wardrobe as she spoke. Her words were more polite than the tones in which they were spoken, and her mouth firmed in disapproval as her eye took in the trail of belongings on the floor.

"Never mind that now; I have changed my mind. Get out my yellow silk. And I shall want the Norwich silk shawl ironed too. You can do that while I bathe. Meanwhile, help me out of these wretched boots."

The maid had been warned by Sir Ralph's man that "her ladyship was in a rare taking" when he had passed her in the hall, but she could have assessed her mistress's mood by the scattered pattern of whip, gloves, and black-plumed hat on the carpet. She kept her eyes lowered protectively as she deposited these items on the bed before hurrying over to remove Lady Tremayne's riding boots. It was going to be one of those sessions when it was impossible to please her ladyship. She set her teeth and prepared to endure an hour of constant carping. It would not be for much longer now, she consoled herself. She had been making discreet inquiries of other dressers to learn if they knew of any lady of quality who might be in need of the services of an experienced lady's maid, one especially skilled in hair design. She did not mean to be turned off without a character before she secured another position.

Lady Tremayne, unaware and equally uncaring of the thoughts going around in her maid's head, succeeded in confounding that damsel's predictions by accepting her services with a minimum of criticism that evening. As her temper cooled, she had become increasingly thoughtful and, for one of her monumental vanity, seemed almost unconcerned about her appearance, acceding to every suggestion put forth by her dresser, a previously unimaginable situation. She dismissed the woman with a wave of her hand at the earlist possible moment, though she made no movement away from the dressing table, where she was inserting long topaz earrings with an abstracted air.

When the exhilaration that accompanied anger had dissipated, Lady Tremayne had found herself seriously analyzing the afternoon's confrontation. Her parting shot at Dominic had been an instinctive retaliation for his reference to her admirers. The more she considered his stunned reaction, however, the more uneasy she became in her mind. Was his reaction due to shock at her accusation or to some sudden knowledge of his feelings for his cousin? What a colossal fool she would be to set him to questioning his feelings for the red-haired chit!

Abruptly she thrust back her chair from the dressing table and rose. She glided over to the window and gazed out on the street below, nearly deserted at this early-evening hour. There was no doubting Dominic's passion for herself at the beginning, but of late had he been less eager to seize her in his arms at every opportunity? She put up a forefinger to smooth out the frown between her brows. If it were true that he was less enamored at present, she would have to accept the responsibility for having mishandled the affair. It had seemed prudent to keep him at arm's length to give herself more space in which to maneuver. Count Levèque had been pursuing her with a vengeance that was promising, but thus far he had not committed himself to the extent of a firm proposal. She was not worried that Dominic would cry off—his rigid code of behavior would preclude such an action—but perhaps she would do well to smooth over this quarrel and throw some sops his way. It might even provoke the count's jealousy enough to prompt him to come up to scratch. If it could be accomplished, she would prefer to marry Levèque. He was an exciting companion, and he would certainly make a more complaisant husband than Dominic. The more she learned of the latter, the more she was inclined to agree with Ralph that he was not the man to allow his wife to go her own way unchecked. Perhaps she had acted rashly in pursuing Dominic to Brussels, but their financial situation had grown too precarious to remain in Vienna, and it had seemed wasteful in the extreme to let such a rich prize escape. Well, she still had her bird in the hand, she thought grimly, and she would see to it that no little chit as green as grass enticed him back into the bush, at least not until she had bigger game safely in her sights.

This afternoon Dominic had accused her of not caring enough for him to become jealous. The irony lay in the fact that her feelings toward Adrienne Castle could best be described as jealousy over her position in Dominic's affections. One didn't have to love a man to resent his partiality for another woman. She considered passingly whether her best course might be to confess to jealousy and undying love, but firmly dismissed the idea. She was too annoyed with her fiancé to put herself in the humiliating position of begging for understanding. Thanks to his ingrained sense of honor, matters weren't that desperate. The most sensible approach was to simply ignore the incident and see to it that Dominic did not feel neglected in the days to come. It might be just the impetus needed to propel Henri Levèque to action. Or the long anticipated battle might take place and be done with so that Dominic would be compelled to set a date for their marriage. If this ambivalent situation went on much longer, she would be quite run off her legs. Today's post had consisted of three bills, including a dunning letter from Madame Henriette. She'd have to order another gown from the modiste to keep her quiet a little longer.

Lady Tremayne gathered her poise about her like a protective cloak as she prepared to leave the sanctuary of her room. The only thing wanting to set the seal on this horrible day would be to have Ralph start criticizing the

way she treated her fiancé. After one last comprehensive
look at her reflection, she fastened a determined smile on
her lips and headed for the door.

To the discomfiture of both ladies, Lord Creighton gave
neither the opportunity to put into immediate action her
plan of conduct with respect to him. Indeed he was
singularly elusive over the next few days. Before Adrienne
could pen a note canceling their ride on the morning after
the review, a message was delivered to her bedchamber
containing Dominic's excuses, citing the press of work at
present for his inability to spare the time to ride with his
cousin. Work must have multiplied alarmingly, for she did
not even lay eyes on him during the next three days. He
was gone each morning before she came down to breakfast, and though he must have dined somewhere during
this period, it was not at his own table.

Lady Tremayne was more fortunate in that her
betrothed did at least put in an appearance at those social
functions that had been on his calendar. When it came to
advancing her plan to allow him a greater share of her
time, however, she was defeated by the lack of cooperation
on the part of the intended beneficiary. Dominic danced
with her at each affair, took her in to supper if she had not
made other arrangements, and paid her the required
number of elegantly phrased compliments on her looks.
He even escorted her home if her brother was not present
to perform that office. But without her quite realizing how
he accomplished the feat, he managed to avoid any
intimacy in conversation, and though he kissed her at
parting, there was none of the ador in his manner with
which he had embraced her a month ago. Since her
beckoning looks and intimate smiles had no appreciable
effect, she was left with no recourse except to bide her time
and pretend that nothing had changed between them.

At first Adrienne experienced almost pure relief at being
spared the ordeal of hiding her love by Dominic's
convenient absence, but such is the perversity of women
that she yet yearned for the danger she most feared. It
might be a torment to see him dancing attendance on Lady

Tremayne, but not to see him at all rendered every day a uniform gray blank.

Which is not to say that she retired to her room to nurse her broken heart in solitude. By now the Castles had been drawn into considerable participation in the active social life of Brussels, and Adrienne could not have turned hermit even had that been her dearest wish. She and Becky paid and received calls with some regularity. Her inherently gregarious nature found something of interest in most humans who crossed her path. If her palms tended to become damp and her breathing irregular whenever the saloon door opened, no one was the wiser, for she maintained a creditable control over her facial expression and refused to acknowledge even to herself that all her senses were straining for the sight or sound of her cousin.

The insouciant Lieutenant Markham was a frequent caller at the house on Rue Ducale, and Major Peters was sometimes able to find reasons to desert Ninove for Brussels. One day he escorted Miss Beckworth and Adrienne to a picnic arranged by Lady Staveley in the lovely beech forest of Soignes south of the city on the Nivelles road. Dominic was not among those enjoying the cool, sweet woodland air, though there were a number of officers present, their red, blue, and green coats providing foils for the pale pastel muslins of the young ladies. In Brussels itself the fine June weather attracted people to the park in droves. Adrienne and Sarah Forrester often strolled along the curving paths, admiring the flowers and feeding the swans that frequented the ornamental water. On a couple of occasions Adrienne or Miss Beckworth took Jean-Paul out for an airing in the carriage, which marked a giant step forward in his convalescence.

On the day after the review, Adrienne had approached Becky about setting a date for their departure to England and had found her open to the suggestion. The ladies were in agreement that Jean-Paul was improved to the point where he could withstand the voyage with no danger of relapse. It only remained to clear the plan with Dominic, which Becky undertook to do at the first opportunity. She had a pretty fair conception of Adrienne's emotional state, though the topic was never mentioned between them. Certainly all references to the engaged pair on Miss Beckworth's part ceased as they directed their energies toward the problem of packing up their belongings, though nothing could actually be done until Dominic was apprised of their intention and had set the wheels in motion.

Adrienne was beginning to chafe at her cousin's continued inaccessibility when Dominic appeared in the saloon late one morning when the ladies were entertaining callers. He had a stylish young female in tow whom he proceeded to present to his relatives. Lady Georgiana Lennox confessed that she had begged Colonel Creighton to effect an introduction to his cousins so that they might be included in the ball that her parents were hosting the following week.

"My mother would have come with me today, ma'am," Lady Georgiana assured Miss Beckworth, "only that she has one of her bad heads this morning and felt she was not fit company for anyone. However, she charged me to present her compliments and deliver the invitation personally to you and Miss Castle. I hope you will come," she urged, turning to Adrienne with a friendly smile. "It should be a lovely party. Mama is determined to eclipse the Duke, who has secured the royal family for his own ball later this month."

Lady Georgiana's infectious smile commanded a return from Adrienne. "If we are still in town we will be delighted to come, your ladyship, but we are making plans to remove from Brussels shortly and may have left by then."

"What nonsense is this?" Dominic demanded sharply, his head spinning back from greeting Major Peters. "Jean-Paul will not be ready to travel for some weeks yet."

Adrienne mustered up a steadying breath and faced her cousin squarely. "Becky and I are agreed that he is strong enough now to make the journey," she returned, her eyes meeting his unwaveringly.

"We will talk of this later," Dominic said with his lazy smile, "after the doctor has pronounced Jean-Paul fit for travel."

Good manners demanded that Adrienne refrain from

continuing the argument in company. She produced a non-committal smile and set about making their new acquaintance feel welcome. This did not prove to be an onerous task. Lady Georgiana was a naturally friendly person with a well-bred ease of manner that never deserted her in social situations. Since part of Adrienne's mind was busy grappling with a new problem, this was just as well. She responded to Lady Georgiana's overtures and bore her share of the general conversation with a smile on her lips that disguised a sinking sensation in the pit of her stomach. Though very little had actually been said, a knowledge deep in her bones told her Dominic was disposed to be difficult on the subject of their immediate departure for England.

Over the next few days Adrienne's foreboding was proved correct. It seemed that Dr. Hume was every bit as elusive as Dominic. Their requests that he examine his small patient at his earliest convenience were met with put-offs and half-promises that still had not resulted in a visit three days later. Coincidence? Perhaps, but Adrienne, rapidly declining into a dangerous mood compounded of unhappiness and impatience, didn't credit it for a moment.

"It's all Dominic's doing!" she declared angrily when Miss Beckworth ventured to excuse the doctor's absence on the probable grounds of overwork. "He is determined to keep us here twiddling our thumbs until it suits his convenience to confer his gracious permission to leave. I've half a mind to simply pack up and go!"

"We could never behave in such a scaly fashion after all that Dominic has done for us!" cried Miss Beckworth, alarmed at the ill-controlled passion in her charge's demeanor. "It would be to sink quite beneath reproach. Besides," she added in a practical spirit, "there is no possibility of such an action; we haven't the resources."

"We are in fact in exactly the same case as we were before we ever set eyes on Dominic!" fumed Adrienne, storming about the room, unable to sit still in her irritation.

Miss Beckworth elected to withhold the contradiction this blatant misstatement merited. She also choked back the sympathy she longed to extend to the girl she loved, knowing it would not be well received. Adrienne needed to fight this battle alone. Acceptance never came easily to one of her passionate temperament. By nature she was a doer, one who would always find a passive role a real penance. Sighing, Miss Beckworth returned her eyes to her embroidery, though her covert attention remained with Adrienne, who was still prowling about, now with a thoughtful frown creasing her forehead. A little pleat formed across her own brow as uneasiness stirred somewhere behind her consciousness. The last time Adrienne had worn that look of deep concentration, the result had been her crack-brained plan to disguise her identity in order to visit a gaming establishment. Her companion could only hope this session of serious mental effort did not spawn an even more outrageous scheme.

16

Miss Beckworth's instinctive misgivings were in-accurate only in that they led her to fear some new action on Adrienne's part that would prove to be inappropriate, dangerous, or worse. Actually it was her original scheme that was again seducing the girl's mind. Inaction was anathema to Adrienne. It was not in her nature to sit back and wait for better times to arrive, nor could she abide being at the mercy of other people's judgments when they concerned her. With the clarity of hindsight she could see that putting themselves in Dominic's hands had been a mistake. Just what options they'd had at the critical moment was a question she preferred not to address at present. It was a lack of funds that had landed them in their dependent posi-tion; therefore, it followed logically that the possession of money would achieve their former independence.

The only avenue open to her to acquire money was, as before, gambling. Her brain was functioning efficiently and coolly now, assessing the probable obstacles and dif-ficulties. The primary obstacle to be overcome was Miss Beckworth, who would fight tooth and nail against her scheme, so it would be advisable all round to leave Becky ignorant of her intentions. She laid her plans accordingly. They were scheduled to attend a card party at the For-resters' this evening. A last-minute indisposition would serve to free her from the obligation. Naturally Becky would be reluctant to cancel on such short notice. Adrienne counted on Becky's unadmitted predilection for General Forrester's society to reinforce her own insistence that her friend go ahead without her.

In the end, matters fell out exactly as Adrienne hoped. She toyed with her dinner and mentioned a slight queasiness when questioned about her lack of appetite. She denied any other symptoms and allowed the suggestion that she might be coming down with something to originate with Becky, even protesting mildly when her duenna prescribed a good night's rest to ward off any invading infections. Becky overrode her insistence that she felt perfectly capable of sitting at a card table and departed for the Forresters' as scheduled, after seeing the girl off to her bedchamber with a cup of camomile tea.

Dominic had sent word earlier that he had ridden to Charleroi and would be away from Brussels overnight. Taking this as a good omen for the success of her venture, Adrienne proceeded to don the golden wig and change into the despised blue gown as soon as the carriage rolled away from the door. Luc and Jean-Paul were engaged in a marathon chess game in the study, leaving the coast clear for Adrienne to slip into Miss Beckworth's room to appropriate some money for her stake. She had turned her winnings over to Becky after the previous gambling adventures. They had not been obliged to disburse any monies since coming to Dominic's house, except for small personal expenses, so there was a goodly sum remaining. She shook off the guilty feeling that assailed her at the thought of helping herself; tomorrow would be soon enough to worry about the morality of her action. For tonight her course was charted. She'd had the foresight to bribe Antoine to call her a cab and keep watch to let her back in on her return. Deciding that she'd made all the advance preparations of a general planning a military campaign, she silently closed the door to Becky's bedchamber and ran softly down the stairs, draping a lace shawl over her head like a mantilla to conceal the blond wig.

Three hours later a jubilant Adrienne was confident that the gods and Lady Luck were sitting at her elbow tonight. She had elected to visit Madame Mireille's, influenced by an impression from her former visit that a greater number of females were among the habitués of this establishment. Perhaps it was the calm of desperation, or simply a new poise acquired through recent social exposure, but she blended in casually with the other guests tonight and was able to select her prospective victim at will. Again she sustained the character of a non-English speaking Bruxelloise. Her opponent, a burly, genial Englishman of early-middle years, was a careless cardplayer, as much interested in conducting a limping flirtation in fractured French as he was in the contest. Adrienne parried his advances cheerfully but mechanically, her primary attention concentrated on her cards. The results were most gratifying.

"Piqued, repiqued, and capoted, by God!" Mr. Hinckley exclaimed at the end of the third rubber. "Young lady, if I had a hat I'd raise it to your skill!"

"Merci, Monsieur Hinckley. Vous êtres très gentil, un vrai gentilhomme." Adrienne's dimples flashed as she smilingly accepted her winnings from her vanquished opponent when he had totted up the score.

"Mademoiselle Giroude, it has been a real pleasure. I trust you will allow me an opportunity for revenge in the near future?"

Adrienne looked up from tucking the money in her reticule, straight into the narrowed eyes of her cousin's betrothed. Her own eyes widened in consternation for a second before she wrenched her gaze back to Mr. Hinckley and murmured a conventional phrase of delight at the prospect of another meeting. Through a veil of curling lashes she saw Lady Tremayne whisper something to the man to whose arm she had been clinging. Panic swept through Adrienne. She muttered an excuse to her partner and rose precipitately, but she hadn't gone two steps when a hand grasped her arm above the elbow.

"Just one moment, if you please, *Mademoiselle Giroude*. I should like a word with you."

Adrienne froze in place, then rallied her courage. She stared pointedly at the hand on her arm. *"Je crois que je n'ai pas le plaisir de votre connaissance, madame,"* she said with unsmiling civility.

Her words had no effect on Lady Tremayme except that she removed her hand. "You may spare your breath to cool your porridge, Miss Castle. I recognized you the moment you smiled, despite that ridiculous wig. There cannot be three such dimples anywhere else in Brussels. What are you doing in this place, and who is your escort?"

"I think that is not your concern."

"It is, however, very much Dominic's concern. I cannot think he will approve of his innocent little cousin's being seen in a gaming house. You seem to have inherited your father's weakness at a very tender age. You also appear to be very successful," she added with a significant glance at the reticule dangling from the other's wrist, "in which case it does seem a trifle *excessive* of you to continue to hang on to Dominic's sleeve all this time."

Angry words trembled on Adrienne's lips as she stared into scornful amber eyes, but at that moment Lady Tremayne's escort reappeared at her side, carrying two brimming glasses.

"Ah, *chèrie,* here you are, one glass of champagne as ordered. Oh, I beg pardon, I did not realize you were in conversation. Allow me, mademoiselle," he said with a smiling bow in Adrienne's direction as he presented her with the other glass. "I shall get another for myself."

Adrienne murmured a startled thank-you while Lady Tremayne bit her lip in annoyance as her escort wove his slightly unsteady way back toward a waiter carrying a tray of drinks. Clear blue-green eyes met Lady Tremayne's look disdainfully. "I cannot think that Dominic would approve of his fiancée's being escorted to a gaming house by another man," she riposted, going on the offensive in her turn.

The older woman drew herself up proudly. "It may interest you to know that Dominic is scheduled to meet me here in ten minutes. Do you care to stay and surprise him?"

Adrienne smiled brilliantly into adamantine amber eyes. "That will be quite a feat of riding, since Dominic left for Charleroi late this afternoon. *Au revoir, madame.* Please make my excuses to your charming escort."

Before Lady Tremayne could react, she found herself holding a second glass of champagne while she was treated to a vanishing back view of a slim blond in an unfashionable blue gown.

Adrienne made her unhurried way to the entrance to meet the hackney cab she had ordered earlier. Not until she had sunk thankfully onto the seat did she dare to relax the control she had imposed on herself during the distressing scene just enacted. To her annoyance, she was shaking all over in a nervous reaction, and her brain was a quivering mass of unpleasant sensation too. What wretched, wretched luck to run smack into Lady Tremayne tonight! She had passed among no fewer than three gentlemen of her acquaintance in Madame Mireille's rooms without earning a second glance from any. Trust that woman to have pierced her disguise! It was just the kind of disobliging behavior one might expect from her, she thought bitterly, arranging the lace shawl over her head with trembling fingers. And finding her ladyship hanging on another man's arm when her fiancé was away was another example of behavior one would expect from a woman of her stamp. *Why* couldn't Dominic see that she would make him an abominable wife?

That had been a nasty scene just now. Lady Tremayne's snide reference to her father had brought her own blood to a rapid boil, after which she could not claim that her own conduct was any more creditable than that of the other woman. It wasn't her place to censure the other's conduct, but she had thrust her oar in anyway and immediately compounded her presumption by letting her ladyship know that she didn't believe Dominic planned to join her at Madame Mireille's. Struggling to be fair, Adrienne tried to bring an open mind to the question of whether Lady Tremayne had lied. Apparently Dominic had gone out of town on short notice. He had sent word to his own household that he would be away overnight. It was barely conceivable that he had forgotten to inform his betrothed, or that a message had gone astray. Adrienne's instinct told her Lady Tremayne had lied, and that she would not care to have Dominic learn that she had permitted other men to squire her around when he was unavailable. On the other hand, she need not have approached her at all tonight if she hoped to keep her own presence from becoming known. Having the advantage of recognizing her fiancé's cousin before being noticed herself, she could have kept out of Adrienne's line of vision thereafter. The rooms had been fairly crowded all evening, so that shouldn't have been too difficult to accomplish.

And yet her demeanor toward that handsome, mustachioed Belgian officer was certainly such that an impartial observer might have taken him for her betrothed. The implications of the question occupied Adrienne's mind for the rest of the drive to the earl's house. In the end she concluded with a newly acquired cynicism that the proof that Lady Tremayne had lied about expecting to meet her fiancé would be if she herself heard nothing further about the matter. If he were informed of her escapade, Dominic would not fail to read her a curtain lecture about setting foot in a gaming house. Lady Tremayne would not inform him of it if she had anything to conceal about her own conduct. If she were indeed the gamester Pamela had insinuated she was, she would wager her last penny that nothing more would be heard of tonight's incident, Adrienne decided as she paid the driver and went up the front steps, to be admitted by the vigilant footman.

"Thank you, Antoine," she said softly. "Has Miss Beckworth returned home?"

"Not yet, Miss Castle."

"Thank you, Antoine," she said again, pressing some money into his hand on her way to the stairs. "Good night."

There was one more detail to be attended to before she could take her suddenly weary body to bed. She replaced the money she had borrowed in Becky's drawer, this time keeping her winnings in her own possession, and entered her own room thankfully. A moment later she stared down at the princely sum of one hundred and fifteen louis as she locked it in her mother's almost empty jewel box. There was no expression on her face and no elation remaining in her heart, though she had certainly enjoyed a brief thrill of triumph when Mr. Hinckley had paid his losses. At the moment, she felt thoroughly deflated. Being ruthlessly honest with herself, she admitted that she had gone to Madame Mireille's this evening in a spirit of defiance and frustration with her present circumstances. As she removed the wig and began slow preparations for bed, she tried to assess what had been accomplished other than the acquisition of a useful sum of money. Not her freedom certainly. In her heart she knew full well she could never repay Dominic's kindness by leaving town without his knowledge or approval. She had managed to alienate Lady Tremayne even more deeply—not that this was likely to cause her any pangs of regret. To date the beautiful brunette had not neglected many opportunities to demonstrate her antipathy toward her fiancé's cousin.

Adrienne slipped into a pale green nightdress of softest lawn. Her eyes sought her reflection in the glass over the dressing table as her fingers tied the satin ribbons at her throat. She looked just as usual, which was a bit surprising since she felt very different tonight, years older than the impetuous girl who had entered this house so reluctantly a few short weeks ago. Life certainly played strange tricks on one. She hadn't wanted to come to Rue Ducale, and now the thought of leaving was like a sword in her heart. They must go soon, of course; their future didn't lie here. She pushed thoughts of the future away, feeling unequal to coping with anything beyond today's misery. Still she acknowledged with relief that the roiling current of frustration and protest that had tossed and swirled her along at will for the past several days had quietened into a stream of dull misery that was navigable, though the cost in courage and dignity would be high. All she had to do was remember that they owed their deliverance to Dominic. He had their best interests at heart, which was a thought to soothe a bruised spirit. Whatever happened in the future, knowing and loving Dominic had been a privilege and a delight, the memory of which she would treasure forever. She climbed into bed that night bone-weary but more at peace with herself than for a long time, and fell instantly asleep.

* * *

It was after noontime when Colonel Creighton entered Brussels by the Namur gate, and fully an hour later before he finished his report at headquarters and headed home to bathe and change out of the clothes he had donned the day before. He was tired, but his fatigue was not the sort to be relieved by sleep. It was mental exhaustion from his unceasing efforts to hold back the tide, in this case the tide of his newly realized love for Adrienne, with the result that always accompanies puny human efforts to combat the forces of nature. It could have been a tidal wave of joy if things had been different, if he had not made an almighty fool of himself two months ago. As matters stood, however, he was a man in a trap, a trap he had constructed for himself and into which he had walked, not just willingly but eagerly, with his eyes open. They were open even wider now, but he could not see an honorable way out of the trap.

Less than two months ago he'd had the world by the tail. There was a precept of ancient folklore that advised caution with regard to what one wished for, because the wish might come true. Well, he had wanted nothing so much as to win the hand of the most beautiful woman he'd ever met, and he had done just that.

Lord Creighton's step slowed and he glanced around in surprise to find himself at the edge of the water staring at the cruising swans. He's been walking through the park to his house without really seeing anything in his path and could only trust that he had not cut anyone of his acquaintance. He altered his course to bring him out near his house, but soon fell back into the same state of frowning reverie. When had the dream world he'd inhabited faded and dissolved? Not immediately after Pamela had agreed to marry him; he was still seeing her through a happy mist at the time Adrienne had come bursting into his life.

Even a man as bedazzled and hungry as he had been for the promise of Pamela's seductive beauty could not long remain blind to the contrasts the two women presented. Perhaps it was his chagrin at discovering that Pamela did not intend to let her engagement prevent her from collecting every available male in her net that caused him to note that Adrienne's charm sprang from a natural interest in humanity rather than a desire to attract an audience. Pamela's admirers were invariably masculine; he had lately come to recognize that she had no real friends among her own sex. Two months ago he'd have accepted that other women were simply jealous of one who cast them completely in the shade. That was before he had come to discern the basic integrity of Adrienne's character that threw Pamela's artfulness into high relief. The generosity and sweetness of the one underscored the vanity and selfishness of the other. He had struggled to retain his original vision of Pamela as the embodiment of a man's ideal woman, but her persistent spitefulness toward his cousin, totally gratuitous and unprovoked, at first shocked and eventually sickened him.

It was entirely through his own stupidity that he was now committed to spend his life with a woman he could not respect. In the throes of his first infatuation he had lusted after her, longed to possess that perfect beauty. Even when he had begun to suspect that she didn't love him, to doubt that she was capable of loving anyone save herself, he had still wanted her desperately. When he took her in his arms, the feel and taste of her inflamed his senses and blotted out doubts and problems. Nobody was without flaws; certainly he was no saint to be entitled to the perfect woman or the perfect union. For a time he had been able to persuade himself that his desire for her was enough to ensure a reasonably successful marriage. He had stopped expecting the moon. Willful self-deception might have carried him through, but thanks to Pamela's spite, even that comfort was now denied him.

The day the Duke had reviewed his reserve troops in the Allée, everything had changed. He had been disconcerted to see Adrienne in the company of his old friend at the outset, but it was the accident that had destroyed his hopes for accommodation with Pamela. She had disappointed and disillusioned him, but he thought he had geared himself to bear it. The knowledge that she had arranged Adrienne's accident had burst that bubble. He had not thought himself capable of such anger toward a woman. He trusted he had controlled it before the others, but he had not been able to resist challenging her with it when they were alone. The quarrel that followed had succeeded in destroying his peace of mind. Out of the blue had come Pamela's accusation that his feelings for Adrienne were more than cousinly affection.

The simple truth of her words had struck him with the force of a cudgel blow. From his vantage point a week later it was difficult to believe one taunting remark could have caused such a bouleversement. More self-deception, most likely.

In fairness to himself he could say with honesty that he hadn't known his affection for Adrienne had been deepening and widening in the weeks she had lived in his house. He had admired her courage and independent spirit from the beginning; the sweetness and integrity of her nature had become apparent only through daily contact. She could make him laugh, her roguish twinkle delighted him, her sunny presence in his house warmed the atmosphere. But he had not known there was more to it than that. And of course there had been Pamela with her enticing promise of passion to further confuse the issue.

Perhaps he could be forgiven for confusing love when it had worn such different faces for him. From the instant of clapping his eyes on that flawless face, of experiencing the magnetic pull of her smile, he had been bewitched by Pamela and had burned with the desire to possess her. Adrienne had aroused quite a different emotion initially. At that bizarre first encounter her fierce independence in refusing to accept charity had imbued him with an equally strong determination to transfer her burdens to his own broad shoulders. It hadn't been pity; one didn't pity gallantry, one bowed to it. He had wanted to take care of her then, and, heaven help him, he still yearned to make her well-being his exclusive and perpetual concern.

This past week had been spent in a grim effort to convince himself that it wasn't love he felt for his cousin, at least not the man-woman sort. He had pointedly kept away from her and had tried to carry on with his engagement, but the fever in his blood had cooled. The joy that used to race through his veins when he took Pamela in his arms was missing and couldn't be called up by her apparent willingness. She was still the most beautiful woman he had ever seen, but now her beauty left him unmoved, and the implication for the future frightened him senseless.

The strain of having to act contrary to his heart's inclination, of being obliged to ignore Adrienne while he danced attendance on Pamela, was taking a predictable and seemingly unpreventable toll on his temper. He had intercepted one or two side glances from fellow staff officers lately, and found himself apologizing for shortness of temper or inattention. It had been a relief to go out of town overnight. For a few hours he had been free of apprehension that he would betray himself by an unguarded look or an unconsidered word.

The respite was over now, bringing no other benefit in its train. The problem had been with him constantly, the long hours in the saddle providing ample opportunity for fruitless cogitation. The solution had been staring him in the face all along, he acknowledged unhappily as he exited from the park, but he had fought against recognizing it. The only honorable course of action was to send Adrienne to England and try to get on with his life. It had been implicit from the start. However, when his cousin had casually mentioned an imminent departure to Georgy Lennox, his reaction had been a cry of protest from the heart. Even now, knowing he must avoid her, his footsteps were speeding up in anticipation of seeing her dear little face and basking in the warmth of her smile. His own lips curved upward as he pictured her vibrant countenance until a strange woman heading for the park glanced at him nervously as she edged around him where he had come to an abrupt halt. A tinge of color crept under his skin as Dominic came back to an awareness of his surroundings and crossed the street with purposeful strides.

He had scarcely closed the door behind him when his eyes fell on the object of his obsessive thoughts. Adrienne, heading toward the reception room at the front of the house, almost dropped the bowl of yellow roses she was carrying.

"G-goodness, Dominic, you startled me!"

The man eyeing her hungrily thought she looked as fresh in her soft yellow dress as the blossoms she clutched. "Hello, my dear. What lovely flowers. A gift from an admirer?"

"Major Peters sent them. Aren't they heavenly?"

"On second thought, I don't believe I like them after all," he said lightly, continuing to feast his eyes on her flower face.

Adrienne gave a nervous little laugh and peered uncertainly at him. "Did you just get back from Charleroi?"

"About an hour ago."

She'd had time for a closer look at his drawn face by now. "Were you riding all night, Dominic? You look terribly tired."

"No, I caught a few hours' sleep at the Prussian camp. I'll be fine after a bath and a change of clothes."

"Of course. I'll send coffee up to your room while you change."

"Coffee sounds welcome, thank you, but only if you'll have it with me when I come down."

She hesitated, seemingly about to refuse. "Please, Adrienne," he said softly.

Her smile was a wavering effort but the aquamarine eyes met his steadily. She nodded. "In the study in half an hour?"

"That will be fine." Dominic paused on the first step as though about to add something, then shook his head and went on upstairs.

Adrienne followed his progress with wistful eyes until he disappeared from sight. Becoming conscious of the heady scent of roses, she retraced her steps toward the reception room, where she deposited the bowl on a table before hurrying to the kitchen with a rapidly beating heart.

In the first joy of seeing Adrienne again, Dominic knew only that he wanted to prolong the moment. By the time he joined her in the study, the fact of his betrothal, his painfully taken resolution to send her away, and the unwisdom of spending time with her in private had all been recollected. Adrienne, looking up from the coffee tray, thought he looked more rested but less approachable than she had ever seen him. The ready smile was missing from his eyes, though his lips parted briefly as he said, "That smells good," and settled into a chair opposite her. He thanked her when she passed him his cup, and busied himself adding cream and sugar. The silence lengthened as Adrienne raised her own cup to her lips.

"How is Luc these days? It seems ages since I have been home for more than a few minutes at a time."

"Lieutenant Gifford says he is making progress with his studies, but his heart is still with the army. Not that he would tell me, but I suspect he spends all his free time listening to the tales of the soldiers who are billeted in town. And of course his tutor is a military man also. There is no escaping the military presence in Brussels."

Dominic said nothing for a moment. Adrienne had ceased to expect a reply when he looked up and nodded. "Brussels isn't the ideal spot for Luc at present." Another silence settled over the room, and again it was Dominic who broke it. "How is Jean-Paul?"

"I am persuaded you will think him vastly improved. The doctor has not seen him recently, though we have sent several messages to him requesting him to call." She leaned forward and said earnestly, "Dominic, Becky and I are convinced Dr. Hume will agree to his traveling to England when he has seen him. Will you please see about a passage for us soon?" As a bleakness descended on her cousin's countenance, she said pleadingly, "You have just admitted that Brussels is a bad place for Luc to be these days."

They exchanged a long look, searching but guarded on the part of both in the beginning before Dominic's expression became more controlled and Adrienne's more beseeching.

"Very well. I'll have Hume over here tomorrow, and I'll set about making arrangements for the journey from Brussels and alert my mother on her end." He summoned up a smile and said with a touch of his former sportiveness,

"There are only a couple of days until the Dutchess of Richmond's ball. Wait until after that so I can claim a last waltz."

Adrienne swallowed once before producing an answering smile. "Of course. I'd hate to miss a last waltz with the best dancer in Brussels." She averted her glance, afraid that he might discern the sudden rush of tears she was struggling to suppress, and rose hastily. "Ex-excuse me, please, Dominic, I . . . I promised Jean-Paul I would be with him at three, and it is past that now. I'll see you at dinner, or . . . no, I suppose you will be dining with Lady Tremayne." She could hear herself babble to cover her hasty exit, but couldn't seem to stem the flow of inanities.

When she reached the door at last, Dominic was there before her to open it. He reached out his hand in the familiar gesture of pinching her chin, then recollected himself. One finger barely touched her cheek as she slipped out the door.

17

Rumors were flying around Brussels. The same could have been said at any time since Napoleon's escape from Elba, but now as the second week in June drew to a close, the reports were mainly concerned with troop movements of the enemy on the frontier. Unconfirmed reports that the emperor had already left Paris to join his army had been circulating for days. Word of a great military review, the so-called Champ de Mai on June 1 in the parade grounds of L'École Militaire, had gone out from Paris to Brussels followed by accounts of a spectacular celebration on June 4, during which the citizens of Paris were regaled with free wine flowing from fountains along the Champs Élysées and an enormous cold collation for all. The day had been declared a public holiday, and the festivities included open air concerts, theatrical presentations and other free entertainments that were capped by a magnificent display of fireworks at night. Napoleon's movements following these fetes were shrouded in mystery and speculation, but one thing was clear. His army was gathering and advancing preparatory to an attack on the British and Prussian forces guarding the entrance to the Low Countries.

Suddenly the holiday mood among the English in Brussels changed to one of apprehension. The town was always teaming with French sympathizers and agents of the Bonapartists, and the Bruxellois themselves were by no means united against a resumption of French control. They weren't universally delighted to be aligned with the Netherlands under the rule of the House of Orange. The stolid native population went about its business, taking little interest in rapidly changing events. The farmers trekked in from the countryside each morning with their produce, and the shopkeepers and citizens continued their normal activities.

Many of the English socialites who had been participating in a Season to rival that of London made hasty preparations to leave the city. The Staveleys were among those fleeing the expected invasion. Lady Staveley and her daughters called at Rue Ducale to take leave of Miss Beckworth and Adrienne and issue a cordial invitation to call on the family when they were settled at Harmony Hall with Lady Creighton. Miss Staveley and Miss Eleanor were much chagrined at being forced to quit Brussels and the legion of soldiers who had made the Season so enchanting, but their parent confided to Miss Beckworth that Lord Staveley had no intention of exposing his daughters to the depredations of a victorious French army. She inquired into the plans of the Castles, but they could give her no definite information on the subject of their own departure except that it would not take place until after the fifteenth, the date of the Dutchess of Richmond's ball.

The uneasiness of the British visitors was infectious. To Adrienne's general unhappiness over her doomed love affair was now added the element of fear for Dominic's safety. She was becoming more adept at dissembling her feelings, but there was a strained look about the delicate features and a dimming of her brightness that represented such an instrinic part of the girl's appeal. The object of her concern was kept increasingly occupied with his military duties so that the ladies caught no more than brief glimpses of him coming home to change his clothes during the two days that preceded the Richmond ball. He dined each evening with the field marshal, and they had no opportunity to inquire whether he had completed arrangements for their journey.

On the afternoon of the ball itself, Dominic sent word that the ladies should go ahead in the carriage at their own convenience, since he would not be free to attend until later in the evening. In due course they did this, though it could not be said that their spirits were an accurate reflection of the frivolous engagement on which they had set forth. Luc had come home full of talk of the French having crossed the River Sambre into Belgian territory. There was an ill-concealed air of excitement and anticipation about the boy that divided the sexes on the question of war and gave an added fillip of uneasiness to the ladies' natural apprehension at such a time.

Adrienne had taken extraordinary pains with her toilette for the duchess's ball. That last unsatisfactory talk with Dominic the other day lingered in her mind and was continually recalled and dissected for hidden meaning in the interval since they had met. All of the customary ease of manner between them had vanished, to be replaced by constraint rising from fettered inclinations and the fear of expressing that which must, for the sake of honor, be repressed. Until that session over the coffee cups, Adrienne had accepted that hers was a one-sided passion that must be concealed and ultimately suffocated for the good of all. The stilted conversation in the study haunted her, played constantly upon a mind struggling to act in accordance with its owner's principles. There had been something in Dominic's unusual want of openness, in his meticulously formed sentences that bespoke an inner conflict. When considered in conjunction with the intensity—one might almost call it pain—with which he had gazed upon her, Adrienne's hard-won calmness of spirit had been threatened anew. Try as she might to put the matter out of her mind, her resolution was not equal to her good intentions. An element of hope that her feelings might possibly be returned in some measure had crept into her consciousness and destroyed her tenuous peace of mind. There could be no mutual future for them; Dominic was irretrievably committed to Lady Tremayne, but still she could not subdue a tiny thrill of comfort in the possibility that her cousin did hold her in tender regard. She was not blind to the dangers of mental self-indulgence along this line, but very soon now she would have removed herself from his life forever. At this moment Dominic might already have their departure all scheduled. This evening could be the last time she would see him before the final parting. Surely she could not be censored for wishing him to remember her looking her best? It was he who had mentioned a last waltz, but she clung to this promise of a few minutes of perfect happiness before their lives, which had merged for a short shining moment, should diverge forever.

Miss Beckworth, closely observing her charge's barely contained excitement, felt her own spirits edge closer to melancholy as the carriage drew near the house the Duke of Richmond had hired on the Rue de la Blanchisserie. Her heart ached for her darling girl. It had been her lot to be a silent spectator to Adrienne's recent misery, knowing there was nothing she could do to alleviate the situation. She could not even speak words of encouragement or sympathy in the face of the girl's obvious intention of battling through her unhappiness alone. She owed it to Adrienne to preserve her dignity. She too suspected tonight would mark their last real contact with Dominic before their departure from Brussels, and it was with a heavy heart and no expectation of pleasure that she climbed down from the carriage to join the procession of guests heading for the ballroom.

The ballroom in the duke's magnificent house formed a wing on the ground floor, quite separate from the family apartments and spectacular enough in appearance tonight to draw forth a gasp of admiration from Adrienne despite her preoccupation. It was papered in an attractive trellis pattern and had been decorated with tentlike hangings in crimson, gold, and black, and royal colors. The night was breathlessly hot and the air was heavy with the scent of hundreds of wax candles competing with the perfume of masses of roses and lilies. More flowers, ribbons, and leaves were wreathed around the supportint pillars. It was altogether a scene of visual enchantment, but tonight the guests provided a jarring note. The young people danced, but many of the older guests gathered in small groups to discuss the rumors of a French advance on Charleroi, not forty miles from Brussels. The company included numerous representatives of the military, from ensigns to general officers, but nobody seemed to know exactly what was going to happen next. And amid all those attendees of rank and prominence, there was one glaring omission. The absence of the Duke of Wellington could not but lend substance to the rumors that the army was getting ready to move out.

For Adrienne, going from partner to partner during the early part of the evening, there was an even more significant omission. She could not prevent her eyes from searching repeatedly for Dominic's gold-streaked head. Though she laughed and chatted with her various escorts, her smile was a mechanical effort and her thoughts never left the man for whom she waited. With the other guests she applauded the members of the Highland regiments who had been induced by the duchess to perform reels and Scottish dances to the music of their pipes, but her eyes strayed to the various exits. Soon after her arrival she had spotted Lady Tremayne, resplendent as always in an eye-catching gown of silver gauze that was nearly transparent. Much later when it became impossible to avoid meeting, the two had exchanged frigid bows and immediately changed course.

It was after midnight, and Adrienne had begun to fear that her cousin had been prevented from attending the ball by the pressure of the military situation, when a whisper went through the room that Wellington had arrived. The chill emptiness settling in the region of her heart stirred into hope again as she caught sight of the field marshal talking quietly with the Prince of Orange and a lady unknown to Adrienne. He looked his usual calm self, and the knot of tension inside her subsided somewhat as her eyes swept the room seeking that beloved tall figure. A group near the French doors dispersed and reformed, permitting a glimpse of a pair of familiar shoulders in an embroidered coat walking purposefully away from her. Adrienne's heart lurched in gladness as she murmured an excuse to her partner, taking a few hasty steps in pursuit.

A regal brunette in floating silver draperies emerged from a group of officers surrounding her, smiling, her hands extended in a graceful attitude. Adrienne watched in agonized fascination as Dominic briefly raised the hands to his lips before taking Lady Tremayne's arm and leading her toward the alcove at the end of the room. Until the movement of the crowd blocked them from her sight, the girl stood there staring after the retreating couple. She drew a painful breath of air into her lungs, but it took a solid bump from behind to reactivate her frozen muscles. After an exchange of apologies, fairly incoherent on Adrienne's part, she spied Becky talking with General Forrester and thankfully headed in their direction.

Lady Tremayne allowed herself to be escorted toward a corner of the room where they could be assured of relative privacy. So far Dominic had not uttered one syllable. She studied the impassive features of her fiancé out of the corner of her eye, thinking him a trifle pale. "Are the rumors true, then, Dominic? Will there be war?"

"Yes," he replied, seating her on a settee in front of some screening palms and taking his place at her side. "We leave in the morning."

"You will take care?"

"Yes," he said again.

They measured each other in a silence that threatened to become permanent, two pairs of eyes seeking something, questioning but not informing.

Lady Tremayne shifted her gaze to the feathered fan in her lap. "You wish to say something to me, Dominic?"

"Yes. I beg your pardon for electing to speak privately in such a public setting, but we seem to have run out of time. Pamela, do you feel, as I have come to feel, that our betrothal has been a mistake?"

The fingers smoothing the red feathers on the fan stilled for an instant before resuming their idle motion. Cool amber eyes lifted to his. "No, Dominic, I have thoroughly enjoyed being engaged to you."

Some violent emotion flickered in Lord Creighton's blue eyes and was gone. He pressed his lips together and continued to examine the lovely face of his betrothed. She did not flinch from his srutiny, and it was he who finally said softly: "I do not think you would enjoy being married to me, however."

Two perfectly arched brows elevated, though the eyes beneath them remained cool and undisturbed. "For shame, Dominic. You are being much too hard on yourself. I am persuaded you will make a delightful husband."

"I am not in the mood for arch games, Pamela. I am asking you to release me from our engagement."

"And I, dearest Dominic, am refusing your request." She was rising from the settee as she spoke. The earl got to his feet mechanically, struggling to reconcile the harsh words he had just heard with the dulcet tones in which they had been delivered.

"Forgive me if I end our little talk now, Dominic, but I am bespoken for the next set and I see my partner approaching." Lady Tremayne smiled sweetly at her fiancé, whose teeth were clenched together to prevent any impulsive words from escaping. He watched impotently as she glided forward toward the Dutch officer hurrying to claim her.

By dint of reminding herself in the strongest possible terms that she hadn't the shadow of a right to be upset by the sight of her cousin singling out his affianced wife for private conversation, Adrienne had recovered her mental equilibrium before Dominic came to claim her for the long-anticipated waltz. She was appalled at her own behavior and could only be grateful that on such a night as this the usual rigid decorum obtaining in public was cracking on all sides, so that her indiscretion might hope to pass unnoticed. Girls who had been gaily dancing and flirting earlier stood white-faced and tearful after taking brief public leave of relatives and lovers. Women wished their sons and husbands Godspeed with heads high and prayers on their lips.

Adrienne had just bidden farewell to a jaunty Lieutenant Markham and was blankly staring into space when her cousin appeared at her side as the orchestra struck up a waltz. He held out his hand without speaking and she put hers into it. A fleeting glance at his face told her nothing. Dominic was smiling at her with his usual kindness. If there had been a shadow of sadness in his blue eyes at first, it was banished by the smile as he took her into his arms and whirled her onto the floor, which had been emptying rapidly. For two whole turns around the room they were silent, letting their bodies and feet take precedence over thinking, mutually seeking to prolong the moment of perfect communion. Dominic looked down at the dark red curls gleaming in the light of a thousand candles. A spasm of pain crossed his features and a muscle twitched in his cheek, neither of which was observed by Adrienne, who was gazing fixedly at the buttons on his coat. Gently he gathered her a hair closer than propriety allowed and they continued their wordless duet until the music ended. As Dominic lingeringly lowered her right hand and removed his own from her waist, Adrienne stared at the palm trees in the alcove behind them.

"Our last waltz."

Adrienne's questioning eyes winged to his in the wake of the quiet words. Dominic's lips smiled but his eyes were somber. Her glance slid away, back to the palm trees, while she endeavored to steady her voice.

"Does that mean you have . . . completed our travel arrangements, Dominic?"

"I'm afraid I haven't been able to do that, my dear. The English are fleeing Brussels in droves, it seems. It will have to wait now until afterward."

Adrienne's complexion lost what little color remained, but she faced her cousin bravely. "After the war, you mean?"

He hesitated. "At least until there is room in the packets once again. Moulton has the authority to make the necessary arrangements, so do not be concerned on that head."

She winced, and the hot tears that had been crowding in flooded her eyes. "When do you leave?" she whispered, blinking them back.

"In a few minutes. I want to say good-bye to Becky."

"And Lady Tremayne of course." Adrienne averted her head, desperately trying to contain the tears that threatened to fall.

"Pamela and I have already said our good-byes." Dominic had kept her standing with her back to the room, and now he lifted a gentle finger and caught one crystal drop from each eye. "Come, let us find Becky." He enfolded the icy cold little hand in his warm one for a moment before placing it on his arm. "Ready?"

The bright head lifted proudly though she did not dare to nod for fear of releasing additional tears. "I'm ready. I won't disgrace you."

"You could never do that, little one."

No more was said until they met Miss Beckworth. She listened quietly as Dominic told her the Reserves would be marching south at dawn and that he was leaving for the front immediately with messages.

"You will see to the children?"

"Of course. Come back safely, Dominic."

The earl smiled at her and turned to Adrienne once more, removing the hand that lay limply on his arm. He raised trembling fingers to his lips and kissed them. "Good-bye for the moment, little one."

"*Vaya con Dios,* Dominic."

A flame leapt into the earl's eyes and it seemed he would pull his cousin into his arms, but he checked the motion as he caught Miss Beckworth's warning look. The line of his jaw went rigid with control, he dropped Adrienne's hand, sketched a bow to both women, and turned on his heel.

The noise of the crowd remaining in the ballroom faded from Adrienne's senses while she stared after Dominic's retreating back, the fingers he had kissed unconsciously pressed against her lips. Never had she felt so alone in her life. A shudder rippled through her body and she drooped visibly.

"Come, dearest, let us fetch our wraps and go home."

"What?" Blind eyes fastened on Miss Beckworth, who put her arm around the girl's waist to guide her steps out of the ballroom.

"It's time to leave. We'll order the carriage and get our wraps."

With automatic compliance, Adrienne obeyed Becky's soft commands. Her tears had dried up for the moment; she was composed but absent in spirit, the older woman noted with mixed gratitude and concern.

It was a matter of a few minutes to go upstairs and locate their light shawls in the ladies' cloakroom. On the way down the handsome staircase at the front of the house they almost walked smack into Lady Tremayne easing her way out of a crowd of protesting admirers with the evident intention of ascending. Adrienne appeared not to see the expression of pure venom that contorted the beauty's face when her glance alighted on the pair. For a second Miss Beckworth feared she meant to speak to them and she girded herself for trouble, but Lady Tremayne evidently thought better of her impulse. She paused fractionally, then proceeded up the staircase without a word. Miss Beckworth relaxed her grip on Adrienne's arm and quickened their pace toward the carriageway.

The ride home was accomplished without a single word being spoken by either woman. Miss Beckworth could conjure up no words of comfort that would not sound trite, and Adrienne had simply removed herself from the scene mentally. Even her oldest friend hesitated to demand entrance to her private world of shadows. As she bade the girl an affectionate good night outside her bedchamber, she decided to leave her to her own devices in coping with her fear and unhappiness, at least for the present. Tomorrow would be time enough to speak of courage and fortitude, and by then perhaps no remonstrations would be necessary. She would see how Adrienne was handling the situation in the morning.

When the morning finally arrived, however, neither woman was prepared for the situation that greeted her. Neither had slept well and the strain was obvious in the shadows under Adrienne's puffy eyes. They met in the breakfast room. Adrienne was already there, absently crumbling a piece of toast with her fingers when Miss Beckworth entered. After a searching look and a brief salutation the latter glanced at the third place setting that was untouched.

"Good morning, Moulton," she said as the butler appeared in the doorway carrying a platter of grilled kidneys and bacon. "Master Luc isn't down yet?"

"Not that I know of, ma'am, unless he went riding early. No," he corrected himself, "that he didn't do because the door was still bolted when I came down."

"I see. No, nothing for me, thank you. I'll just have coffee."

As the butler poured the dark liquid from a silver pot into the cup she was indicating, Miss Beckworth's forehead puckered and she bit her lip thoughtfully. "Moulton, would you ask Antoine to inform Master Luc that breakfast is ready?"

"Certainly, ma'am."

Adrienne spoke for the first time as the butler left the room. "He has most likely gone in to see Jean-Paul before coming down."

"Most likely," agreed her companion, but she did no more than sip at her coffee until footsteps were once more heard outside the hall door.

One look at the perturbed face of the young footman had Adrienne going paper white and clutching at the edge of the table for support. Miss Beckworth, scarcely less pale, reached out a hand for the envelope Antoine was extending to her.

"His bed hasn't been slept in, ma'am!" blurted the footman.

Neither lady looked at him. Miss Beckworth tore into the note with clumsy fingers and Adrienne fixed huge frightened eyes on the sheet of paper that emerged. Someone's harsh breathing could be heard in the hiatus.

"Oh please, Becky, no!" whimpered Adrienne brokenly when her companion looked up at last, her eyes blank with shock.

"He has taken the place of a sick private in the Ninety-fifth Rifles and gone with the army," said Miss Beckworth.

18

An almost unrecognizable Luc Castle passed a green
sleeve over his face to clear away perspiration and tried to
recall what day it was. It had been Thursday evening when
he left, stealing out of the house after Adrienne and Becky
had driven off to some ball or other. From the talk about
town that afternoon he had felt sure that the army would
move out before morning. His friend Josh Thornapple of
the Ninety-fifth, who had been teaching him to use his
weapon these past days, had fallen ill the night before and
was intermittently delirious with fever when he had visited
him where he was billeted with a Belgian family. The idea
of going off in Josh's place had been born at that moment
and was full grown by the time he had returned to
Dominic's house for dinner. Knowing the family would
never understand his yearning to be part of the upcoming
battle, he had confined his explanations and good-byes to
the written word. When the drums had started beating he
was completely dressed in Josh's uniform with his gear all
ready. The Belgian housewife nursing Josh had tried to
dissuade him from going, but he had paid her no heed.

At the start it was greatly exciting to form up in the
Place Royale amid the trappings of an army on the move
and march off with the others in the predawn grayness,
down the Namur Road, through the gate of the same
name, south to meet the enemy. He had done a lot of
marching since then under far less salubrious conditions.
As an activity it had palled even before they had reached
their ultimate objective that first day. They had lingered
for a time in Waterloo village before being ordered south
to a crossroads called Quatre Bras where fighting was

already in progress. His first encounter with real warfare occurred when he nearly tripped over the body of a soldier when moving to take up a position. The sight of the young man, not more than a few years his senior, lying on the ground with his eyes open and a gaping hole in his forehead, had turned Luc sick, but there had been no time to indulge his weakness. The Ninety-fifth had been thrown into the fighting, which lasted until dark. They had bivouacked in the fields that night, though he certainly hadn't slept well. In fact, he couldn't remember when he had last been rested, well-fed, dry, and safe.

At this point it seemed his whole life had been spent defending this gravel pit near the Charleroi-Brussels highroad, first from waves of French infantry, then from cavalry attacks. He'd lost count of the number of cavalry charges that had moved up the slope in an awesome precision that chilled the blood but quickened the admiration. So far none had succeeded in breaking through the squares to open up the British line.

Wellington's hodgepodge army was strung out over a three-mile front above some sloping fields around Mont St. Jean, where they had retreated—was it only yesterday? How could he ever forget that march that started out in dry conditions and turned into a mud- and waterlogged trial of endurance when summer thunderstorms turned the fields and roads into quagmires. Only the oldest Peninsular veterans had been able to sleep last night. The rest of his comrades had merely waited for morning, wet and shivering in the inundated fields of uncut corn and rye. He still wasn't completely dry but he couldn't complain of being cold any longer. The temperature on the battlefield was reaching hellish proportions after hours of fighting in the summer heat. His senses were dulled from overexposure to the sounds of artillery firing in his immediate vicinity and the appalling sight of growing mounds of enemy corpses in front of the allied position. Men on either side of him in the square had fallen, but so far he had escaped with a slashed sleeve and a stinging saber cut from a French cuirassier who was falling from a bayonet thrust at the time. A semiclean handkerchief was binding the wound at present, thrown down to him by a passing staff officer and tied around his arm by a fellow rifleman.

The waiting between attacks was almost worse than the attacks themselves because there was time to think about the fear, discomfort, hunger, continual raging thirst, and the imminence of one's own death. The fighting had commenced in the early afternoon, but that seemed aeons ago. It was almost impossible to tell the time of day, since the smoke of battle obscured the sun, if indeed the sun was out. It had rained earlier, he recalled. The enemy was forming again at the bottom of the slope in preparation for yet another charge. The defensive squares were thinning out with each attack, though more real damage was done by French skirmishes as a prelude and in the wake of the actual charge. The Ninety-fifth had lost both colonels, its major, and two out of three captains. The Duke himself had lingered to steady them during the last attack, but still they stood and still the French challenged the squares all along the center of the line. The Duke was everywhere assessing the situation, rallying the defenders, calling in reinforcements where defenses were collapsing, in constant communication via his aides with the situation all along his line. Once or twice Luc had caught a glimpse of his cousin riding Trooper, but pride had kept him from bringing himself to Dominic's attention. The incurious men of the Ninety-fifth had accepted him as one of them, though he had seen raised eyebrows that first day. For their own protection they made sure the men on each side of them understood their assignments.

The French were coming again. One of the ADC's had told the men it was Marshal Ney who was directing the battle. He had managed to reform remnants of the cavalry for another charge. Luc could feel the ground under his feet move to the slow steady beat of the horses' hooves as they breasted the slope. The British gunners waited to fire until the last minute, bringing down the front rank of charging horses before they abandoned their pieces temporarily to take shelter inside the squares. It had been happening for hours, the same dreadful war dance, starting with the drone of enemy artillery, giving way then to the rhythmic hoofbeats, rising in tempo with the shrill battle cry of *"Vive L'Empereur"* sweeping along the wave of attackers, and ending with a mad crashing as horses met bayonets and horsemen tried to drive through the ranks of the defenders. It had become a recurrent nightmare by now, but it seemed once again he would wake unharmed as the charge failed to break the square despite the bitter fighting.

Luc turned his head to follow a cuirassier whose charge had carried him into the space between two adjacent squares. In so doing he looked straight into the eyes of a mounted staff officer riding across the cuirassier's path. Dominic drew up in shock and Luc saw his own name forming on his cousin's lips. At that instant the Frenchman fired, and to Luc's horror, Dominic fell forward. He found his own Baker rifle at the ready and pulled the trigger, noting with satisfaction blunted by fear that he had struck the cavalryman in the back of the neck. He was already running toward Dominic when a lieutenant grabbed his arm.

"Get back there, man! Stand firm! It's not over yet!"

"*My cousin*! He shot my cousin, and it was *my* fault!" Luc struggled in the grasp of the officer, the strength of his desperation pulling the larger man forward.

"Whoa there! That's one of the Duke's aides!"

"He's my cousin Dominic, I tell you! Colonel Lord Creighton!" Luc was still tugging to release his arm as he plowed forward to where Trooper was pawing the ground with Dominic slumped over in the saddle.

The lieutenant had come with him, and together they supported the limp body of the rider and eased him to the ground.

"He's alive," said the officer after a cursory examination. "The ball got him in the leg." He glanced up at the boy, who was ashen beneath the dirt and sweat of combat, and his jaw dropped. "How old are you, lad?"

Luc didn't see the lieutenant's astonishment at the answer; his attention was all for the man on the ground.

Dominic was not a prepossessing sight at that moment. A bloody bandage tied around his forehead testified to an earlier wound and his complexion was colorless under the grime. He was unconscious, scarcely seeming to breathe. As Luc looked down at the powerful figure, now so helpless, pity and guilt overwhelmed him and he began to shake convulsively.

"Put your head down, quick!"

"I won't pass out, sir. I'm going to stay with him." A hint of steel stiffened the boy's face and voice as he met his officer's eyes.

"You do that, lad. I'll give you a hand getting him into a square to wait for a surgeon to attend to him."

Luc's relief at this tacit acceptance of his desertion of Josh Thornapple's duty was a transitory emotion soon forgotten in the rampaging worry about Dominic's condition. It seemed an age before the regimental surgeon could spare a minute to examine him, and then his verdict shook the boy to the core.

"The leg will have to come off. He could bleed to death if I tried to take the ball out here, and the kneecap is probably shattered."

"*No!* I'll take him back to Brussels to his own doctor. He'll remove the ball."

The busy surgeon shrugged. "Have it your own way. He may be strong enough to stand the trip, though the pulse is irregular."

Luc hesitated, almost paralyzed by the responsibility that lay on his shoulders, but the surgeon hadn't waited around to see if he would reverse his decision. The supply of wounded that sanguinary afternoon was seemingly endless; his services would be required around the clock. The boy was kneeling there, staring worriedly down at his cousin's still face when a familiar voice demanded:

"Is Colonel Creighton here? I was told he was brought in here."

"Major Peters, over here!" called Luc, scrambling to his feet as hope and relief stirred in his breast.

"Good God, boy, what are you doing here?" The major's unbelieving eyes swept the concerned face gazing up at him and took in the uniform at a glance. "No, don't tell me!'' he added peremptorily as he dismounted. "Where is Dominic? Is he badly hurt?"

Luc led Major Peters over to where Dominic lay on the ground. "The surgeon says his leg must come off, the bullet is in the knee, but I told him I would take Dominic back to Brussels and let Dr. Martin see if he can save the leg."

The cavalry officer had been making his own inspection of his friend's wounds while the boy was speaking. The line of his mouth was grim, but he said, "Good for you, lad. These damned sawbones are knife-happy!"

"The only thing is, sir," offered Luc hesitantly, "there is some question of whether Dominic can stand the trip, and I do not quite see how I am to convey him home."

"I'm told the roads north are already clogged with supply wagons, deserters, and wounded, and it can only get worse. This little affair is not over yet by a long shot. There will be another charge any moment now, and if the Prussians don't get busy soon it could get pretty uncomfortable back here."

"Then you advise me to take him away now?"

"I'll try to get word to Nelson, his groom. There's probably no hope of getting hold of anything on wheels, but I see you have Trooper here. Nelson will have the other horses. If you have to tie him on a horse and walk back, do it."

"If only his constitution is strong enough to survive the trip. If he dies I shall feel like I murdered him—it was my fault he was hit!" Luc cried in an agony of anxiety.

"Steady on, lad. If I know Dominic, he'd much rather chance the trip than concede his leg to these butchers."

"Right as usual, Ivor."

Both whirled to stare down at the man at their feet. His voice was no more than a thread, but intelligence gleamed in the pain-filled eyes.

"You'll be right as rain presently, old fellow," Major Peters said in a confident manner, awkwardly patting his friend's shoulder.

Dry cracked lips twisted into an attempt at a smile. "Get

me home, Luc," Dominic said before he fainted again.

It would have been a challenge to locate in all of Brussels on that terrible June 16 any persons whose state was more pitiable than that of Miss Beckworth and Adrienne. For several minutes after discovering Luc's absence, they were too stunned to be capable of coherent speech or thought. Adrienne knew only that she was resisting rising hysteria, that each breath had become an almost Herculean achievement. She was battling for air like a person fighting his way to the surface of the water after falling overboard. At last she gasped:

"We must *stop* him! We must make him return!"

"How? He has been gone for hours. The Ninety-fifth was forming up even as we left the ball last night." Looking perfectly distracted, Miss Beckworth was kneading her forehead with the fingers of one hand while she continued to stare at the paper she held in the other.

"General Forrester!" exclaimed Adrienne, exploding out of her chair. "Perhaps he has not yet left Brussels. He'll find Luc for us and send him back." The girl was at the door before she finished speaking, rejecting out of hand Miss Beckworth's suggestion that they should send the footman with the message. "No, no, I must speak with him myself!"

She was back within the hour. No words were required to inform her companion that her mission had not met with success. She slipped into the small sitting room like a pale ghost of her former self and made a negative movement of her head when Miss Beckworth raised anxious eyes to hers.

"The general left shortly after dawn himself."

Though entirely sympathetic, Sarah Forrester had not been able to offer any advice as to how to make contact with an army on its way to an engagement for the purpose of expropriating one of its most anonymous members. She had, however, somewhat diffidently ventured to suggest that the time might pass more rapidly for Adrienne if she were to participate in the preparations that would be necessary for the care and comfort of the wounded.

The distraught girl had jumped at the opportunity to throw herself into a vital task. She'd have been eager to assist in any case, but now she yearned to be frantically busy as a means to preserve her reason against the on-slaughts of a disordered imagination.

"I truly think I should go mad confined within these four walls just waiting for news, Becky."

Watching the girl's agitated pacing as she explained, Miss Beckworth was inclined to accept this statement at face value. She was grateful to Sarah for providing work that would use up some of Adrienne's undirected energy. It was agreed that Miss Beckworth would remain at Rue Ducale for the present to watch over Jean-Paul, though she would hold herself in readiness to assist the other women as the need arose.

For those who waited in Brussels for news of the battle, all sense of time was lost during that anxious period following the dawn departure of the army. On the surface life went on as usual for the citizens, but even they were aware of the listening attitude, a feeling of emotional distance from everyday activities. The foreigners sought each other out, gathering in small groups to seek or exchange information and speculate on the outcome of the expected battle. Many were involved in frantic attempts to leave the area. Anyone owning horses or vehicles could name his own price as these commodities became totally inadequate to the demand. Moulton hired extra men to guard the earl's stables around the clock. The roads to Antwerp became choked with travelers evacuating the capital.

By late afternoon the distant rumble of cannonading could be heard in the city. The reports coming into town were confused; the one clear fact emerging was that an engagement of sorts was taking place somewhere south of Waterloo village, which was about ten miles from Brussels. The firing stopped eventually and they settled down to an uneasy night, their rest disturbed by the rumble of artillery trains heading south. Just before dawn a troop of retreat-ing Belgian cavalry came racing through the town on their way north to the Nivelles gate, causing a minor panic with

their shouts that the French were coming. The hours that
followed proved this rumor unfounded, but the wounded
from the previous day's fighting at Quatre Bras did come,
under their own power or in the military tilt carts, and their
plight brought visitors and citizens alike into the streets to
render what aid they could, even if it were only to offer
water and provide shade for those dying in the cobbled
streets in the pitiless blast of summer heat. The sun's disappearance in midafternoon was a welcome relief until it was
rapidly succeeded by torrential rains that impeded efforts
to get the wounded into the shelter of the hospital tents
being erected outside the city gates.

The uncontrollable tension as each new group was
searched for a glimpse of one or the other of those beloved
faces took its inevitable toll on Adrienne and Miss Beckworth. A painwracked young rifleman with an empty left
sleeve told Adrienne that the Ninety-fifth had not only
been engaged in the battle of Quatre Bras, but had covered
the retreat north to Mont St. Jean, just south of Waterloo.
"First in the field and last out of it" was the Ninety-fifth's
motto, he informed her with a brave attempt at jauntiness
that twisted her heart. As the afternoon wore on she
struggled constantly to control pity, horror, and impending nausea at sights and sufferings she could never have
envisioned a day ago. And always there was the underlying
dread that stalked her soul. The services the women could
render were so slight, the materials at hand so pitifully
inadequate, but they persisted doggedly until driven inside
by the drenching rain allied to physical and mental exhaustion.

Adrienne was too fatigued to do more than pick at her
food that night, but though her aching body cried out for
sleep, such was her emotional torment that she rose from
her bed on Sunday morning more in need of repose than
when she had lain down upon it. Word of a Prussian
defeat at Ligny on the sixteenth and their retreat to Wavre
cast more doubt than ever on the eventual outcome of the
war. Informed opinion held that Lord Wellington's patch-
work army could never defeat Napoleon's experienced

troops without aid from the Prussians. Bonaparte had struck at the point between the allied armies to divide them and prevent his troops from having to face the enemy's combined forces. That the battle would be resumed that day was universally assumed, but no sounds of firing reached the town with the wind in the wrong direction. The hours dragged by while the women waited in painful suspense that was exacerbated by their work among the wounded who continued to pour into the city. By all accounts it was the bloodiest battle in memory, with staggering numbers of casualties on both sides. By six P.M. when Miss Beckworth insisted that Adrienne return to the house for a rest, the outcome of the fighting was still unknown by those wounded who had managed to make their way back to Brussels. They reported the conditions of the roads to be bad everywhere and impassable in places where overturned wagons and abandoned supplies would have to be cleared away.

The women retired indoors, too depleted in energy to make any efforts at conversation while doing less than justice to their dinner. It was too early to go to bed, so they resumed their vigil, mostly silent now, each keeping her deepest fears to herself from a superstitious dread that vocalizing them might cause them to happen.

The street was fairly quiet until almost nine o'clock, when the sound of horses outside brought Adrienne out of her chair and down the stairs at a dead run. She was right behind Moulton as he swung back the entrance door, her face mirroring anxiety and hope, her hands unconsciously pressed to her pounding heart. For a split second she failed to recognize the tattered and dirty figure standing on the step; then she shrieked, "*Luc!*" and rushed forward to throw her arms around him, almost rocking him off his feet. "You're *safe*! Oh, thank God!"

"I've got Dominic outside," said the boy, regaining his balance with difficulty as he stepped back from his sister's embrace. He still hadn't looked directly at her, and a chill began creeping over Adrienne's body.

"He's not . . . ?" Her mouth hung open but she could

produce no more sound and was unaware that Miss Beckworth, alerted by her cry, had come downstairs and now slipped a supporting arm about her waist.

"He's alive but not in prime twig," said Luc, again in that dulled tone. "The trip here tried his endurance pretty high. He's been unconscious for the past couple of hours."

Before the youth finished speaking, three of his four listeners had deserted him. Moulton, Adrienne, and Antoine were rushing outside to where Nelson still sat his mount, supporting the earl, who was slumped in front of him. Two riderless horses stood nearby.

The eyes of the two persons remaining in the hall clung together in wordless communication until the boy's composure cracked. "If Dominic dies it will be my fault, Becky. What am I going to do?"

A suspicious moisture shone in Miss Beckworth's eyes but her voice was serene and confident. "Do? Why, see to it that he recovers, of course. We shall all do that."

His lordship's household sprang into action for the relief of the master, as Adrienne, the unheeded tears sliding down her face, led the procession upstairs, lighting the way to the earl's bedchamber with a candelabrum she had seized from the entrance hall. She was searching for a knife to cut his boots off when his batman gently but firmly put her outside the door despite her furious protests that she intended to nurse her cousin.

"And so you shall, miss, as soon as Antoine and me have got the colonel into decent nightclothes," that individual said calmly.

"Try not to hurt him," she pleaded. "He looks so dreadfully weak."

"We'll be as careful as possible," promised the man, closing the door on her remonstrations.

Adrienne stood irresolute, staring at the paneled door for a few seconds until Becky's voice roused her. Luc had insisted on being the one to go for Dr. Martin, sending Nelson off to the stables to see to the horses. Adrienne received his information with an absent nod.

"Becky, Dominic looks half-dead. That head wound is still bleeding, judging by that filthy bandage."

"It isn't the head wound that is of greatest concern, my dear. Luc said the field surgeon was going to amputate his wounded leg. That's why he brought him home."

An anguished moan escaped Adrienne's lips before she clamped her teeth together. Only when she was sure she had herself under command did she speak in a quiet voice of utter conviction. "Nobody is going to cut off his leg. I shan't allow it."

It was over an hour later that Luc, still in his ragged uniform, slipped silently into his cousin's room to report that he had been unable to contact Dr. Martin in person and had been forced to leave an urgent message at his house. By this time Dominic was lying between clean sheets, the grime washed off and the disgusting bandage on his head replaced by a fresh covering. However, his stertorous beathing and ashen complexion were enough to inform the boy that any visible improvement was merely the result of soap and water.

"Has he regained consciousness at all?"

"No." Adrienne subjected her young brother to a thorough inspection and her heart was wrung with compassion. He had escaped serious injury, thank heavens, but he was certainly not unmarked by his experiences. As he pulled up a chair nearer the bed, she urged, "Please, Luc, you must rest. There is ample hot water for a bath and plenty of food. We'll talk tomorrow. I'll send Antoine back to the doctor's later."

He shook his head. "You don't understand, Adrienne. It's my fault Dominic was wounded. He pulled up his horse when he recognized me, and a cuirassier shot him. How can I sleep until I know he's all right?"

"Don't talk fustian, Luc! Who knows how many other bullets may have just missed Dominic today, equally fortuitously?"

The bleary-eyed youth blinked stupidly but was prevented from attempting a comeback by the entrance of Miss Beckworth, who announced that a bath and a meal awaited him. Too weary to protest convincingly, Luc allowed himself to be led away by Miss Beckworth. She returned an hour later to say that he was already in his bed, and to persuade Adrienne, though with little hope of success, to do the same while she sat with Dominic. As expected, the girl refused to leave her cousin's bedside. Her wan face brightened momentarily on learning that Antoine had volunteered to station himself outside the doctor's house so that he might explain the urgency of the case to him immediately on his return. She accepted the laudanum Becky provided to quiet Dominic should he begin to thrash about in pain, and resumed her vigil.

Over the next few hours her eyes rarely left his face, which was quiet for a time while he was sunk in an exhausted stupor brought on by the jolting journey from the battleground. Greedily she memorized every plane and ridge of that beloved countenance against a future that would separate them. Her fingers longed to follow her eyes along the sensitive curves of his lips, and she curled them into her palms to resist the temptation. After a while he began to move about in his sleep, and spasms of pain flickered across his features. Adrienne got up and leaned over him to retuck the covers around his shoulders. As she drew back she found herself staring into burning blue eyes inches from her own.

"Hello, little one." His voice was weak, but he knew her, and a swift glance around acquainted him with his surroundings. He tried to smile. "So Luc did get me home?"

"Yes. Is the pain very bad, Dominic?"

"Nothing to signify," he lied, moving restlessly. "Did we win?"

"Win?" Adrienne looked blank for a second, not having spared the war or its outcome a thought since her cousin had been brought home. "I don't know. We are waiting for the doctor. Perhaps he will have news. Would you like a drink, Dominic?"

He nodded, and Adrienne strained to raise his shoulders a few inches so he could drink. The action seemed to use up his strength for a time and his breathing grew more difficult, but after a moment he said with a little twist of his lips, "I'm glad we had that last waltz."

"It *wasn't* the last one! Dr. Martin will save your leg. He must!"

Dominic smiled a little at her ferocity and made a tiny gesture of comfort with his hand. Adrienne took the hand in hers and they remained thus until sounds in the hall at about two in the morning indicated an arrival.

Events moved swiftly from the doctor's entrance, which was followed in short order by Adrienne's exit from the sickroom. She left under protest, having flatly refused to comply until Dominic, whom she believed to be sleeping once again, added his voice to the doctor's ordering her removal. She went no farther than the corridor outside his bedchamber, where she paced compulsively during the hour and a half it took Dr. Martin to remove the bullet with the assistance of Moulton and Crimmons, the earl's cool and capable batman.

The gray-faced doctor, himself almost groggy with fatigue on his emergence, did not give her the reassurance she craved. The earl had endured the operation with exemplary fortitude, but the chance of infection was great and he must resign himself to the eventual loss of the leg if his body could not throw off the infection. Meanwhile, he concluded brusquely, having been given a heavy dose of laudanum for his own good, the patient would likely sleep for some hours, and he would strongly advise Miss Castle to do the same if she intended to be of any use in the days to come. At this point the doctor accepted Moulton's escort downstairs, where a carriage waited to take him to his well-earned rest.

Adrienne, who had listened to the physician's gloomy prognostication in mute but smoldering rebellion, at least possessed the sense to accept his advice with regard to herself. After a quick visit to the sickroom seeking confirmation that Crimmons would remain by his master's side through the night and call her at once at any change in his condition, she took herself off to her own room, pausing only to bring Becky, who was still wakeful, up-to-date. It wasn't until she had climbed wearily into bed that it dawned upon her that she had forgotten to inquire about the outcome of the battle. The passing thought that the enemy might be at the door any moment was not sufficiently terrifying to keep her aching body from making up the sleep it had missed recently.

Adrienne was still sleeping at nine the next morning when a carriage pulled up to the front door. Antoine, on his way to do an errand for the housekeeper, opened the door just as Sir Ralph Morrison, with one hand under his sister's arm, pulled back the other hand that had been about to bang the knocker.

"Good morning, sir, madame," said the startled footman, recovering his wits.

"We have come to see Lord Creighton."

"I regret that his lordship is unable to receive visitors, madame," replied Antoine, addressing the speaker. "Would you care to see Miss Beckworth?"

"No, no, we won't disturb Miss Beckworth," said Lady Tremayne. "We came to inquire for Lord Creighton. Is it true that he has been wounded?"

"Yes, madame."

"How serious is it? How is he?" she demanded sharply.

"The doctor fears that it will be necessary to amputate his leg."

Lady Tremayne recoiled with a gasp, a look of revulsion contorting her features. She seized her brother's arm and dragged him back a step.

"Does your ladyship wish to leave a message?"

"*No!* No, thank you. We'll call at a more convenient time. Come, Ralph."

The young footman stared impassively after the departing callers as they climbed back into the hired vehicle. Not until it moved off did he turn and go about his business.

An hour later, a small package, accompanied by a letter addressed in a feminine hand, was delivered to the earl's residence and placed with the small pile of mail that had accumulated in the period of his lordship's absence from Brussels.

During the next few days the post was the last thing on

the minds of those residing in the stone mansion near the park, as all their combined energies were employed in assisting the master in his desperate battle to survive his wounds in the wake of the great victory at Waterloo. As the doctor had foretold, infection invaded the site of the wound, and fever and delirium followed. For want of any more efficacious treatment, hot fomentations were applied to the leg around the clock. At first the earl's condition grew steadily worse and the issue of removing the leg hung in the balance, with the doctor favoring that more prudent course, while Dominic's relatives urged waiting a bit longer to give his strong constitution a chance to master the infection. By the third day, Adrienne felt the downward spiral had been arrested, and she waited anxiously for the doctor's visit, hoping for confirmation that Dominic's tumultuous pulse was steadier and his leg less inflamed. If the Belgian physician could not entirely agree with her reading of the situation, at least he was persuaded it was safe to delay a decision for another twelve hours.

The earl's attendants redoubled their efforts to bring the fever down with increased sponging of his heated body. Adrienne was engaged in this task that evening after the doctor's visit when her patient began to mutter incoherently. This wasn't a new development; he'd had periods of delirious ravings all along, mostly about the battle just fought. Sometimes phrases and snatches made sense, but they were never uttered in conscious awareness. Dominic had called out to herself and to Lady Tremayne on occasion too, but even when his eyes were open they showed no recognition of persons or of his surroundings.

The muttering increased in frequency. Tonight it appeared to be concerned with Lady Tremayne. He seemed to be begging her to do something. Adrienne doggedly continued to bathe his face in the tepid lavender water, soothing him with hands and soft words while she made a determined effort to blind back the tears that seemed always near the surface these days. Naturally it was Lady Tremayne who would occupy his dreams. She was his fiancée, after all, though to Adrienne's knowledge, the woman's name had not once been among those who had called to ask about Dominic's progress. If only he would get better, she could see him in Lady Tremayne's arms without shedding a tear, she vowed, and then berated herself for trying to make deals with the Almighty.

Under her ministering hands, Dominic moved his head from side to side, his lips contacting her palm. "If you'd come closer, I could kiss you properly."

Without conscious thought, Adrienne leaned over and covered his mouth with her own. She froze in consternation when the lips under hers firmed and began to move against her own in a fashion that sent shock waves of sensation shooting through her body. Her eyes flew open, but Dominic's remained shut.

"*Adrienne*! My dear, that is so unwise of you!"

A hot tide of color surged into Adrienne's cheeks as she jumped back and stared at Miss Beckworth coming in to take over the late-night shift of nursing. "I . . . I know, Becky. I'm sorry. I don't know what came over me, but Dominic is still delirious. He . . . he'll never know." She was rising to her feet as she spoke in a breathless fashion.

The women's eyes met as Miss Beckworth walked over to the bed, her skirts rustling softly. "I'm thinking of you, dearest. I believe we must leave Brussels as soon as Dominic is out of danger."

Adrienne lowered her lashes to conceal the pain that shafted through her at this pronouncement. After a moment she said dully, "You are correct, of course. I'll speak to Moulton tomorrow."

Miss Beckworth followed the girl's exit, a troubled expression on her comely countenance, before seating herself beside the bed.

In the big bed, Dominic's eyelids flickered once, then closed.

19

Only those sounds indigenous to the natural world disturbed the hush in the far corner of the garden on this lovely day in midsummer. Bees were going about their business in the flowerbeds beyond the hedges and crickets were chirruping monotonously. An occasional whir of wings indicated a bird's passage. Beneath the spreading branches of a handsome chestnut tree a girl seated on a rustic swing moved idly back and forth from time to time, but mostly she just sat quietly, the only human element in the peaceful scene.

The Castles had been at Harmony Hall for a full month now. The kindness of their reception by the countess, the pleasure she took in their company, had quickly expunged all of Adrienne's doubts and forebodings with regard to her father's family. That she was Dominic's mother was enough to predispose Adrienne in Lady Creighton's favor sight unseen, but it had been a case of mutual liking from the moment the travel-weary little party had drawn up before the open doors of the rosy brick edifice that was the earl's family home, to see his mother awaiting them in the entrance.

Tall, slim, and attractive with fair hair lightly spinkled with gray and the smooth skin of a younger woman, Lady Creighton was easily recognized as the source of her son's good looks. She also possessed in full measure her son's openhearted generosity and interest in people, allied to a graciousness of manner that made her a delightful hostess. She had made them all welcome and set them at their ease within five minutes, but her blue eyes kept returning to Adrienne, and at last she had put out an impulsive hand to

touch one gleaming ruddy curl beneath the bonnet of chip
straw.

"It's just like Matthew's hair was thirty years ago," she
said softly, smiling at the bemused girl, "and your eyes too
are so like his, but you must favor your mother in features,
my dear, for that delicate chin never came from the Castles,
nor those dimples. Despite the coloring, the boys have
more of Matthew's cast of countenance, especially Luc."

The girl on the swing smiled to herself as she tried—
and failed—to recall the nervous dread with which she had
approached Dominic's mother. Lady Creighton had made
them all feel at home, including Becky, in whom she had
discovered a compatible nature. If she could not summon
up the anxiety, she could well recall the relief that had
spread through her that the initial meeting had gone so
pleasantly. She had been so oppressed in spirit herself at
having to part from Dominic that the journey had made no
impression on her. Even now she could barely recall any
details except that Jean-Paul had withstood the trip well
and Becky had suffered from seasickness during the
channel crossing. Moulton had made all the arrangements
for them, concealing his surprise behind an impeccably
wooden facade, but she had felt like a heartless wretch for
deserting Dominic when he was so ill. The fever had
broken that night, fortunately, the night she had kissed
him, but she wasn't going to think about that. Becky had
taken upon herself the task of informing Dominic of their
intention to leave, and Adrienne had never inquired as to
what actually passed between them. She herself had not
even seen her cousin the following day, having obeyed
Becky's instructions to supervise their packing while she
took over Adrienne's share of the nursing. She had gone
about the preparations with a heavy heart that she tried
conscientiously to conceal. After all, Dominic's life and leg
had been spared; there was so much for which to be grateful. Becky reported that, though extremely weak, he had
been improved enough to insist upon being shaved, and
had even felt able to glance through the pile of mail that
had accumulated over the past week. When Adrienne had
gone in to bid him farewell two days later, she had found

him in so cheerful a frame of mind she had been hard pressed to try to match his mood. He had stressed his relief that his cousin would be able to give his mother a comfortable firsthand account of his progress to allay the anxiety that would follow on the receipt of his letter. He had forbidden Moulton to inform her ladyship of his wounds when the doctor had operated on the night of the battle. Adrienne had experienced a sharp pang of conscience as she realized that she had been too wrapped up in her own reaction to Dominic's danger to spare a thought for his parent.

She pushed one foot in its blue kid sandal against the worn place in the grass and backed up on tiptoe, releasing the swing to go forward again as she recalled Lady Creighton's relief and thankfulness at learning about her son's narrow escape. On the subject of the full recovery of the leg she had, unhappily, been unable to reassure the countess, and from the lady's disgruntled snort after reading her son's latest letter, it seemed Dominic had neglected to keep his parent informed as to his progress.

A little sigh escaped Adrienne as she lazily pushed the swing. She felt so cut off from Dominic. She had accepted that he would no longer be a part of her life, but she longed for some news of him, at the same time dreading that it would most likely be word of his marriage to Lady Tremayne that would arrive. In the beginning of their visit Lady Creighton had questioned Adrienne and Becky eagerly about her son's fiancée, but the questions and references to Lady Tremayne had ceased tactfully when she found her guests strangely reticent on the subject. Adrienne had braced herself again today when the countess had cheerily announced the reception of a letter from her son, but there had been no mention of his upcoming marriage. She herself had received a letter from Sarah, and Becky had been in communication with General Forrester, but they had written from Paris and had nothing to say about Dominic. Perhaps he was already married to Pamela even as she sat here mooning. It was time to quit mooning and focus her attention on their future. The quiet weeks at Harmony Hall had been a marvelous respite that had seen Jean-Paul restored to health, but they were no closer to a plan for the boys' future.

The man coming around the corner of the hedge was able to feast his eyes on the delectable picture presented by a red-haired girl, hatless, in a snowy white muslin gown with blue ribbons trailing down behind her to the grass as she moved rhythmically to and fro, in and out of the dappled patches of shade provided by the huge tree. Her complete absorption in her thoughts allowed him time to discover that her expression of wistfulness, almost unhappiness, was at variance with the harmonious visual composition.

"Hello, little one."

Dominic had the exquisite pleasure of witnessing the radiance that transformed Adrienne's countenance briefly at his unexpected appearance.

"Oh, Dominic, you're limping!" she said, sobering abruptly and bringing the swing to a halt. "Does it hurt much?"

He laughed with pure joy. "No, not at all. I'm just grateful to be walking again."

Adrienne had reexerted her control in the interim. "Is Lady Treymayne with you?" she asked, her expression carefully polite.

"No, and to be quite accurate, Pamela is no longer Lady Tremayne."

The color that his sudden appearance had brought to her cheeks drained away at once, leaving her deathly pale. She moistened her lips. "Then you are . . . already married?"

"Not I—Pamela!" he said with emphasis.

"I . . . don't understand."

"Pamela became the wife of the Comte de Levèque last week in Brussels."

For a second Adrienne simply stared in disbelief; then her compassion was stirred. "Oh, Dominic, how awful for you! I'm so sorry!"

"Well, don't be. Only one thing could make me happier than seeing Pamela wed to another man."

He certainly *looked* happy enough. Adrienne felt herself relaxing slightly. "And what is that?"

"Seeing *you* married to *me*!" Dominic said simply. To his chagrin, Adrienne looked away from him swiftly, but not before he had seen the soft lips quiver.

"What is it, my love? Is the thought of being married to me so repugnant?"

She faced him then, but her eyes were guarded. "Are you asking me to marry you because Lady Tremayne jilted you, Dominic?"

He swooped on her then, releasing the hands that were grasping the swing's ropes. "Come out from there so I can show you why I want to marry you after I apologize for such a *maladroit* proposal."

The light in Dominic's eyes ignited a response in Adrienne's as she came willingly into his embrace. For a long moment he stood there savoring the feel of her in his arms while he lost himself in the warmth of those soft, southern-sea eyes. "Will it atone for my clumsiness if I tell you that I asked Pamela to release me from our engagement at the Richmond ball? It was not quite the action of a gentleman, but knowing she was not in love with me and was encouraging another man, I felt justified in asking for my freedom."

"Why did you not tell me then, Dominic? I was so desperately unhappy that night."

"Because she refused to release me. It wasn't until the day after the battle that she sent back my ring with a note saying she had reconsidered my request and was acceding to my wishes." He grinned at the expression on Adrienne's face. "Now, let us be charitable, darling. She may simply have regretted trying to hold an unwilling fiancé." He put a finger over the lips that had parted indignantly. "Now that I have apologized for such an unpoetic proposal, do you think I might show you *why* I want to marry you?"

Adrienne nodded shyly, but there was nothing shy or reserved about her reaction to his kiss. The feel of his mouth on hers produced the same explosion of sensation that had disconcerted her the first time their lips had met. This time she responded joyously, abandoning herself to the mysterious delights of the senses. She could have remained in that kiss forever, but Dominic raised his head all too soon to stare down at her, slightly shaken. "And I thought you were still a child!" he murmured, readjusting his thinking with effort. "That was certainly an improvement on our first kiss."

Adrienne grew very still, her eyes huge and questioning. "Wh-what do you mean?"

Dominic smiled at her tenderly. "You thought I was delirious, and I let you. Things were in such a muddle then. I shouldn't have done it, of course, but I came out of a nightmare where I was trying to explain to Pamela that it was you I loved, and there you were just inches away. The memory of that kiss is what kept me sane these last interminable weeks without you. I didn't know it was possible to miss someone so much. I didn't really know what love was until you burst into my life."

The oblique reference to his former engagement was not lost on Adrienne. There was nothing childish in the candid gaze raised to his as she said quietly, "I knew I was in love with you when you picked me up after Bijou threw me, Dominic, but I couldn't believe you could ever prefer *me* to Lady Tremayne. She is so very beautiful."

His arms tightened about her in instinctive protest. As he shifted his weight to relieve the bad knee, the swing came into his line of vision. "May we sit for a moment?" Seeing the spasm of pain cross his face, Adrienne made no demur when he sank onto the swing, pulling her onto his lap as naturally as if they had belonged to each other forever. He set the swing moving with one foot, saying nothing for a moment while he cradled her more comfortably in his arms.

"There is no denying I thought myself madly in love with Pamela in the beginning. *Now* I can see that it was merely an infatuation with her beauty and popularity that couldn't stand up to discovering her real nature, but no one could have told me that at the time. I'm not proud of myself for such stupidity, but there's no escaping it." He stopped the swing and lifted her chin with gentle fingers so she could read his eyes when he asserted, "I know the difference now, my one and only love, please believe that. You began to weave your way into my heart right from the first moment, and in case you might wonder if there is any element missing in what I feel for you," he added in some embarrassment, "you have only to feel my heartbeat when I am close to you."

Meeting his eyes steadily, Adrienne laid her hand over his heart and felt it racing. Their eyes locked together in a look as old as time. "I thought I would have to woo you slowly," whispered Dominic. "Instead you overwhelm me."

This time it was Adrianne who ended the long kiss out of the sheer necessity to draw an unrestricted breath. "I think you must love me," she said somewhat unsteadily, "to take on such a totally ineligible bride."

Dominic chuckled and tucked her head beneath his chin as he resumed the slow swinging. "I have already been warned about your lack of dowry and accomplishments, and find the subject a dead bore," he said firmly.

"I also have two penniless brothers to establish."

"*We* have two penniless brothers to establish," he corrected.

"And there is Becky. I could never desert Becky after all she has done for us."

"I could dwell happily under the same roof with Becky forever, my love, but I believe General Forrester has other plans for her future."

"No, *really,* Dominic? I was almost sure he loved her!" Adrienne tilted a sparkling face to his and was promptly kissed in reply.

"Any more objections or impediments to our immediate marriage?"

"Your mother?" she mentioned hesitantly.

"My mother is eager to welcome her new daughter whenever we decide to leave this delightful but uncomfortable perch."

Adrienne bounded off his lap, dimples in evidence and eyes full of mischief. "Weakling!" she teased as she extended a hand to help him rise.

The stiffness of his injured leg became more apparent as they walked slowly through the garden toward the house, hand in hand.

"It may be that we really have had our last waltz, my darling," Dominic said apologetically. "I hope you won't mind too much."

A fierce protective love surged through Adrienne, but she said with an airy wave of her hand, "We'll just find something else to do together."

About the Author

Dorothy Mack is a native New Englander, born in Rhode Island and educated at Brown and Harvard universities. While living in Massachusetts with her husband and four young sons, she began to combine a longtime interest in English history with her desire to write, and emerged as an author of Regency romances. The family now resides in northern Virginia, where Dorothy continues to pursue both interests.